MOUNTAINS
AGAINST
THE SUN

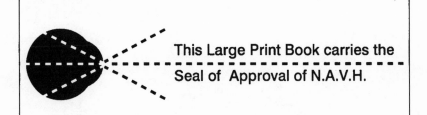

This Large Print Book carries the
Seal of Approval of N.A.V.H.

MOUNTAINS AGAINST THE SUN

PERRY HOLMES

Thorndike Press • Thorndike, Maine

Published in 1998 by arrangement with
Golden West Literary Agency.

Thorndike Large Print ® Western Series.

The tree indicium is a trademark of Thorndike Press.

The text of this Large Print edition is unabridged.
Other aspects of the book may vary from the original edition.

Set in 16 pt. Plantin by Juanita Macdonald.

Printed in the United States on permanent paper.

Library of Congress Cataloging in Publication Data

Holmes, Perry.
    Mountains against the sun : a western story / Perry
Holmes.
        p.   cm.
    ISBN 0-7862-0778-7 (lg. print : hc : alk. paper)
    1. Ranchers — Nevada — Fiction. 2. Murder —
Utah — Fiction. 3. Nevada — Fiction. 4. Utah —
Fiction. 5. Large type books. I. Title.
[PS3558.O366M68   1998]
813'.54—dc21   98-30796

To my Mother and Father
who left their indelible mark on so many lives
. . . and to Peg
who endured the many hours

Chapter One

In an unmapped and seldom traveled expanse of wilderness in this southwestern corner of Utah Territory the night wind howled out of the Wah-Wah Mountains. In spring and early summer it always began just after sunset — a great current of chill air, spawned among the towering eastern peaks capped with winter's snow and drawing moisture as it surged down and across the descending shoulders of the lofty range to accumulate as ground fog in the plunging cañons and sudden valleys of this dramatically configured land. Riding the frigid airstream was a heady, wine-like pungency of pine resin that a stranger, recently arrived off the high, arid desert of the neighboring Great Basin country, might consider unique and welcome. But to the inhabitants of Mountain Pass the capricious gusting of the wind and the clinging fog were an old story. On evenings such as this it was their habit to seek the comfort of warm fires and stout walls.

Three hours had passed since sunset. The new moon cast a sallow light that failed to penetrate the condensed mist and illuminate the landscape beneath it. Full darkness draped its somber shroud over the weathered buildings along both sides of the town's central street. Narrow alleys led away from the street at intervals, snaking between various buildings to meander through rear lots and ramshackle sheds to a fringe of tree stumps that marked the beginning of the pine forest.

Mountain Pass in 1875 was not a crossroads of any importance, for it lay along no frequented cattle trail or commonly traveled byway. Sandwiched between the Old Spanish Trail farther south and the widely used California Trail distantly northward, it guarded no established pass through the Wah-Wahs but lay quietly, tucked between a fold in the hills at the knees of the formidable mountain barrier. The little village provided a convenient water hole and source of supplies to a scattering of far-flung ranches, itinerant miners and trappers, or infrequent travelers who stumbled into this primitive region. With the arrival of nightfall many of the town's business establishments were closed. A sturdy cross-piece of hewn pine clamped together the iron-strapped double gates of the blacksmith shop, while the bolted doors of Tinker's Mercantile, Dunn's Emporium, and Jim Skinner's Feed Barn rattled forward and backward on their hinges from the alternating pressure or suction of the fickle gusts. In the parlor of the two-storied Staghorn Hotel the flame from a hooded night lamp flickered unsteadily. Down at the foot of the street, in the yawning arch of the livery stable, a coal-oil lantern swung freely from an overhead beam, spreading its weaving, fan-shaped stain of light over the dusty street. On the extreme northern end of town, properly positioned behind a white picket fence, squatted the village church, unadorned peeled logs topped by a cone-shaped steeple with a bell in it. Adjacent to the church and outside the fence was a dry goods store, its entrance marked by a spiral-streaked barber's pole, leaning drunkenly to one side. The store's proprietor, the Reverend Alonzo Pike, was both the town's barber and clergyman. On the Sabbath he preached the Gospel, but weekdays, while his wife minded the store, he practiced his tonsorial art in a lean-to bathhouse at the rear. The town's main thoroughfare terminated opposite the church. Only a pair of saloons, three-quarters of the way down the street and facing each other on diagonally opposite corners, showed any stir of activity.

Neither the Gilt Edge nor the Sage Hen

was particularly busy but had not as yet closed their storm portals against the night. Only slatted wooden batwing doors swung in the entrances, separating the patrons from the elements. Out of these harbors spilled the stale incense of tobacco smoke, the reek of whiskey, the growl of men's amiable bickering, their bawdy laughter, and the rake of their boots. At hitching racks ranged along the street outside, their top bars gnawed and nearly chewed in half by numberless horses having been tethered there, some two dozen ponies waited passively, backs humped and heads down, their tails turned into the blustery stream of air that whined down the alleys and whipped around the buildings' corners, raking up powdery motes of dust and scattering bits of trash.

One citizen was already preparing to retire, but no thick walls sheltered him, for he had no cabin and no stove. His lodging was at the foot of the alley, bordering the Gilt Edge, and consisted of what was left from an abandoned Conestoga wagon. Someone had long ago stripped away the undercarriage, leaving only the bed and a few hickory-bowed frames supporting tattered remnants of a canvas canopy. The once-proud prairie schooner was home to

Verne Posey who crept here each night. He was the town drunk.

At one time Posey had a measure of pride and self-respect, working for one of the larger ranches upstate and standing alongside other men as their equal. But whiskey was his poison, and, in spite of noble intentions, he unfailingly would soak up liquor until his paycheck ran out. He began losing one job after another, each succeeding position of lesser duration as word spread, until eventually he found no steady employment of any kind. He lost all contact with old friends, created no new ones, and now occasionally performed menial chores for Skinner and some of the other merchants. Henry Tinker, who owned the Mercantile and remembered what Posey had once been, assigned him errands and gave him jobs of short duration. Sometimes Posey washed dishes at the restaurant in exchange for leftover food from the kitchen and sporadically would swamp out the saloons to work off his whiskey bill.

Tonight Posey's slow-paced routine had been further dulled by earlier samplings from a flask of whiskey, and he lay contentedly beneath a thin blanket, hugging the bottle under his arm. Remnants of waste lumber had been nailed up to reinforce the decaying walls of the wagon bed, and discarded planks, wedged overhead, supported the tarpaulin, giving him a roof of sorts. The aged timbers had dried out and were warped, permitting the incessant wind to knife between them. Posey rolled clumsily about, trying to ignore the cold and find some warmth against the night. He fumbled for the old buffalo robe near his feet and dragged it over the threadbare cover, burrowing himself beneath this as he would a comforter.

His peace, however, was short-lived. Insistent low sounds from the alley denied him slumber. He threw off the dirty covers and raised himself on one elbow, peering through a gap between the stringers. The dark alley presented a muddy screen through which he could not see. The dry shuffling sounds persisted, very near yet beyond his vision. Then, without warning, the wind shifted, and the gray veil separated enough for a diluted light to seep through, making it possible for him to distinguish a pony, standing saddled and waiting on dropped reins, mincing the ground with back hoofs, clinking its bridle, and grinding on the iron bit. It was a palomino marked by starkly white stockings and matching white-blaze forehead. The markings, and their uniformly pale color, were particularly unusual. Posey gaped at the horse until the ground fog, continuously agitated by the nagging wind, cut off his vision. He slumped back, dully considering what he had seen, uncorked his bottle, and drank a quarter of it without drawing a breath. He tugged at the robe and drew it up to his chin, closed his eyes, and promptly forgot the entire incident in a fitful slumber.

On the opposite side of the alley in the office of the jail Sheriff Amos Burns was in a swivel chair behind a scarred desk. On one corner rested a wire basket stuffed with papers and reward dodgers. A coal-oil lamp and a bottle of whiskey along with two short glasses sat in the middle of the desk. At the junction of two walls a pot-bellied stove threw out its heat, the flame of a burning pine chunk showing through the isinglass window.

The sheriff was a large, deep-chested man beyond middle-age, his pugnacious features square and blunt beneath a grizzled mantle of silver-gray hair. A handlebar mustache, trimmed in flowing frontier style, half hid his upper lip beneath a prominent nose. Tom Yeager, his deputy, had just entered from the street. Yeager, a younger and roanheaded man, lingered inside the doorway long enough to remove his cartridge belt and holstered revolver, hooking them over a wooden peg. He carried a rifle which he stood in a gun case, shrugged out of his coat, and hung it with his hat on a wall rack of deer antlers. He ran a hand through his unruly hair, gave an immense yawn, and stood for a moment, stretching his limbs in a deliberate and faintly indolent manner.

Burns, with a tolerant half smile, took advantage of the lapse to reach into his desk for a cigar. He rolled it between his thumb and forefinger, and made some ceremony of trimming it with his pocket knife. He dug for a match and raked it across the desk, then wiggled it under the cigar until he got a hot coal glowing, exhaling billows of smoke. "Damn' cold night," he remarked. "How was your trip?"

Yeager lowered his lank frame into a chair on the opposite side of the desk, pursing his lips in a long and drawn-out sigh. He was tall and string-shaped, clean-shaven with a ruddy and unlined face. "We followed their trail to the state line," he replied. "The cattle were driven over the border and probably sold to somebody in Arizona. A couple of lawmen from Tucson took up the chase where we left off. We'll hear from 'em in due time." His eyes fell on the bottle and glasses. "What's the celebration?"

Burns reached over and uncorked the bottle. He poured two generous helpings and curled his thick fingers around his stubby glass. He pushed the other glass across the desk. "I got news today that calls for good liquor, and I been savin' this expensive stuff for just such an occasion. They had a necktie party two days ago down at the Saint George jail. Jack Slade was hanged."

A smile left Yeager's face, then returned broader than before. "I'll be damned. Never thought the law could move that fast." He shifted in his chair, took up his drink, and sipped the whiskey slowly. "Down Texas way they'll be glad to hear about that. Slade robbed a couple of their banks and gunned down a few of their citizens before he came here."

"That judge in Saint George is tough," Burns observed. "We need more like him. Soon as the jury brought in a guilty verdict, the old boy passed sentence. They strung Slade up the next day." He used this as an excuse to take another turn at the bottle. "This is the best rye in town. Drive the chill from your bones." He proposed a small toast. "Here's to crime and punishment. Slade ran with a bad bunch and was one dangerous customer, but you brought him in without a shot bein' fired. It was a nice piece of work."

His young deputy accepted the praise casually and took another sip of Burns's choice liquor. The combined smell of raw whiskey and cigar smoke strengthened in the little room, and both men fell comfortably silent.

Burns leaned back and made a steeple with the tips of his big fingers, choosing his words very carefully. "Tom, you take some time off and leave these parts. I can manage without a deputy for a spell. Go fishin' or take a trip back to Nevada where you grew up and visit your old friends. I been hearin' things I don't like." He sat forward and spread his broad hands fanwise on the desk in front of him, frowning thoughtfully at the big knuckles, driving his words home. "You remember when Jack Slade came into this country with three of his chums and holed up in Winona Basin? I found out that all four were professional gunslingers, probably on the dodge and damned dangerous. The three still up there know it was you caught Slade, and, now that he's dead, it's my thinkin' they'll be after your hide."

This drew a quick-tempered response from Yeager. "To hell with them. I can take

16

care of myself. None of that bunch scares me at all."

"Nobody said you're afraid. That ain't what I'm talkin' about. Didn't Slade threaten you, say his partners would see you in hell?"

"Sure," agreed Yeager, "he talked tough, but they all do. Slade bragged his bunch would break him out of jail right here, too, but they didn't."

"They couldn't because they didn't have time to arrange it," said Burns. "A couple of deputies from Saint George happened to be in town and hustled Slade out the followin' mornin'." His cigar had gone cold, and he thumbed a match into flame and steadied it under the cigar's tip. "Listen to me. We haven't had anybody around here as mean as this bunch since the Rafter brothers in 'Sixty-Five. You don't know how these fellers think or what they might try. I want you gone."

Yeager's face was flushed and angry, and he was primed for further argument. He took his glass in his cupped hands and began to swirl the amber contents, staring down at the circular motion. Watching him, Burns sympathized with the conflict going on in his deputy's mind. He had hired Tom Yeager two years before. Having never married, he had come privately to regard his deputy like a son, a sentiment he took considerable pains to conceal. Yeager had an abundance of obstinate pride, a quality Burns admired, but he also nursed a hard-headed stubbornness that sometimes extended beyond Burns's reach, as it did now.

"Tom," he said impatiently, "you're bull-headed as hell. Granted that runnin' ain't your style, but this is different. Those three have you marked, and you don't have eyes in the back of your head. They're seasoned gunfighters. You're not. And the match-up ain't even. Far as they're concerned, your tin star don't mean a damned thing. Besides," he added with a gruff attempt at humor, "good deputies are in short supply, and I'm too old to break in somebody new."

"If you're that worried, organize a posse and we'll go into the basin and round 'em up."

Burns lifted a broad hand, dismissing the remark with a gesture of annoyance. "You know better than that. Where you been lately? If we had some kind of legal charge against any of the three, it would give us a reason to try, but I don't have one. The difference with Slade was we had an enforceable Texas warrant for him. Then he obliged us by comin' down here, outside the basin and alone. Sure, he was blind drunk and that made it easier to serve him and haul him in, but everything was done legal and proper." He paused to let his words sink in. "Even with a posse we couldn't get in the basin without big trouble. I know them folks. Everybody, even the women, would grab a rifle and put up a fight. Sure as hell some girl, or an old-timer, or a fool kid, would get shot. Besides, I hear Ben Lenifee's posted guards with rifles on both the east and west entrances."

"You hear a hell of a lot," commented Yeager dryly. "When did that happen? I thought the old man was a God-fearin' Bible-thumper who liked things nice and peaceable?" He paused a moment, then added: "Who told you that?"

"Never mind where I get my information," retorted Burns. "I got good ears. For a week there's been a man on both the east and west roads. Old Ben don't want Winona Basin to get a reputation so outlaws run there for shelter. Slade and his bunch were enough." He sat up straight in his chair and slapped a palm sharply across one thigh, his patience exhausted. "Damn it, man, you been around long enough to know the history hereabouts as well as me. Why should I have to repeat it? The folks in the basin never gave us any trouble until those four *hombres* moved in. Now I understand it ain't peaceful there any more. Everybody's spooked since they found out Slade was wanted for murder." He leaned forward across the desk, biting down on the cigar. "One of the three is named Lenifee, a distant cousin of Ben's. That's how they got in the basin, because he's kinfolk. If you're from Tennessee, that's important. Ben realized too late they're cheap gunmen, and, by puttin' a look-out on the only two ways in and out, he's makin' sure no more of their friends show up."

Yeager's stiff cheeks reflected his displeasure.

Burns nursed his cheroot before he spoke again. "Kid," he said wearily, "hear me. These *hombres* are bad business. I know you ain't afraid of 'em but play this one my way. Pull out first thing in the mornin' and put some distance between you and here. Come back in a month. I'll have somethin' figgered out by then. In the meantime who knows, maybe Ben will have found a way to get rid of 'em." He thought he saw a break of feeling in Yeager's sullen exterior. "I say it again. You did a fine job with Slade, and the right parties will hear about it. Mebbe you'll get a raise. Now pack up and clear out. Enjoy yourself and come back in a month."

As far as the sheriff was concerned, the discussion was over, and his joviality returned. A smile creased his leathery face. He picked up his glass and got out of his chair, coming around the desk and standing next to Yeager. The latter had not entirely conceded and was even briefly tempted to offer further argument, but in the end he swallowed his displeasure and glumly rose to his feet. Solemnly the two men clinked their glasses together.

The bullet, exploding through the glass, destroyed the prevailing quiet of the town as it splintered the window pane and ripped into the back of Yeager's skull. His head jerked obscenely from the concussion, and he reeled unnaturally, took a step, and crumpled across one corner of the desk. His body hung briefly there in tangled suspension, then seemed to unravel all at once, and he fell prone, heavily. There was a momentary twitch; then he was still.

Burns dove for the lamp. A second slug, coming through the window, caught him in mid-air with a solid thud as it tore through the left side of his chest, near the shoulder. It flung him sideways, and he skidded to the

21

floor, carrying a chair with him, rolled over twice, and tried to rise. A dark blotch spread across the front of his woolen shirt. A windy sigh broke from his throat, and he dropped flat on his chest, his face twisted to one side, losing consciousness.

The sound of the detonations in close proximity and the shivery cascade of glass shards raced along the street, slamming off the store fronts, rebounding in a ricochet of turbulent echoes. The wind picked up the reports and hurled them into both saloons, abruptly halting all conversation and setting off a chain reaction.

In the Gilt Edge a man's bellowing shout lifted above the raised voices. "What the hell was that all about?"

"Two shots, right outside," cried another, his yell soaring over the clamor, "busting hell out of somebody's window."

Two dozen pairs of boots struck the floor at the same time as the crowd rushed for the exit and spilled into the street. Across the way the Sage Hen disgorged its own flood of men who fanned out and took up the hue and cry, searching for the source of the shots. Somebody spotted the destroyed window at the sheriff's office, ran over, and looked inside. What he saw there immediately increased the bawling and the uproar.

Lights winked to life behind the shaded windows of nearby cabins, their furtive streaks making only a little impression on the darkness. A man darted from the livery stable and sprinted up the street, swinging a lantern.

Verne Posey was rudely awakened by the two quickly spaced shots and at first lay immobile, annoyed by the disturbance. His tarpaulin roof fluttered in the wind, wound around the twisted staves, and raised a steady flapping sound. Above it all his ears clearly picked up the nearby rustle of agitated movement. He struggled up on his elbow and squinted through the crack, observing the taut shadow of a man slide out of the blackness and mount the palomino. Posey was unable to distinguish any of the man's features, but he was in obvious haste and, once in his saddle, wheeled the horse about and rode to the end of the alley, fading into the trees.

Posey sank down on his bedclothes and considered what he had seen. He couldn't identify the phantom rider and had no particular interest in doing so, but he idly wondered about the gunshots, and his thoughts kept returning to the horse. He heard men calling and answering; a welter of voices and heavy shouting rose above the wind's howl, followed by the pounding tread of many feet, running down the alley. Posey, no longer interested, drew his blankets close around him and took another long and satisfying pull from the bottle. Drowsiness returned to spread warmly through him, and his eyelids grew heavy. He flung a hand over his face, sealed his ears to further distractions, and fell back into slumber.

Chapter Two

The spring sunlight poured out of the eastern half of the sky, and the bright, glazed air was already warm. Summer's crushing heat had not yet parched the sagebrush, and the ferment of spring growth sparkled everywhere. The creosote bushes which dotted the floor of the Shoshone Valley, itself broadly spread between two ranges of dun-colored mountains, shimmered in yellow-flowered profusion. To the east rose Wheeler Peak, lofty and majestic, a perfect cone of snow shrouding the summit. Robb's Creek was born in those high snowbeds, a creature of seasonal extremes, storming down the mountainside in quicksilver cataracts during the rainy season, flowing shortly through spring and early summer, eventually vanishing altogether in a marshy sink thirty miles to the south.

Frank Allard and his foreman, Ray Bliss, were rebuilding a section of the plank bridge over the creek, a mile or so below Allard's ranch house. They had been working steadily since early morning when a far-off fumarole of dust rose on the horizon. As the funnel grew nearer, the shape beneath it eventually materialized out of the desert mirage into a horse and a rider who continued toward them until he drew abreast and halted. The caller was Fuzzy Doyle, a long-time acquaintance of both men. He was a short, wiry little man, saddle-warped and rail-thin with a weather-beaten face, parched and dried by the sun. Unkempt strings of hair ran lawlessly down his scrawny neck, hanging to shoulder level from beneath the brim of a salt-encrusted hat. Whiskers sprouted from his jaw, growing in every direction. The ends of his rusty mustache and the corners of his mouth were brown-stained from the generous plug of tobacco, pouched in one cheek. His restless eyes, half hidden by a perpetual squint, were bright.

Allard and Bliss ceased work, glad for the respite. Bliss was no hand to waste words. Using a thumb, he pushed his hat back from his forehead, lighted a cigarette, and said nothing. Allard remarked genially: " 'Mornin', Fuzzy. What brings you out here?"

Doyle hooked one leg around the saddle horn and folded his hands on the pommel. He had come on an errand he deemed of some importance and took his time working around to an answer. He said: "Should be a good year for you fellers. Lots of natural forage all the way down the valley." He had the curiosity of a magpie, and his roving eyes settled on the bridge. When he saw the new timbers recently nailed in place, he inquired innocently: "Havin' trouble with your bridge?"

His mild face showed nothing more than a simple curiosity, but Allard bent a withering look in his direction. "Use your eyes, Fuzzy," he said. "It washed out during the winter. Ready to fall in the creek."

Doyle relieved himself of his tobacco chaw, bit off another from his battered plug, and revolved it from one cheek to the other with a furtive tongue while the three waited out an interval of silence.

Allard had his own style of subtle humor to match Doyle's and presently commented: "It occurs to me that you may know something about bridges."

"Matter of fact, I do," Doyle declared carelessly. "Built lots of 'em in my time. Too bad I'm in a hurry. Otherwise I'd help."

Doyle's patronizing attitude provoked a quick gust of irritation in Bliss, and he laid a frosty stare on the little man. "You lazy runt," he said. "You ain't in no hurry, and you got no place to go. Get off your bronc' and give us a hand."

It had been Doyle's purpose to get a rise out of Bliss, and he was secretly pleased. He pointedly ignored the suggestion and turned his attention to Allard. "I got a letter here for you, Frank. The stage driver left it at the hotel a couple days ago, so I brought it out. Looks like it had a hell of a trip."

He began a search of his pockets, finally unearthing a grimy envelope which he handed down to Allard who took it from him and seated himself on a rock. He slit the envelope by running a thumbnail along the seam and spread the enclosed paper on his knee.

April 21
Frank Allard
Shoshone Valley Ranch
Somewhere south of Ely, Nevada

Hope this letter finds you. Not sure I got your location pegged. Your old friend and my deputy, Tom Yeager, was bushwhacked and killed two weeks ago. I got a slug in my shoulder and can't go after the drygulcher myself. Tom used to tell me you two was pretty close. If you still remember what a good man he was, maybe

you'll come see me. I could use some help.

My cabin is on the high side of the trail, three miles north of Mountain Pass, with firewood stacked against the walls. Show up at night, don't go thru town, and don't tell anybody about this.

Amos Burns
Sheriff Moapa County
Mountain Pass, Utah Territory

Some men have a way of absorbing trouble or punishment without visible signs, and Frank Allard was a man of closely guarded emotions. Fuzzy Doyle, watching from his saddle, observed no discernible change in Allard's expression, but Bliss, wiser and more perceptive, knew what to look for and recognized subtle signs that gave him away. Only twice since working for Frank Allard had he seen similar indications of trouble in him — a stiffening of muscles that lifted his shoulders and tightened his jaw, accentuating the prominent cheekbones and compressing his lips into a taut, thin slash across his face. Allard read the note a second time with more care. The blunt letter had caught him unprepared, and in a single moment threatened the carefully planned design of his life. His friendship with Tom Yeager marked a relationship going back to his beginnings.

He folded the letter neatly along its creases and slipped it into his shirt pocket. He placed his elbows on his knees and rubbed his big hands together, the vertical lines of his face deepening and drawing tight. Life had not always been entirely kind to Frank Allard. The letter's message jogged unwelcome, bygone memories. The flames of smoldering resentment toward a pitiless world that had crushed his parents' spirit and cut short their lives flared up in his memory — and now Tom. He waited for some resurgence of hope to lift his spirits, but none came. Deeply perturbed, he grew restive and climbed to his feet, aimlessly tramping through the desert scrub. He came upon the bleached and coyote-picked skeleton of some large animal and irritably kicked the bones aside, startling a jackrabbit that exploded from its hiding place beneath the carcass and bounded off in a series of vaulting hops. Out of habit he stopped and fumbled to locate his pipe, packed, and got it burning, the smoke having a calming effect on his nerves.

A pair of broadly spaced slate-gray eyes

looked unsmilingly upon the land, grown bleak and ice-cold now as the goodness and flavor of the day washed out of him. He scowled out across the sand, shading his eyes against the reflected flashes from millions of tiny mica particles buried in the gravel, a tall and narrow-hipped man of twenty-eight with a wiry precision about him, endowed by nature with a muscular physique intended for hard usage. The punishing desert weather had gouged sun-squint furrows near his eyes on deeply bronzed cheeks, and his boldly chiseled features evinced a mixture of physical vitality and a rashly impulsive disposition.

The surge of nostalgia, once started in his mind, showered him with a stream of images, reviving his association with Tom Yeager and carrying him further back to his earliest years as an only child on a hardscrabble ranch at the foot of the Ruby Mountains in the remote desolation of northeastern Nevada. Some of the time-worn images were sweet and soft-hued, like dried and fragile flowers pressed in an aged book. Others were old injustices, still burning, which he had deliberately banished from his mind because they were dismal and depressing. Now they flooded back in poignant detail.

His parents were middle-aged when he was conceived, quite by accident, and his birth was greeted without enthusiasm by his father, for it meant another mouth to feed in a dirt-poor household. He had known almost nothing of paternal warmth and affection from the dour and round-shouldered father who had sired him, an embittered man whose attempt at ranching had proved an outright failure.

Allard's adolescence ended early, his boyhood years spent among rough and workworn men from whom he received an education about a brutal world in which he dared not falter. This had hardened him and gave birth in later years to the principles that ruled him, an inflexible code of give-and-take in which every man made his own judgments and was responsible for his own failures or successes, accepting equally the rewards or penalties, asking no help and caring nothing for outside advice. Because of the disciplined shell of toughness he displayed outwardly, many would be surprised to learn that buried within Frank Allard was a second facet to his character. He was a product of contradictions, possessing dual surfaces, a stubborn individuality set against a keen sensitivity. On one hand, what he saw as life's injustices had carved its lasting brand of distrust and rebellion where daily living itself was a harsh test of survival. On the opposite side dwelt a rarity among the hard-bitten ranchers along the border, an individual capable of mawkish sentimentality and a profound veneration toward women of all stations, the latter being a trait deeply embedded in him long before by his mother. This was his soft point and his weakness.

She had been born in Virginia of gentler stock, a woman of some education who had married his father in the hope of bringing him up to her own level. But, when they migrated to the edge of civilization on the western frontier, it proved to be a life as remote as possible from her previous circumstances. Her daily routine, on the knife edge of scarcity, involved a good deal of suffering without much happiness, but she was like many other women of her generation with an uncomplaining fortitude, reserving her tears for the misfortunes of others and meeting every adversity with quiet courage and gentle patience. Her influence on her only son had been huge, and it was entirely because of her untiring efforts and her faithful tutelage that Allard had been exposed in a small way to a graceful side of living he otherwise would never have known.

There had been absolutely nothing on the Allard ranch to excite ambition for knowledge, but, determined that he would not grow to be an illiterate man without any schooling, his mother taught him early to read and write, and much more. Over the years she supplied regular instruction from a dusty collection of schoolbooks, at first reading to him and turning the pages over and over with her care-worn hands until she was satisfied that he understood. Later, he read them himself, and those dog-eared volumes now occupied permanent space on a shelf in his ranch house. He would keep them always, for they represented to him a shining memorial to his mother's devotion, but the difficult memory of her privations also stayed with him and had left their bitter tracks on his heart. At one time his mother had been a beautiful woman, but the severity of the country and the harsh range life eventually proved too much for her. When she died, he was far too young to be safely left on a failing ranch with a detached and elderly father, a man broken in spirit whose desire to continue living without his wife was swiftly fading.

It was about this time that Tom Yeager's family had filed on a stretch of rangeland bordering the Allard property, both spreads some two hundred miles to the north of where he now stood. There were no other ranches for miles in any direction, the country still young and largely unsettled, boasting less than four inhabitants to the square mile. Like himself, Yeager was an only child, and the two had drifted into a companionship that the subsequent years of separation had left undimmed.

Haunted by memories, Allard ground his teeth over the acid-sharp sting of certain recollections and tipped his head up to gaze sightlessly into the distance, moved by a disquietude that always accompanied such thoughts. His half-closed eyes roved northward, and he shaded them with his hand, observing the familiar outlines of his ranch buildings, low shapes above the plain on a spur of benchland. The shimmering illusion of desert mirage made small details indistinct, but he could see outlines on the little plateau, sheltered and watered in the middle of a grove of enormous cottonwoods. The sight reminded him of a day five years earlier, when, far to the north, he had stood alone and hatless on a low hill overlooking the dreary desolation of the old ranch at the foot of the Rubies. A newly cut headboard rose bravely on a freshly turned mound of earth where he had buried his father next to his mother. On that day he had bid farewell to a largely joyless youth and a period of his life which had, until now, been expunged from his memory.

The sad and worn-out spread had been disposed of to pay off the mortgage and accumulated debts, leaving no surplus. Shortly thereafter he and Yeager had left the region and signed on as cattlehands with an established outfit north of Pyramid Lake, near the Idaho border. It had taken Allard five careful years to accumulate a stake, whereupon he quit his job and came down alone to the Shoshone Valley, finding there a fertile stretch of country where he began a small operation with some twenty head of beef. Something definable, yet difficult to explain, had motivated him in the building of this spread. A stubborn insistence to run his own ranch and a passionate faith in himself kept pushing him, and he found that he gained a strange and malicious satisfaction from the daily struggle to succeed. It fulfilled a demand within him for lasting self-esteem, stemming from his early days when nothing mattered so much as the simple ability to stay alive. His Spartan toil had paid off, and today he was modestly independent, the sole owner of an unpretentious layout with a crew of two full-time 'punchers and a manageable debt.

Yeager's death pumped him empty of all other feelings, for it effectively severed his final link to the past. With his one remaining close friend gone, he felt himself changing in a curious way. Previous aspirations seemed less meaningful as tentacles of an oddly felt desolation reached out to grasp him. For the first time in his life he felt absolutely alone, lacking the close friendship of a living soul, but then his bitter and fatalistic anger rose up, and he spurned the dismal realization with a shrug of his shoulders.

Two years ago Tom Yeager had appeared on his ranch, unannounced and with his gear rolled behind his saddle, bound for southern Utah, a job offer in his pocket to become a deputy there under Sheriff Amos Burns. He had dropped by to say so long to his old sidekick, and they lounged in the porch shade for an hour, reminiscing through the years, laughing over the good times, soberly recounting the bad. Yeager was enthusiastic and buoyed with expectation about his new venture, afterwards departing southward into the desert, his figure dwindling in size and finally fading into the trackless plain. It was the last time Frank Allard had seen Tom Yeager.

The relentless sun, by now high in the

heavens, was pounding down on the desert, grilling the exposed parts of Allard's body, and roused him from his musings. He pulled off his Stetson to wipe the white rime of dried perspiration from his hatband, and, when he did so, the sweat collected beneath it ran down his forehead and stingingly into his eyes. His pipe had gone cold, and he sought the sparse shade of a lone cactus to knock the dottle from the bowl by beating it against his palm, then repacked it, and coaxed it alight.

Always a man of quick decision, he seldom paused to deliberate when faced with hard choices, but in this case the racing mainstream of his thoughts galloped ahead with such intensity it denied him the opportunity for calm analysis. Striving to be objective, he asked his conscience to find some justification if he should fail to heed Burns's appeal. Was it, after all the elapsed time, wholly reasonable for him to pull stakes and travel into an unknown country on a dubious summons from a man he had never met? He had a moment when he doubted the message and the originator, but the letter appeared genuine, and the sheriff's name was the same one Yeager had mentioned two years ago.

All he owned in the world was his ranch,

and he placed it in great jeopardy if he abandoned it for any length of time. Some men, in the face of such a drastic step, would have dismissed the letter's call. But there are times in a man's life when all logic collapses, and he falls back upon the instincts that are strongest within him. The simple human elements of friendship and fidelity surmounted Frank Allard's practicality, and he could not escape Yeager's dead hand lying heavily on his shoulder. Long gambles were nothing new to him. He had been faced with complexities before and ended up doing what he felt had to be done with no doubts and no regrets.

In this case it was the way Yeager had died that finally swayed him. A lawman's life itself was a perilous occupation, and, if his friend had perished in the line of duty, it would have been borne as a hazard of the profession, a tragic consequence he could have endured. But to be cut down by an assassin's cowardly bullet was the wrong way to die, and the unknown assailant still rode free. The trail was growing colder, giving the killer an edge, and nobody was running him to earth. It was this absence of swift justice from a system he despised that helped make up his mind. He shook off the lethargy of brooding resentment and fell back on the simple precepts by which he lived. He rose, retracing his steps to where the others waited.

"Ray," he said, addressing Bliss, "I'm going to town." He pointed to the bridge. "Get Mateo to help you finish here. I'll be back around dark."

Fuzzy Doyle had been hanging back, hoping for some news. His inquisitive face was half concealed by his hatbrim, and his jaw moved perpetually as he worked on his plug. When Allard said nothing to enlighten him, he wheeled his horse, preparing to leave. Allard held him with a word.

"Settle down, Fuzzy, while I run up to the ranch house for a couple things. I'll ride to town with you."

Together, Allard and Bliss moved to their horses, staked out close by. They saddled swiftly and swung aboard, heading toward the ranch buildings at a fast lope. Doyle was in no hurry to leave and dropped off his pony to stretch out on the grass, bordering the creek. He pulled his hat over his eyes, and, when Allard returned forty minutes later, he was sound asleep, sweating heavily and snoring through his mustache. At Allard's hail he awoke with a choking snort and climbed on his horse. He bit off another chew, the taste of the tobacco brightening him, kicked the pony into motion, and they rode off together, following the road to town.

It was mid-afternoon when the pair pulled into Rimrock, a drowsy cluster of wooden and adobe shanties, flung carelessly on the sun-baked prairie at the foot of a sandstone bluff. Sage smell and a flour-fine haze combined in an atmosphere that had no movement at all, clogging their nostrils and reddening their eyes. Although well past its meridian and dropping swiftly in the western sky, the sun was still potent, turned blood-red by the powdered heat. They drifted up a street drained of life, coming to a tie rack in front of the town's only saloon. The board overhang offered a small shield of shade, and a dog lay under it and flopped its tail without getting up, sending a small plume of dust into the air. Out in the open a lone chicken, oblivious to the heat, scratched in the dirt. Doyle dropped off his mount with a groan. Beads of sweat glistened on his cheeks and droplets ran off his chin.

"By God," he croaked, ineffectually shielding off the sun with a raised hand, "it's hot enough to fry your brains. Too early in the year for this much heat. I got to have somethin' to drink 'fore I die. Join me?"

41

Allard shook his head. "Not yet. A few things to take care of first." He watched the peripatetic little man's bowlegged shuffle propel him into the saloon. He rode to the stable and surrendered his mount to the glum hosteler who squatted there in a patch of shade. He retraced his way up the street to a frame building whose ground floor was occupied by the general store, rounded a corner, and climbed an outside staircase, ascending to the second story, each worn board creaking and swaying ominously the moment he laid his weight on it. When he arrived at the second-story landing an open doorway faced him with a faded sign above it.

R. R. BRIGHT
ATTORNEY-AT-LAW

Allard entered the small office, airless and stifling, plainly furnished with a roll-top desk and table, four chairs, a standing bookshelf crowded with law books and a coat rack. A doleful man of middle-age in wrinkled shirtsleeves, long and spare and somber, rose from a swivel chair behind the desk and offered Allard a damp, oversized hand, shaking it limply. His smile of welcome creased a face dominated by an unusually

42

high forehead that broke off to a severe, bony nose.

"Frank," he said, his words lighting up the gloom of his deep-set eyes, "good to see you. How can you travel in this heat?"

He resumed his seat, turning to face Allard and fanning himself with a sheaf of papers. He was dressed in dark trousers and a sweat-begrimed shirt that clung wetly to his gaunt frame. Allard sank in the opposite chair, removed his hat, and swung it back and forth, ineffectually agitating the stagnant air.

"Ralph," he said, getting right to the point, "I'm pulling out tonight on a trip that will take me away for a time. What happens to my property if I don't return?"

Bright was momentarily taken aback. "Sudden isn't it, Frank? You in some kind of trouble?"

Allard hesitated. He was inclined to show Bright the letter, but habitual silence about his affairs was part of a pattern adopted long ago, and Burns's admonition for strict secrecy had been quite plain. He said, "No," rather sharply. When he saw Bright's expression change to one of chagrin, he realized he had been overly curt and that the lawyer had reason to expect him to amplify, so he added lamely: "Just tending to some personal business for a friend, Ralph. But what would happen to my ranch if I didn't make it back?"

"You got any living relatives?" inquired Bright.

"None," said Allard.

Bright looked at him keenly. "No distant relations of any sort, perhaps some family living in the East?"

Allard shook his head. "No, nobody at all." The admission seemed to touch a tender spot, and he stared at Bright with a deliberate steadiness until the lawyer shifted uncomfortably and busied himself rearranging the articles on his desk.

"Didn't realize that, Frank," he said. "Ever make out a will?"

Allard again shook his head. "Never have."

"Then it's time you did. If you die without one and have no relatives, after a statutory length of time, providing nobody files a claim to satisfy a debt, your property would escheat to the state of Nevada."

"You can say it simpler, Ralph," said Allard. "If I don't have a will on file, the state winds up with everything?"

Bright nodded. He started to add something else, but Allard showed him a wire-edged impatience that changed his mind.

He nervously tapped his fingers on the desk top and broke off his glance, waiting for the other to continue.

"Then write one for me now," resumed Allard. "I don't owe the state or the general public a damn' thing. Can you have it ready in an hour?"

"If I don't die from heat stroke, I can," replied Bright, mopping his face and hands with a damp handkerchief. "It will be a simple one." He swung around at his desk, dipped a pen in the glass inkwell, and squared a sheet of paper before him. "What are your assets?"

"My spread and my bank account are all that I own. The mortgage on the ranch is coming down, and there's no reason to consider foreclosure. If I don't come back in a couple months' time, you sell the place for what you can get, pay the bills, and divide what's left between Ray Bliss and Mateo Rozas, my two hired hands. I got nobody else." He felt the weight of Bright's silence as the man regarded him. "Put that in the will, too. Bliss gets two-thirds, Rozas one-third."

Bright penciled appropriate notes. "That's straightforward enough. I'll have it ready for your signature in an hour." He swiveled his chair around and absent-mindedly lifted a hand to his forehead. "By Christ," he groaned, sponging his brow. "If it's this hot in May, what will it be like in July?" He unbuttoned his shirt part way down the front, picked up a sheaf of papers, and fanned the air in front of him. "Why the hell did I open a practice in this God-forsaken furnace? Can you tell me?"

His shambling discomfort drew a grin from Allard. "You're the only lawyer in the territory, Ralph, and you can pick your spot. Why don't you set up shop some place else?"

"Yeah, where? When the weather turns hot, there's no place in the whole damned country to escape it."

Allard drew a fat, white envelope from his pocket, reached over, and laid it on the desk. It had been carefully tied with twine and the knot sealed with candle wax. "One thing more," he said, regaining Bright's attention. "I put this bundle of papers together one night and been saving it out at the ranch. You hang on to 'em. Everything about the place is explained inside."

His haste to get rid of matters that Bright considered important bothered the lawyer. Allard was clearly anxious to put this bit of business behind him and be on his way, so Bright picked up the envelope, sliding it into a drawer. He kept hoping for some additional explanation about the whole affair, but, when Allard offered none, Bright was compelled to inquire farther. He gnawed on the end of his pencil and drew a deep breath. "Got another question. If you never come back, how will I know what happened to you?"

Remembering Burns's official position as sheriff, Allard said: "I don't expect this to be a one-way trip, but, if it happens that way, you'll be notified." He rose to his feet, wiped the sweatband of his hat with his bandanna, and clapped it on his head, scanning Bright with a mild glance. "See you in an hour."

Outside, he went directly to the bank and spent a half hour with Arthur Davis, the local manager. His second stop was the general store where he bought supplies and filled a gunnysack with them. He left the sack at the livery stable, and, when he reappeared at Bright's office an hour later, dusty and thoroughly dried out, he found the latter sprawled at the open window, his shirt unbuttoned to his belt and pulled out of his trousers, inviting any elusive breeze. Beads of moisture dimpled his forehead and brought a pink stain to cheeks already puffed from the heat. He had a glass of water in his hand and took a swallow, but the liquid was lukewarm and tasted like dust. He spat it back in the glass. "The damn' water is hot as the air and full of alkali. It probably corrodes your stomach, but I got to drink something." He nodded toward his desk. "Your will is over there."

Allard perched a hip on the desk's corner and took up the document. It was in a neat, clerkish script on two pages, and, as he read it, the significance of the occasion, which would forever alter the grooved routine of his life, caused him to hesitate. He could still change his mind, but, once embarked on this mission, there would be no way to sidestep whatever followed. He would then become the central actor in a flow of events he could neither predict nor foresee, and probably not control. He might have to subordinate his independence to the will of someone else, and the very thought that anyone other than himself might have an influence over his fate was repugnant, for he was one who bridled at any sort of outside authority. He took up a pen, dipped it into the inkwell Bright had set before him, and affixed his signature to the bottom of the second page in rapid, sweeping longhand, leaving it on Bright's desk to be witnessed.

"Ralph," he said, "keep this here with ev-

erything else. Papers get lost at the ranch."
He got to his feet and stood silently for a
moment, as if reluctant to leave, his expression totally unreadable. Bright waited ex-
pectantly for an accounting he thought
might be forthcoming, but finally Allard
only inclined his head and said: "See you in
church."

He wheeled from the room and, descending the precarious staircase, came once
more to the street. His errands completed,
he marched directly over to the deserted saloon where, much to the amusement of the
lone bartender, he drank three glasses of
beer without pause, still unable entirely to
slake his thirst. Doyle had disappeared, and
the barkeep was hot and bored. He swabbed
his damp cheeks with the bar rag and commented idly on the weather. He drew a glass
of beer for himself and buried his lips in the
foam, swallowing the contents with high rel-
ish.

A man appeared in a doorway, bearing
the barkeep's dinner. At the sight a feeling
in the pit of his stomach reminded Allard
that he had eaten nothing since breakfast,
and he left the saloon at once, crossing to a
Chinaman's restaurant where he sat up to
an early supper and then lingered over a
third glass of warm tea to enjoy a short idle-

ness with his pipe. When he was through, he laid his money on the table and went outside into the evening's blandness, a comfortable ease coming over him as his nerves gradually unwound and his muscles lost their tension. The food and liquid had restored him, and he felt energy returning to his body. The day was dwindling down, the sun just dipping below the western range and the sky beginning to change from blue to orange. Soon twilight would be running across the flats, coating the landscape in a copper-like brilliance.

The blistered earth beneath his feet began to lose its heat, and he strolled along the street, watching giant-toothed shadows climb the scarred eastern bluffs at the same speed as the hidden sun descended below the opposite rim. Once he reached the stable, he got his horse and lashed the sack of supplies behind the cantle. The hosteler was lighting a lantern to hang in his makeshift office. He gave Allard a short glance and said: "Mighty hot day for so early in the year, Frank," and moved off.

Allard swung up and turned from town, increasingly impatient to be underway. He pushed the chestnut at a rapid clip through the increasing shadows, reaching home around nine o'clock. Except for a single light in the bunkhouse the place was wrapped in soft moonlight, and the resonant hum of insects rode the still, tepid air. When he rounded into the yard and dismounted at the corral, Bliss and Rozas rose from the shadows to meet him.

Rozas took charge of his horse, and Allard dropped the burlap bag on the steps. He entered the house to light a lamp, afterwards returning to the porch and taking his usual seat in the rocker. His two hands settled themselves on the steps and smoked in silence. He saw their cigarette ends glow and die in the darkness as they waited.

When his pipe was burning properly, he stretched his legs out, considering at length the things he was leaving. This was the hardest moment, with his ranch and all that it represented spread around him. The smell of sagebrush was comfortable and familiar. By the brightness from a full moon he could see the far-off silver-lined borders of the desert, stretching southward beyond his vision. His thoughts roamed far beyond the porch, and he tried without success to strengthen a hope that, once his undertaking was accomplished, he could resume his former life without change or interruption, but little doubts kept questioning whether he could ride into trouble and ride out again. Another thought was the possibility that this trip was a fool's errand. The manhunt could end with his own destruction. Although Burns's letter had imposed silence on him, he couldn't decide whether or not he should reveal the purpose of his journey to the two men he was entrusting with his ranch. As with Bright he was partially disposed to do so, not entirely convinced that withholding the information was the wisest course in view of the risk he was running. Yet, having already once settled this matter within himself in Bright's office, he pulled his pipe from his mouth, reversed it, and tapped the ashes into the palm of one hand.

"Boys," he said, "I've got to make a ride that may keep me away for some time. Maybe a couple months." He looked through the darkness at Bliss. "You're boss here, Ray, while I'm gone." When neither man spoke up, he went on. "I've arranged for you to pick up your pay on the first of each month from Arthur Davis at the bank. I expect to be back before fall round-up, but, if I'm not and you need to hire a hand or two, see Davis for the extra money."

Rozas, a Mexican with limited knowledge of English, sat expressionless and turned his head to Ray Bliss for guidance, the only *gringo* he knew and trusted. Bliss was a man nearing forty who had been with Allard for four years. Medium-size and wire-tough, with a face browned by the weather and showing the knocks of a hard and active life, he had no soft edges about him. His eyes were never fully opened, giving him a shrewd and watchful look, and Allard really knew very little about the man. He had never spoken of his past or inquired about another's, but he was the best hand with cattle Allard had ever seen. During his tenure he had proved steady and unswerving, and Allard trusted him.

Bliss digested the news for a while, then flicked his cigarette into the darkness, rose, and put his back to the porch. His low voice came out of the shadows. "Frank," he declared, "I work for you and your personal business ain't my affair, but I know you pretty well, and somethin' in that letter was mighty important. Never seen you move this sudden and go off alone. I been out there on the trail by myself, and it gets lonesome. How about takin' me along?"

Allard knew what an effort it was for Bliss to express himself at such length. It was the nearest to genuine concern that the man had ever offered. "Ray," he said, "I trust you more than I trust anyone. But this is something for me to tackle. Think you two can run the outfit without me?"

"The ranch will be here when you get back," Bliss said. He had offered to come along and presumed to say no more. He rolled himself another cigarette, withdrawing into his habitual reserve.

Allard turned to Rozas. "Mateo, throw a pack saddle and this sack of supplies on the bay. I want a rifle boot on my saddle. Find what canteens we got. I want plenty of water. Give Wash all he can drink and a bag of oats, then bring both horses up to the porch."

He reëntered the ranch house where he spent a half hour assembling his outfit. When he emerged, both animals were at the steps. He lashed everything on the pack animal, then made a second trip inside for his Winchester and a final look around. He turned up the wick in the lamp and carried it with him from room to room in a last review of those time-worn articles with which he had lived for so long. He stopped occasionally to contemplate particular objects gathered over the years, each one recalling events once crowded with meaning: the worn leather sofa, the gun rack, the mounted mule deerhead on the wall, and in the living room over the stone fireplace the ancient daguerreotype of his parents, carefully preserved and brought down from the home ranch. It was the last sentimental thing he had done, and now the venerable photograph caught his attention. He approached it, holding the lamp close to memorize each detail, as if he had not seen them all before. It was a strange thing how these accumulated material things no longer heartened him, as they once had, and the depression settling over him left no doubt that the old satisfaction was gone. It was as if, when this last tie to the past was severed, it brought home to him the lonely vacuum toward which he had been headed in his solitary existence.

He stopped in front of a wall mirror and eyed his reflection critically, surprised at how hard his features had become. The fierce anticipation with which he was accustomed to greet each new day had left him now, and he foresaw his future as a barren span of years, without a wife, family, or even a close friend. On the frontier there was always a scarcity of women which had limited his contact with the opposite sex as much as his own chosen lone-wolf way of life. There were few eligible girls in that far-off corner of the state, and he had never exerted special effort in that direction, content to build and expand his ranch to the exclusion of any other pursuit. The loneliest feeling in the world belonged to him now. Reluctantly honest with himself, he knew he had turned sour, like a bad horse.

He set the lamp on the mantle, blew it out, and left by the front door, crossing to the horses. He settled his weight firmly in the dip of the saddle on his mount and sat there for a moment, his head swimming with a thousand small things. Then he gathered the pack horse's lead rope in one hand, lifted his own reins with the other, and sloped away into the night, striking southeasterly toward the desert's broad expanse. Ray Bliss, standing guard at the bunkhouse, threw up an arm in farewell, and, long after Allard disappeared, his motionless figure remained in the doorway, gazing sightlessly across the wasteland, his own thoughts cutting a disturbed track through his mind.

Chapter Three

Allard halted around midnight after two hours of steady travel and made dry camp in a shallow, rock-free coulée. The moon was long set, and the swollen hemisphere of night was a cloudless immensity above him, washed by the ghostly glow of starshine from a million remote pinpoints of reflected light. He was affected, as he always was, by the mystical lure of the desert and the sense of enchantment at the enormity of the universe. The stars offered sufficient light for him to unsaddle and picket the horses. Kneeling and searching the ground with his hands, he located a spot of soft sand, still warm from the day's heat, and dropped his bedroll on it. He scraped out a depression for his hips, folded his coat for a pillow, and stretched out on the blanket with a long sigh.

Protective darkness had awakened all the desert's nocturnal life. Animals and birds were all around him, and he heard the familiar rustlings of furtive little prowlers. Somewhere in the distance a coyote's mournful chant lifted to the great arch of space, and he listened pensively to the lonesome bark.

The mournful call touched him in a strange way; in it he imagined a kinship between himself and another orphaned nomad. His spirits dipped, and he fell into the melancholia that had been eating away at him. When he made an attempt to arouse his brain and contemplate past events, all he saw behind his eyes was a blurred series of shadowy ghosts. He reached for his blanket, wrapped it around him, and made one more half-hearted effort to estimate their meaning; but weariness finally overtook him, and they dissolved into a great nothingness, and he slept.

It was still dark when he arose. He boiled his coffee, fried his bacon, and was on his way. Both horses were fresh, and in the cool predawn grayness he covered a substantial distance before a corona, containing every color in the spectrum, developed over the mountains. Suddenly the sun popped into view to fling its lustrous heat on the land, and, to spare the animals, he immediately adjusted his rate of travel to a more leisurely pace. His initial progress took him steadily southward and eastward in a fast-warming atmosphere, and occasionally, in the far distance, he spotted a band of wild horses or caught the sudden blur of a coyote in pursuit of a rabbit. In the glow of late afternoon a flock of nesting ravens swooped and dove above his head. To break the tedium of long hours in the saddle, he whistled between his teeth or smoked his pipe until it grew rank and tasteless between his lips. At times he played his harmonica and sang snatches of long-remembered songs. He talked to the horses, and sometimes spoke aloud to himself, as if conversing with someone a dozen feet away. When he realized he was carrying on both ends of a conversation, he wondered with wry amusement if senility were overtaking him.

The glare of pure desolation stretched around him from horizon to horizon, a desert ocean of low clumps and yellowing grasses, running outward into the distance. He swelled his lungs full of the spiced air in an atmosphere so pure and clear that objects a day's journey away seemed far closer. To Allard, the infinite abundance of untainted air to breathe was a necessity he could not do without. This was the way people were meant to live, for man was created to enjoy the luxury of uncluttered space.

As the days rolled by, one much like another, he moved steadily down the broad reaches of an austere wasteland, palisaded by a continuous succession of copper-colored, north-south mountain ranges. They rose suddenly from the desert floor, their crenelated, washboard surfaces sometimes distinctly etched, at other times rendered indefinable by the oscillating screen of desert haze. In the distance ahead he could distinguish the dim outline of white peaks.

The high desert he traversed was a flatland frosted with gleaming stretches of alkali salts and dry lakes across which, at his approach, the speeding shapes of antelope fled. One day he came to a section where weather-worn cinder cones and isolated monadnocks pocked the sand like giant black anthills, formless hummocks of ash thrusting their tips through the soil, single remnants of some ancient volcanic past. Everywhere spring was in full profusion, and the silvery sheen of gray-green sagebrush stained the landscape. An occasional creosote bush or the crimson cluster of Indian paintbrush bloomed proudly.

His systematic progress now began to carry him through increasingly unfamiliar territory, but he had a natural orientation for the country and never doubted his general direction. On the tenth day the landscape altered in a more dramatic fashion. Evidence of nature's relentless erosion appeared in the form of steeper gulches, no longer bone dry but with little side streams flowing at the bottom of flower-strewn cañons, sharply gouged from the earth's crust. Some of these chasms he skirted to more passable ground, riding alongside until they wandered off on a different heading. Others, lying precisely crosswise in his route, he was forced to traverse head-on, breaking new trails down precipitous inclines strewn with schist, then ascending the next slope at a snail-like pace, both time-consuming and hazardous work for the horses. In this varied and little-known region each day introduced new vistas. He rode beside impressive sandstone mesas with colored layers of cream and red dancing through a mirage of heat waves and skirted solitary buttes, towering hundreds of feet above him. Stipa grass grew profusely, and scattered piñon pines stood as advance sentinels to the brooding mountains, no longer indistinct purple outlines in the distance but looming closely ahead.

Early on a morning two days later he entered the mouth of a cañon and found himself in a shadowy forest of virgin aspen and Douglas fir. A fine-edged breath of sweet wind scoured out of the cañon and strengthened against him, speaking of a richer, damper climate beyond. During his journey he had encountered no living soul except one morning, three days prior, when he happened into a desert wash and came upon a prospector, breaking early camp. The miner, who was heading in the opposite direction, had swapped talk, commented on the weather, and given Allard general directions to Mountain Pass. He followed those instructions now, keeping a distant pinnacle between his pony's ears, striking ever higher into the mountains.

Sunset caught him deep in the recesses, and he soon found there was no lingering desert twilight here, for night hovered just behind the next ridge. True dusk lasted only a few minutes, and darkness, as always in these mountains, came with remarkable speed to drop its black curtain over the landscape like the sudden slamming of a cellar door. One moment he could distinguish an object at two hundred yards; moments later the same object was a vague shape at a distance of twenty feet. It contributed to an odd uneasiness about this alien country and pushed a thready ruffling along his nerves. That night he gathered an extra armful of twisted manzanita limbs and threw them into his campfire, building it bigger than usual close to a long-fallen tree. He ate his supper with his back against the trunk, using it to reflect the fire's heat.

The following day he resumed his travel toward the grandly colored peak that vanished when he dipped into a hollow and reappeared as he gained higher ground. Around mid-morning he came across the crusted furrows of an old wagon trail, the vagrant tracks overgrown with weeds, and he followed the casual road until it petered out at the base of a bluff. The steep slope, facing him, showed no break in its sheer wall, so he shortened the lead rope to the pack horse and tackled the climb in a pattern of switchbacks, traversing back and forth in criss-cross fashion, making sharp turns on either side before reversing himself. In this time-consuming manner he beat his way up and over the crown, descending the far side to a shallow creek which he crossed, noting, as he did so, the cold temperature of the white-laced water.

On the riverbank he stopped for lunch and rested the horses. Then he resumed his climb to a second and higher ridge, now very close to the naked peak that towered like a great beacon. When he reached the crown of the ridge, he was greeted by a flower-fringed alpine meadow whose lush mantle of green was a splash of lighter green against the deeper emerald hue of the forest. From this vantage point he commanded a sweeping panorama of the broken tangle of puckered mountains, pushing eastward to the eventual summit of the range. Behind him, looking westward, the mountains sloped down and back to the flat openness of the Nevada desert. When he stood up in his stirrups for a better view of the adjacent cañon, his exploring eyes spotted the irregular scatter of rooftops below him, cramped between two low-lying hills. Aware of no other settlement in the area, he believed he had at last reached Mountain Pass.

It was nearing four o'clock, and the sun was sinking steadily toward the western rim, its light beginning to slant at a more acute angle across the rugged geography of this diverse land. During daylight's final hours every fissure and gorge turned into a sea of violet haze, shrouding the depths and converting the raised spires into spectacular beacons of iridescent light. In spite of his preference for the desert, Allard was struck by the majestic beauty of this wild country. It raised a challenge to him and freshened his anticipation for what lay ahead. With two weeks of hard travel behind him his destination was finally within reach, and the first link of his chain had been forged.

Burns had instructed him to wait until dark before approaching the cabin. Therefore, with a little time on his hands, he awarded himself the luxury of a temporary respite. Across the meadow a mountain spring bubbled from the earth, giving birth to a little creek that wandered lazily over the lea. He dismounted to let the horses drink, and, while they muzzled into a clear pool, he walked upstream, removed his hat, and stretched belly-flat beside the water. It was sweet and cold on his tongue, lacking the brackish taste of the desert. He drank until he was satisfied and then drank again, rinsing each mouthful around in his cheeks before swallowing. Remembering what the horses had been through, he pulled the pack saddle from the bay, unsaddled the chestnut, and stripped off the harness. He drove two picket pins in a patch of graze and hobbled the animals with extra rope. A full two hours remained until nightfall, and he unrolled his blanket beneath a fir, stretched full-length on it, and let his eyelids fall.

The dry cropping of the ponies as they browsed the meadow woke him, and he appreciated that he had dozed. He was in no hurry and lay, watching the last of daylight fade. High above his head the tops of the trees slowly lost their definition against the sky, melting into the fast-darkening heavens. The sonorous scrape of crickets rose from the grass in familiar harmony, and a chorus of frogs swelled along the creek. The unfailing wind, sweeping down from the peaks, quickened and grew suddenly colder, wiping away the day's warmth.

He rose to bridle and saddle the horses, caught up his blankets, and began his descent into the valley, following a single, down-sloping ridge until it forked into several lesser spines, one of which he blindly chose, steadily losing elevation. A chasm, felt rather than seen, deepened on his left, and now and then he caught a glimpse of faint lights on the cañon floor. He hugged the contour of the hogback which ran in a long slant toward the winking pinpoints that flashed and died and reappeared.

A narrow wildlife path emerged from nowhere, crossed the ridge, and headed directly downhill. He dipped into it and followed as it contoured around a timbered prominence and ran all the way to the cañon's floor. He found himself at the edge of a well-used road with the scattered lights of Mountain Pass directly ahead and drew in to consider the town. Shielded in the dark cover provided by the giant conifers, he was able to identify the pale emptiness of the main street, running northward and bisecting the town. He knew that his present location was on the south side of town, and Burns's note had specified his cabin to be some three miles distant, off the north trail. He made a right turn and rode a wide loop to skirt the village, keeping in the timber and returning beyond the town to his original northward course, paralleling a road on his left, running in the same direction.

There was no trail to follow in the opaque timber, and, appreciating that the sharp ears and keen eyes of his horse were better than his own in penetrating the darkness, he gave the animal its head to pick a way among the trees, supplying only gentle guidance ever northward. On the spongy carpet of needles the muffled hoof falls raised only hushed echoes, and suddenly Wash's ears flew forward as a deer erupted in their path with a rush of sound and went crashing away through the brush.

Allard's meandering detour took him through stands of young fir trees where the cloying musk of balsam was strong in an atmosphere turned frigid. The sharp chill bit through his shirt, prompting him to dismount and paw through his gear until he found his heavy coat. He shouldered into it and muttered under his breath: "Colder here in summer than winter back home."

He remounted and resumed his patient

march, keeping fifty yards from the north trail, constantly listening for whatever message the wind might bring. On two occasions his ears picked up the hard run of horses, coming along the trail, and each time he pulled up in the liquid shadows and waited silently until the riders swept past, not proceeding until the last echoes of their traveling died in the night.

The faintly acrid taste of woodsmoke in his throat provided the first hint of habitation somewhere ahead. The sensation grew stronger as he progressed, and suddenly the watery flicker of a light winked ahead of him, dancing and vanishing behind the trees. He dismounted and walked between the horses, leading them to the edge of a small meadow. In the center of the open space the sagged image of a shed emerged from the ground as a darker smear, and on the opposite side he saw the faint hulk of a cabin against the trees. The glow he had noticed came from vague slivers of light escaping around a single shuttered window. At the margin of the clearing he stopped and surveyed the cabin, standing motionless for a full five minutes, his ears alert to the night. He could see nothing moving and heard no sounds save the rasp of his own breathing and that of the horses and the sigh of the steady wind through pine boughs. Satisfied, he carefully advanced into the open, drifting closer to the cabin until he could identify the tiered rows of cordwood racked against the outer walls. When he saw the wood, he knew this was Burns's cabin.

Chapter Four

Allard veered off across the little field and led the animals to the shed, coming against a back-sloping wall without an opening. He hooked his way around a corner, finding there an entrance with a half open door sagging resignedly on one leather hinge. He shoved the door fully open and pulled the horses into the Stygian interior, conscious at once of the fetid stench of horseflesh and manure. He probed with fingertips across a rough partition and slid into a stall where unexpectedly his hand fell on the rump of a horse. The startled beast threw a whistling blast out of its nostrils, stamped the ground, and moved away to the far wall where it stopped and grew silent. Allard backed out and changed direction, groping his way along until he found an empty stall where the rank smell of the shed was sweetened with the odor of fresh hay, guiding him to a bin. He sightlessly explored further, located a pitchfork, and filled the feed boxes, unsaddling both animals.

When he was finished, he worked his way back to the entrance and went outside, cautiously crossing to the silent cabin. Although at dusk from atop the ridge he had watched the waning moon in its last quarter throw off its faint sliver of light, here on the cañon floor a coagulated mist clung to the soil. Unable to see he took careful, precise steps until he reached the porch. He mounted the steps, making no special effort for silence, and rapped smartly on the door, receiving no response. He knocked a second time with more force, thumping his knuckles roundly on the wood and calling out: "Hello, the cabin!"

A man's voice, guarded and wary, muffled by the closed door, issued from within. "Who is it?"

"I'm from Nevada," he announced. "Name's Frank Allard. Got a letter from you in my pocket."

The sound of a bolt being drawn back scratched along the door's inner side and the same voice, more positive than before, said: "It's unlocked. Lift the latch and push."

When Allard laid his shoulder against the door and shoved it inward, the protesting hinges squealed. He stepped over the threshold into a small, strongly scented room. The brightness temporarily blinded his night-tuned eyes, and, when his vision cleared, he found himself facing a high four-poster bed. It was occupied by an older man who lay recumbent under a mound of carelessly thrown blankets, his back braced by a bank of pillows against the headboard. A cast-iron stove, two chairs, a bureau, and a table alongside the bed completed the sparse furnishings. To serve as a temporary latch-string some fishing line had been rigged from one bedpost across the room to a hole in the wooden bolt, itself fastened to the door's inside surface. The bolt could be slid sideways from the bed by pulling on the line; this had made the scraping noise Allard had heard from the porch. The man's knees were drawn up tent-like under his bedclothes and balanced between them, held steady by one hand, was a large revolver aimed squarely at Allard's midsection.

By the subdued half light from a bedside lamp he could see that the man's cheeks were drawn sockets, hollowed to the point of emaciation. His skin had a gray coloring, and the puckered flesh on his face and neck hung in loose folds. He was extremely thin, his white hair uncut and his abundant beard and mustache untrimmed. He had recently made some attempt to shave for part of one jowl was scraped clean. A rip in the neck of his nightshirt revealed a discolored bandage binding one shoulder and encasing the upper half of his body. His big-boned wrists were stringy and thin, and, although he gripped the gun in one hand, the pistol's barrel never wavered, and behind it the flinty blue eyes in their recessed pouches scrutinized Allard with suspicion.

The cabin was in monumental disorder. Parts of harness and a saddle gathered dust in one corner, a heap of soiled laundry perfumed the air in another, and a stack of encrusted dishes lay in a pile on the bedside table. Everything essential to the old man's immediate needs had been dragged next to the bed, within arm's reach. Two doorways in the opposite wall apparently led to a spare room and a kitchen, but both were black and silent, and it was obvious that he was alone.

The man on the bed challenged him with a question. "Who did you say you was?"

"Name's Frank Allard. You Sheriff Burns?"

The effect his words had on the older man was noticeable. Above the sweep of his mustache some of the strain faded from his face, and his tautly held shoulders settled lower against the cushions. "Let's see the letter," he grunted. "Throw it down on the blanket."

Allard opened his coat and pulled out the envelope, sailing it over to the bed. The man glanced sideways, recognized it, and then laid the revolver beside him on the bed and scrubbed one hand across his whiskered cheeks in a sudden gesture of weariness. "Got to take a chance on you," he declared. "Guess you're the right feller. You match Tom's description, and that's my letter. Never knew if it reached you or not. I been a mite jumpy since the shootin'."

"I left the same day it arrived," said Allard. "Took me two weeks to get here." He approached the bed and took Burns's proffered hand. There was no strength in the old man's clasp. Burns mustn't have been eating regularly and was too enfeebled to take proper care of himself. "When's the last time you had a good supper?" Allard asked.

"Been some time," admitted Burns. "Don't feel much like cookin'."

"I could stand a square meal myself." Allard waggled a suggestive thumb at the dark doorways. "If you've got grub in there, I'll rustle up a feed for both of us before we palaver."

"Ah." Burns managed a faint smile. "That would hit the spot." He leveled a finger at the nearest doorway. "That's my kitchen. Coffee and spuds in the cupboard, bacon in the cooler. Henry Tinker sends supplies out from town every week, but this damn' shoulder keeps me from doin' anything with my left hand. I ain't got any close neighbors." What was left of his vitality bled away, but he was still troubled by another thought that caused him to raise off his pillows. "Anybody see you come in?"

"Don't think so. It's black as coal outside, and I stayed off any trails. My horse and pack animal are in your shed."

Burns nodded and lay back, now apparently satisfied. Allard shucked out of his coat and hung it on a bedpost, unbuckled his gun belt and draped it over the coat. He took up the lamp and ducked through the first doorway into a small kitchen, finding there a blackened cook stove with nickel trimmings, a table, two chairs, and a chopping block. A row of packing boxes were nailed up on one side of the room for cupboards, and next to the back door leading outside a cooler had been cut through the wall.

The little space was rancid with the sour odor of tainted food and old grease. Allard unlatched the rear door, pushed it open, and carried the lamp outside, there coming upon a covered well with a hand pump and bucket alongside. He removed his shirt and washed in cold water, shook the dust from his shirt, and put it back on. He half filled the bucket and selected an armload of pine chunks, carrying them inside. He kindled a fire in the stove, put on a pot of coffee, and heated enough water in a tin basin to scrub an accumulation of unwashed pots and pans. He foraged in the cooler, threw out some spoiled vegetables and a wheel of moldy cheese. He located the side of bacon and several potatoes which he peeled and sliced. He put everything on the stove, and, while it heated, he lit a second lamp, returning with it to the other room where he cleared off and set the bedside table.

The sheriff had been dozing, but he opened his eyes and silently watched with an elderly man's critical eye. When the coffee was ready, Allard carried a cup to the bed where Burns accepted it, parted his mustache, and greedily swallowed a hot mouthful through his whiskers. He smacked his lips, blew on the liquid, and then finished the contents, his spirits climbing immediately.

"Feel better already," he announced, wiping the ends of his mustache. "Mighty fortunate you showed up, otherwise I might have skipped dinner."

He kept shifting around on the mattress, twisting his hips and pulling at the quilts, each movement evoking obvious pain. He inched his way over to the side of the bed, picked up his knife and fork, and was ready to eat when Allard emerged from the kitchen to lay his meal before him. The latter pulled up a chair, sat down opposite, and the two men, both obviously hungry, ate without conversation. Between mouthfuls Burns continued to study his visitor with a growing interest. Signs of Allard's hard travel were evident on his person. He had washed his face and hands, but his thickly matted hair and his eyebrows were floured with travel dust. Two weeks' growth of whiskers darkened his angular cheeks, and above one eye an earlier scar traced its irregular line toward his ear. The sheriff considered himself a good judge of men and concluded that Allard was equipped with a combination of characteristics especially suited for this kind of rough business.

After completing his meal and drinking a second cup of coffee, Burns repositioned himself on the bed. He sat upright, rubbing a back muscle that had been crushed against the headboard, and mounded his pillows behind him. The food had returned a flush of color to his cheeks, and a trace of his spirit returned. In the meantime Allard cleaned off the table and took the dishes into the kitchen. When he reëntered the room, Burns looked up and grumbled irritably: "Confounded bed. Can't git comfortable no matter which way I turn." He waved one arm at the chair. "Sit down and tell me about you and Tom. Grew up in Nevada together, didn't you?"

From a pocket of his coat Allard fished out his pipe and a pouch of tobacco which he proffered to Burns. "You smoke a pipe? Try this Kentucky Burley."

Burns shook his head. "Pipes are too damn' hard to keep lit," he said. "Always runnin' out of matches."

Allard got his pipe burning and leaned backward as far as the upright chair would permit. He pitched his tobacco pouch on the table and drew long on the pipestem, exhaling a mouthful of smoke that floated over the bed and seeped into Burns's nostrils. The tempting fragrance prompted the sheriff to drag himself within reach of the table and take a half-smoked, half-chewed cigar from an ashtray. He stuck it in one corner of his mouth and groped unsuccessfully among his blankets for a match. Allard produced one, scraped it alight, and stretched forward, holding the flame steady for Burns who puffed vigorously, turning the cigar slowly until the tip glowed redly. He rolled the cheroot around between his lips, a broad peace wreathing his face. Then he pulled it aside and resettled himself against the bank of pillows with a grunt of satisfaction.

"Go ahead," he said, bluntly. "I'm listenin'."

Allard opened his mouth and started to speak, but his first words were interrupted by a fit of dry coughing from Burns. The spasms wracked his thin frame, and, when they ceased, he wiped his mouth with the back of his hand and crumpled loosely on the pillows. He experienced some trouble regaining his wind but waggled his fingers in an impatient gesture for Allard to begin.

He did so, scratching his memory for facts long past and took sufficient time to summarize for Burns his long association with Tom Yeager, from their boyhood beginnings in the foothills of the Ruby Mountains up to the day Yeager left Nevada. While he spoke, a wilder wind whipped up outside and seemed to tear at the cabin walls. Somewhere on the roof a loose board began to vibrate, raising a banging racket. He raised his hand and listened carefully, establishing the source of the noise. Believing nothing was unusual, thereafter he followed Allard's narration without further interruption.

When Allard was finished, Burns merely grunted and commented dryly: "That was a lonesome stretch of country to grow up in." He lay, silently chewing on his cigar, and then cast a brief glance at his visitor. "Imagine you both been in a fracas or two."

Allard nodded. "We had a few good scraps, when we were younger. Saloon scuffles, nothing serious."

Burns's face shown whitely against his pillows. He raised his eyebrows, gave Allard a quizzical look, and asked a curious question. "Ever kill a man?"

"No," said Allard.

"Ever been in a gun fight?"

"Never have," admitted Allard. "A couple of times in Elko we did a little shootin' just to make noise, but nobody got hurt."

He had the patient attention of a man long accustomed to his own company but was increasingly irritated by Burns's persistent questions. He was growing tired of talking and displayed a little of his quick temper by a terse statement of his own. "I've said enough. Now it's your turn. Tell me what happened to Tom."

Burns cleared his throat, and his eyes clouded over as he recalled the events on that night. The tragedy had marked him, leaving its permanent scar, and Allard saw a profound sadness come over him, the breakage beginning to show on his face. When he finally spoke, it was in a wistful, dreary voice.

"I liked that boy," he muttered, "a hell of a lot. He was like my own son. I was groomin' him for my job. What happened punched a big hole in my life, and I feel kinda responsible."

His statement drew an immediate glance of censure from Allard, and Burns felt the weight of a quick, penetrating stare. He tried to find a better way of saying what he felt so deeply, but speech came slowly and was full of dark self-reproach.

"That night we were sittin' in my office. It was after dark, and the street was quiet, not much of a crowd in town. I was worried the kid might be a target for a gang of hardcases and had talked him into leavin' the territory for a spell. The bushwhacker was hiding outside in the alley. He shot through the window and killed Tom with one bullet. The boy never had a chance. The second slug got me here in my shoulder. A couple of inches lower and I'd be dead too." He rubbed his jaw with a thin, white hand and chewed glumly on what remained of his cigar. "With me laid up, there was nobody to run down the killer, and it'll be some time before I get another deputy. Law enforcement is spread thin in these parts, and the trail's gettin' cold. That's why I wrote to you." Something deeper was eating away at him, and his lusterless eyes narrowed. He shook his head morosely. "I been thinkin' about that, too."

Before he could enlarge on the statement, Allard interrupted him harshly, his words intolerant and forceful. "I left a damn' good ranch in Nevada and came here for only one reason. To get the ambusher that killed Tom. Nothing else interests me. You know who did it?"

"Yeah," said Burns, looking up at him apprehensively. "I'm sure it was one of three men."

"Three men? I understood from your letter that you knew who fired the shots."

His hard glance carried such intensity that Burns felt its heaviness and hastened to elaborate. He wearily held up a hand and said: "Hold on, my boy. Let me tell you about this territory, then you judge for yourself. Winona Basin is due east of here, a natural bowl plumb in the center of the mountains, like a single egg in the middle of a nest. The Wah-Wahs ain't a big range, pretty high in spots but not very wide. The only people livin' there are the Lenifees, an old Tennessee family that wagoned west some years ago, along with a collection of kinfolk and friends. They're different folks who keep to themselves and over the years never caused me trouble. All that changed recently when four gunslingers showed up and settled in. They brought bad reputations with them, and one is evidently a distant cousin of old Ben Lenifee. Ben's the head of the family. He founded the valley community and rules it with an iron hand.

"With this distant cousin was Jack Slade. He was wanted for murder and bank robbery in Texas. I had a warrant for him, but it ain't all that simple to ride into Winona Basin and ride back out again. Tom and I held the warrant and waited for Slade to get thirsty and come into town. We knew he would because Ben disapproves of alcohol in all forms. He's strong on religion and keeps booze out of the basin, but this gang drinks heavy and don't give a damn for Ben and his rules."

Allard asked: "Are these folks Mormons?"

"Naw," said Burns, "the Lenifees ain't Mormons. They're from Tennessee hill country with old clan laws stricter than the

Mormons. They keep with their own kind, marry each other, and have big families. Unless you're a blood relation or a damn' close friend, you ain't welcome in the basin." The two men traded glances in the ensuing silence, and Burns continued. "Winona Basin is a mountain fortress, protected by cliffs five-hundred feet straight up. There's only two ways in and out, one from the eastern side of the Wah-Wahs and one from here. They watch those roads. If we tried to force our way in, everybody up there would grab their rifles and fight like hell. Some innocent folks would get shot, maybe women or kids. It made more sense to wait for Slade to come out."

Prolonged speech continued to aggravate the sheriff's lungs. He coughed again, wincing with the pain of each shuddering convulsion. He dragged over a towel and daubed at his eyes, then transferred his weight from one hip to the other, altering his position on the mattress. Allard could tell by his drawn face that the gunshot wound was punishing him hard. He went into the kitchen, returning with a cup of water, and listened to the sucking sound of the sheriff's lips on the rim. When he had drained the contents, Burns reached over, placed the cup on the table, and went on with his story.

"One night Slade came to town for whiskey, jes' like Tom and me figgered, had a large night, and wound up drunk in the street. He was in no shape to put up a fight, and Tom hauled him to jail without a shot bein' fired. But now," — he tapped his chest for emphasis — "I bleed a little right here every time I think about it and wish to God I had arrested Slade myself." He made a weary gesture with his arm, shivered, and drew the comforter up to his chin. He looked at Allard. "You cold?"

Allard shook his head but got up and went outside through the kitchen, reappearing with an armload of wood. He dumped it on the floor next to the stove, selected two chunks, and thrust them into the firebox, stoking up the coals with a poker.

"East wind always has a nip in it," lamented Burns. "But this year's worse than usual. We're too close to the summit."

Allard returned to his chair, waiting for Burns who kept pushing himself around on the bed and finally got back to his tale. "When Ben Lenifee and his family left Tennessee, they headed west on the Oregon Trail with a wagon train and a flock of relatives and a few friends. They went through Fort Laramie and South Pass and got as far as Fort Bridger where Ben's wife came down with cholera and died. When that happened, the fire went out of the old boy, and he changed plans. She wanted to travel to the West Coast and settle in Oregon or California, but, after she was gone, Ben and his bunch dropped out of the train at Bridger and headed south. They got this far and turned across the mountains where they stumbled into the basin by accident. Wasn't shown on any map and didn't even have a name. Ben stopped right there and named it after his wife. It's been called Winona Basin ever since. I been in there only a couple of times, and my memory is a little rusty, but it's a damned pretty valley. In the last five years more of the Lenifees' kinfolk have joined 'em until there's mebbe a hundred or more people livin' there."

The room was warming up, and some of Burns's color had returned. A fresher expression played across his cheeks. He threw off the top blanket and spoke in a lighter tone. "You ain't a bad nurse. Want the job full time?"

"Not in my line," Allard said, pointedly rejecting further wandering from the subject. "Keep on with what you were sayin'."

"I'm gettin' there," growled Burns. "We kept Slade in Mountain Pass overnight. Our jail ain't good for much except holdin' drunks. Slade's friends figgered to bust him out and probably could have, but we moved too fast. A couple deputies from the marshal's office in Saint George happened to be in town, and they took him back with 'em the next mornin'."

"Slade still in jail there?"

Burns shook his head. "No, he ain't. The jury brought in a guilty verdict, and they stretched his neck. Two days later somebody shot Tom and me."

"You sure it was one of Slade's three partners?"

"I'm dead certain. One of them pulled that trigger. It happened right after Slade was strung up, and nobody else had reason. My mistake was sendin' Tom out with the murder warrant, but in Slade's condition that was the easy part, and it never occurred to me they'd lay for him. What's more, the town was quiet that night, and nobody saw nothin'. No witnesses at all."

Allard's features had frozen into a hard mask, and he gave Burns a tough look, full of reproach. "Who are these three *hombres?*"

"Well," replied Burns, holding up three fingers and touching them individually, "there's Emmett Hanks, Pinto Daly, and this shirt-tail relation, Cat Lenifee. He was their ticket into the basin, but he's nobody you'd want to know. He's originally from Tennessee and fought in the Confederate army. That's where he met up with the Allison brothers." He looked at Allard keenly. "Ever hear of them?" Allard shook his head, and Burns went on. "Any lawman can tell you about those two, especially Clay. He's the coldest killer you'll ever meet, bloodthirsty and mean as a snake when he's drunk, which is most of the time. Earned himself quite a reputation with his gun. Last I heard, he's somewhere in Texas, and I hope to hell he stays there. There's a few stories about Clay Allison. I'll tell you one that happened a couple years ago when he was travelin' with Cat Lenifee in New Mexico. Allison killed a man named Charlie Kennedy in Confax County. After Kennedy was dead, Allison cut his head off, impaled it on a pole, and rode with it into Henri Lambert's saloon in Cimarron where they all got drunk. How's that for fun?" He looked at Allard with a distasteful expression and kept going. "That ain't all I know. Not long ago he got some more kicks by ropin' a fella named Cruz Vega and draggin' him to death. If Cat Lenifee is anything like him, then he's an alcoholic killer capable of anything."

Allard listened, and his composure never changed, but an inner revulsion crawled up through him. "How far is Winona Basin from here?"

"Two hours by road," said Burns, "due east as the crow flies. The mountain ranges hereabouts run north-south and so do the Wah-Wahs. They're two hundred miles long and fifty miles across with this natural basin in the middle. I know it ain't easy to figger, but it's a different world in that place. With a guard on each gateway nobody rides in or out that Ben don't know about. He let Cat and the others move in, but that's gone sour, and he don't know how to get rid of 'em."

Allard's pipe was cold between his lips. He tamped the dead embers with a fingertip and scraped a match along his pant leg, cupping the flame over the bowl. A network of fine, short wrinkles furrowed the skin near his eyes, and he showed Burns a bleak glance. "How many Lenifees are there?"

"Besides Cat only three," said Burns. "Ben and his two kids, a son, Chester, and a daughter, Joyce. The rest are distant relations with different last names. The only time we see anything of the Lenifees is when the daughter comes to town for supplies. She's a fine-lookin' gal, spunky as hell and dead loyal to her family. I don't think she knew anything about this dirty business."

"I came a long way to find the drygulcher that shot Tom Yeager," Allard said shortly. "How do you propose I get into the basin?"

"I been doin' some thinkin' about that. I made a mistake, sending Tom out for Slade, because it set him up, and I don't want to make another. I can see you're a rough cob, but you ain't a gunfighter. You never killed anybody, and you'll be up against three professionals who have. The odds are bad, and I don't need anything else on my conscience. I wish to hell I never wrote that letter, but I wasn't thinkin' clear." He scowled down at his hands, an old fighter whose spirit refused to accept his infirmity and whose combative instincts were not entirely quenched, but his watery eyes, grown weary and apprehensive, rose to meet Allard's and stayed there, the anxiety in them plain. "Fork your bronc' and go back to Nevada."

"I guess you don't know me very well," Allard replied bluntly. "I've come too far to quit. One way or another I'm going in there."

"Wish you wouldn't," Burns lamented with an old man's pessimism. "I didn't stop to consider what you'd be up against when I asked for your help."

Allard yawned and stretched his arms, paying no attention to this last remark. "I could use a couple hours' sleep, and pull out of here around daylight. Before I go, I'll cook up something for you."

"Don't bother. Fresh grub is due out tomorrow. I'll be all right." He had another recommendation to put forth that he knew Allard wouldn't like and was uncertain how to broach it. But it was too strong to suppress, and he sat up in the bed. "Hate to have you do more ridin', after comin' so far, but there's only two roads into the basin. The shortest way runs straight from Mountain Pass to the west entrance, but you can't go that way. If somebody found out you was here in town, they might connect you with me."

"You got a better idea?"

"It is my belief that the best chance to talk your way in for a night or two might be as a traveler comin' from the east that got lost in the Wah-Wahs. You could be on your way to California. Ben ain't got much hospitality when it comes to strangers, but, if you blunder in cold, they might take pity and put you up. Never know about those people. I can't think of any other way. It will be a tough ride over the divide, but you've come this far without bein' seen, and you better do it right. Take grub from here for five or six days and leave your pack horse in the shed. The Mexican boy that takes care of my cayuse won't ask any questions."

He was faced with the dismal prospect of another week in the saddle, but Allard, by responding to Burns's letter, had placed himself in the sheriff's hands, and it seemed unwise to second-guess him at this point. He buried his aggravation with difficulty and gave a resigned shrug.

Burns rested on his mounded pillows, totally devitalized from the emotional strain. "Frank," he said gravely, "one last thing. If I deputized you, it might offer protection in some situations. I considered doin' that. But more likely a star would cramp your action. I can't put a halter on you when you're headin' into trouble. Go at it your own way. My life was good until this happened, and, before I cash out, I want to see Tom's murderer lyin' dead or danglin' at the end of a rope. Go get him any way you can. You got my blessin'."

With that he ceased speaking, rolled over, and turned his face to the wall. Allard went into the kitchen where he scraped together enough provisions for another week's ride. He carved some steaks from a haunch of cold beef, hard-boiled a dozen eggs, and trimmed the mold from a wedge of cheese. At the back of a shelf he saw a real prize in two forgotten cans of tomatoes. He took one, together with a loaf of stale bread, and rolled everything into his pack. Burns had dozed off, so Allard lowered the wick and spread a blanket on the floor of the adjoining room. The planks were hard and made a poor bed, but, when he stretched out full-length and let his muscles go loose, fatigue washed over him like a giant wave, and he slept.

Chapter Five

The unyielding floor awakened Allard while the windows still showed darkness, and he hauled himself painfully to his feet. There was no warmth in the room. He was stiff and sore in every joint, and the chill from the cold boards had cramped his muscles. He lit a lamp and carried it into the other room where Burns was snoring loudly. His first inclination was to leave the sheriff undisturbed, but something persuaded him to have a final word. When Allard shook him by the shoulder, Burns strangled on his snoring and sat up. Groggy from sleep, he groped for Allard's hand and held it between his thin, white fingers. He stared up from the bed, his eyes wide open, his pupils large.

"You're walkin' into danger, son," he whispered in a thin, reedy voice. "I wish I could go with you."

Allard pressed his hand, dropped it, and gathered up his gear. He wheeled from the room and crossed at once to the shed. The predawn hush of a dull and lowering morning, frigid and misty, hung around him. The moon had paled, and a faint grayness in the eastern sky offered ineffectual help within the unlighted shed. He saddled the chestnut purely by touch. He tied his bedroll to the cantle strings, forked hay into the bins for the bay and for Burns's animal, and left two full water buckets in their stalls. Then he led his horse from the lean-to and swung aboard, heading in a northeasterly direction through the dismal, weeping conifers.

Allard was in a depressed frame of mind, soured by the gloomy weather and the dreary prospects of more tiresome days in the saddle. His thoughts returned to the cabin and dwelt long on the sheriff's last words of warning. If the older man was right, his prospects for success held small promise. The search for Yeager's killer had widened from a single man to any one of three, and he wore no star to protect himself if he ran into trouble.

To reach the eastern passage into Winona Basin, Allard had to describe a great half circle, crossing the spine of the Wah-Wahs from west to east. The clinging ground fog eventually lifted, and a bright sunshine slanted out of the eastern sky, bringing into light a massive network of mountains whose farthest peaks were lost in the smudge of distance. His journey took him through territory where there were few footprints and no marked trails, his first days entirely spent climbing through evergreen stands of pine and fir.

When he sometimes encountered sets of tracks, worn bare by wildlife, he followed them until they played out against a shattered cliff or at the rim of a severely cut cañon. At such times he would alter his course to one side or the other, breaking trail through rock-choked gullies where bursts of wildflowers bloomed on the river banks. He crossed suitable fords where whitely frothed water scoured over polished stones, thereafter resuming his ascent over inhospitable ground.

His climbing eventually lifted him above the timberline, and one clear morning he achieved the crest of the divide from where he had his first view of the Wah-Wahs' eastern side, a formidable expanse of rolling country solidly covered with pines that unfurled beyond his vision in a labyrinth of timbered ridges and cañons. The air at the top was thin, and he wasted no time there, turning downgrade into an area where ancient pressures had stacked the upthrust rocks in vertical layers. The earth here was a devil's landscape of tortuous stone ridges and scored gullies, ravined by nature's relentless erosion and covered with a jagged undercrop against which the horse's hoofs struck sharply. When he dropped back into the timberline, he found himself in a zone where there had once been a violent storm. Capsized trees lay askew, piled across one another in a maze of rotting trunks, forcing him to pick his way carefully between scrub and rock and fallen branches.

He had only Burns's broad directions to keep him properly headed, but he used the sun's orbit as his compass, moving unerringly eastward and steadily losing elevation. As each afternoon wound down, the fast-closing angle of the setting sun draped the landscape in glorious colors, a sequence of contrasts that ignited both sky and rock, transforming each lordly crag into a glowing pinnacle. When its fireball finally vanished behind the western rim, twilight's first violet eddies rushed forth like an incoming tide to swallow every peak within view. As soon as the sun disappeared, the temperature in this rarefied atmosphere plunged dramatically, and Allard made camp early, banking his fires with sufficient wood to sustain a bed of coals until dawn. When supper was finished, he lay in his blankets, watching the world fade into total darkness, observing the slow creep of the moon's wafer-thin sickle inch along its trajectory, a desert-bred man removed from his spacious freedom of the open plain and feeling strangely out of place.

The thready feeling that tightened his nerves he attributed to his craving for a return to familiar soil, but for him today's sunsets were not the same as yesterday's and would never be again, nor was he the same man he had been before receiving Burns's letter. Some essential element was missing, and each time he tried to reach into his history and recapture the old smells and tastes, none was there. Progress through the rough country was agonizingly slow, but it afforded him ample time to review his undertaking in light of what he had learned from Amos Burns. Tom Yeager's remembrance bound him forever, and now the dying faith of an old man also rode on his shoulders, and then he understood something else about himself. The quick, combative pride that dictated his actions also ruled his mind and governed his decisions, whether they were ill-considered or not. His prompt election to heed Burns's letter had been deliberately made, but now, when his thoughts ran forward to situations he was likely to face, he reviewed his poor prospects and had his bad moment of gray foresight.

A rough-and-tumble man, full of strong individualism, he was no greenhorn to conflict and trouble, surrendering to no man and never retreating from an argument. That same pride had pushed him into many brushes with danger, but the actual encounter with mortal, chilling fear for his life was foreign to him. If he succeeded in penetrating Winona Basin, he would come against men to whom death was commonplace while his life had been that of a cowpuncher and rancher, not a gunfighter. He knew his limitations with a six-gun and recalled Burns's queer question — "Ever kill a man?" — and at last understood the reason. He looked down ruefully at his rawboned fists, brown and callused like a farmer's by years of physical toil. They were big hands, strong hands, but not suited for swift gun play, and he did not delude himself into believing he could match the dazzling speed of a veteran gunfighter. He normally carried a revolver to protect his life and property, but he had never been forced to use it in a life-and-death encounter. He also knew the reputations of such frontier badmen, tales which spoke of a wild, terrifying rapidity of motion followed by the unerringly fatal bullet, but his mode of living had run in another direction; he had traveled a different road and knew little else about them.

One morning, not pleased with such thinking, he stopped and dismounted, removed his gun belt from his pack, and strapped it about his waist. He hefted the gun in his palm, feeling its familiar weight, spun the cylinder, and dropped it into the holster. For a half hour he worked on his draw, snapping shots at rocks or stumps, disappointed at his lack of speed and accuracy, and acknowledging that he was long out of practice. Thereafter, he trained on a daily basis, facing an imaginary adversary and snatching his gun out of his holster with the greatest speed of which his muscles were capable. He didn't delude himself into believing he was a match for a hardened professional, but after each session he felt more comfortable with his improving proficiency. Further, he knew that a few days' drill would be of little help in a showdown with a gunman skilled in the art of killing and gave considerable thought to the possibility of his own death by the sudden burst of a bullet. This by no means deterred him from proceeding to his unavoidable destination, but in a small way his improving dexterity pleased him, and he felt he was no longer completely unprepared.

On the morning of the fifth day after leaving Burns's cabin his downhill travel flattened out on the level floor of a rolling vale, gouged from the middle of the mountains as if by a giant scoop. A box cañon struck into the northwest, tapering inward as it marched toward a prominent peak. Therefore he set his course in the opposite direction toward the suggestion of a gentler valley beyond. The landscape unrolled in front of him as smoothly rounded contours of glistening grass and subtle splashes of flowering color spotted between stands of fir, box elder, and the omnipresent pines. He stopped in a patch of shade and made a brief lunch of beans and black coffee, afterward continuing through a day so brilliant and undiluted that every feature of far off objects was revealed in sharply etched detail, looking much closer than they really were.

He read signs of increasing travel and observed hoofprints from various directions merge into a wider trail which he followed with a growing feeling that the main artery lay somewhere close at hand. In the middle of the afternoon he rounded a bend and came abruptly upon it, a well-beaten wagon road winding over the grasslands. To his left it curled eastward, leading away from where he believed Winona Basin to be; therefore, he turned into the afternoon sun and held to the road which continued westward and a little south, running alongside a small serpentine brook that coursed through thickets of lazy willows. There was only a light breeze on the floor of the bowl at this time of day, and it was quite warm. The silent sun poured into the trapped cañon air with relentless intensity, and a film of dust from the dry roadbed lifted behind his horse, hanging there long after he passed. Water ran clear in the adjacent creek, eddying into darkly still pools fringed with reeds and marsh grasses. Blackbirds circled overhead in loose formation, shrilly cawing as they wheeled and dipped into the rushes. It was a lush country, peaceful and immensely satisfying to Allard who had now been in the saddle twenty days straight.

The warm sunlight felt good through his shirt after the coldness on the summit, and he basked in this bit of comfort, content to allow his horse to drift leisurely. The road shortly left the stream and began a series of turns, snaking around low hillocks that disturbed the otherwise flat symmetry of the valley. On all sides, framed against the heavens, plummeting cliffs loomed above the treetops, narrowing in the direction of his ride to pinch in the secluded bowl and effectively seal it off from the world. In the grassy open spaces he saw stacks of meadow hay and the rusty hues of square-bodied Hereford cattle at graze. He anticipated the eastern pass into Winona Basin to be no great distance ahead, and, when he arrived there, a confrontation with the guard was sure to follow, and he had not as yet even the filmy tendril of an idea what he would do or say. Burns had told him it was doubtful the Lenifees would grant asylum to any wandering stranger, and the more he thought about his assumed rôle of a wayward traveler, the more implausible it seemed. He couldn't turn back and was unable to think of any better scheme, so he rode along stoically, like a gambler throwing his lot to the unpredictable vagaries of fate, and ceased to worry.

From behind him a single new sound rose and swelled into a louder noise that destroyed the quiet of the afternoon. When it quickened and grew closer, he identified the racket as that of an oncoming wagon. It was out of sight at the moment but fast approaching and gave him only a brief moment in which to adopt a course of action. Not wholly sure what to expect and still casting about for any kind of circumstance that might gain him entry, he pulled to a halt in the middle of the trail and sat idly on the leather, both hands folded over the pommel.

A span of buckskins materialized around the bend, hauling a spring wagon at a driving rush, the road behind offering up its dry powder in a swirling mushroom of dust. Handling the rig with consummate skill was a lone girl who balanced, slim and graceful, on the high seat, her hands tightly clasping the ribbons and her shoulders bending in harmony with the wagon's rocking and swaying motion. Unable to maneuver around Allard, she jolted to a halt with a jarring squeal of brake blocks and glared at him, clearly annoyed.

"Can't you see you're choking off the whole road?" she demanded impatiently. "Move your horse."

Her flare of anger freshened the color on features as arresting as Allard had ever beheld on a woman. He smiled in open admiration and swept his hat from his head with a single, automatic gesture. It was an unstudied act of courtliness that produced a noticeable reaction in the girl who gave him a glance he never understood. She was evidently unaccustomed to such courtesies and studied him with a closer interest, her earlier annoyance partially thawing.

Allard judged she was in her early twenties, clad in bib overalls and a shaggy man's shirt which fell carelessly away from her throat and failed to conceal the well formed symmetry of her body. She was narrow-waisted and held her back very straight. A knotted rawhide sling, tight beneath her proud firm chin, ran to a sand-pale hat, and from under the narrow brim a pair of lively and watchful eyes gave him a careful appraisal. She was completely self-assured and carried herself with a level of confidence that hinted of a temperament as aggressive as his own.

Allard reined his horse to one side and moved off the road. "I'm sorry to delay you," he said. "This road lead to Mountain Pass?"

"This road would eventually take you to Mountain Pass," she replied tartly, "if you could use it, but it runs through Winona Basin. That's where my family lives, and my father allows no strangers inside." When she mentioned her father, it was almost in reverence, but something about this stranger drew her interest. "Who are you, and what are you doing here?"

"My name is Frank Allard. I'm traveling west to Nevada and maybe California. Been a while since I slept in a bed, and I was hoping to make Mountain Pass by nightfall."

A deeply-rooted distrust of unknown persons prevailed in her attitude, and her eyes said she didn't believe him as she balanced his words. He sounded like just another vagabond who had drifted into the basin by accident, but he didn't show the dissipation or wear the ragged outfit of a vagrant wanderer.

"You're running from the law, I suppose."

"No," he responded, "the law's not after me. I'm just riding through."

"You can't escape from anything by just riding," said the girl, disbelieving him and for some reason constrained to offer him advice. She gave no clue as to whether or not she accepted his explanation, but he discerned a faint shade of change cross her features as she reflected on his explanation and developed her assessment of him. "You better turn around and take another route." Then she chose to repeat her former admonition. "I told you, my father doesn't allow travel through the basin."

"That will be a bad break for me," acknowledged Allard. "But I've come too far to turn around without a try. I'll talk to him."

"Suit yourself," said the girl, shaking her head firmly. "You can try, but you won't have any luck."

In spite of her unwillingness to offer him any encouragement, her mere presence lifted Allard's spirits and caused him to smile. "I'm obliged," he said, "but, if you're headed home, I'll follow and take my chances."

The girl's feelings were divided, and for reasons she did not immediately understand, something was making her uneasy. She drew on her gloves, unlocked the brake, and flipped the reins, sending the bangtails away at a smart trot. Allard watched the rig groan down the road and disappear behind a choking banner of dust, the powdery ropes building and dropping from the spokes of the spinning wheels. He shook his mount into motion, trailing after the wagon.

The road wound through pastures of alfalfa, hawkweed, and wild geraniums. A little stream spilled from the timber on his right, meandering down the valley in the direction he was riding. He passed through a stand of aspen, skirted one more bend, and came abruptly upon the buckboard which had pulled to a dead stop. Through a gauze-like screen of dust he saw the girl crouched beside the near horse, holding one of the animal's hoofs in her hands and looking at it closely. He rode up beside her and halted.

"It's a stone bruise," she declared, rising

and dusting herself off. "This poor animal has gone lame." She swung back and lifted the hoof again, probing it with a slender forefinger. When she struck the bruised area, the horse snorted, threw up its head, and jerked its hoof from her hand. "I could use some help," she admitted, her voice calm and unruffled. "From here to the ranch house in the basin is three miles. Please go there and have somebody bring out another horse. The eastern gate is just down the road, and, if you tell the man there what happened, he should let you pass. I could make it home with only one horse, but they are used to pulling as a team, and it would be easier this way. Ride on and find my father, Ben Lenifee, or my brother, Chester. My name is Joyce Lenifee."

At her words Allard dismounted and walked over until he stood next to her. She was tall for a woman, standing higher than he had suspected, the edge of her shoulder brushing his upper arm. Her eyes were not afraid, and her glance forced its reserve steadily against him. He extended one hand, capturing hers. "Miss Lenifee," he said, and smiled openly, "I'm pleased to make your acquaintance."

The touch of her palm went through him like a cool wind. She evidently believed that his mannerisms were genuine and not feigned, for she returned him a short nod before withdrawing her hand. Then she retreated to the wagon with her full guard up and waited for him to speak. After many days in the saddle he was a hard-looking specimen, but his self-effacing manner continued to draw her reluctant interest. Conscious of her close regard, he was all at once aware of his unshaven and scraggy appearance. He lifted a hand to his lower face, running it over the growth of beard stubble, and said with some chagrin: "I haven't been near a razor for a week and might scare the ponies, but let me have a look."

He stepped over and put a shoulder into the horse's flank, lifted the injured hoof, and inspected it carefully, then dropped it. "Bad bruise in the frog," he agreed. "This horse can't go any farther in harness."

The girl seemed to be at the mercy of strong cross-currents. Her voice was rapid and concerned: "You'd better go. I'm already late, and my father will wonder what happened to me."

He couldn't remember how long it had been since he had conversed with a woman. Politeness forbade him to stare, and so there was considerable embarrassment in him for continuing to do so. The impact was not entirely lost on her, but she acknowledged his appraisal with no outward display other than a delicate flush that stole across the sun-dusted shading of her cheeks.

"I really must get home. Please go."

"I have a better idea," said Allard, "and it will save time. Wash has been in harness before. If I unhitch the lame horse, can he make it home by himself?"

She listened to his words and nodded.

Allard unhitched the animal and turned it loose. Then he stripped his gear from the chestnut and dumped it into the bed of the wagon, thereafter backing the animal into the traces and hitching it to the rig. Wash balked at first and braced his feet, giving Allard a bad moment, but finally got acquainted with the other horse and stood docile and quiet, whereupon Allard hooked the straps. He said to the girl: "Better let me handle the reins. He knows my touch."

She offered no argument, accepting his recommendation without comment. She turned to climb on the wagon whereupon Allard slid a hand under her elbow and lifted her up in one swift motion. The color on her cheeks deepened, and she kept her head turned away from him, her eyes averted. She murmured: "Thank you," and established herself on the right edge of the seat, keeping the full width between them.

Allard climbed to the seat, settled himself on the hard board, and unwound the reins. He kicked the brake handle out of its iron ratchet with his boot and began to talk to the horses, jiggling the reins and coaxing them into motion. After a couple of false, plunging starts the wagon took off with a lurch, and the pair settled to a steady pulling and rattling progress.

The next several miles were covered in a protracted silence. Allard had his hands full, holding the unfamiliar team, and the girl made no sound. On a single occasion he stole a glance at her. The ride had deepened her breathing, and a vein in the soft line of her throat pulsed rhythmically to the beat of her heart. She continued to gaze straight ahead. Allard broke the silence between them. "Will there be trouble for you if we arrive like this?"

She shrugged her shoulders, and Allard saw a hint of apprehension in her eyes.

"You have been helpful with your horse," she said. "That may make a difference." She dropped her head and murmured in a soft, barely audible voice: "Sometimes my father can be difficult." Then she continued: "This road is not a route to California. How did you happen to find it here in the middle of these mountains, if you're not running from the law?"

"Stumbled on it yesterday, when I was working my way over the mountains. It's pretty country, and I'm in no big hurry."

"You're probably lying," she said in a tone of dismissal and turned her back to him with a gesture very much like despair. Then he heard her say at the bottom of her breath: "You're just like the others. I sometimes wish. . . ." Her voice trailed off, and she said nothing further.

Chapter Six

The notch through which they entered was a narrow cleft in the sheer walls of the high-rimmed sandstone cliffs striking up to the sky. It confined the opening to little more than the width of the road, and a man stood atop a boulder watching them, his arm cradling a rifle.

The girl threw up a hand in signal. "Ted," she called. "It's all right."

The man inclined his head and waved them onward with a sweep of his arm. They passed through the slim cut and entered Winona Basin, a sequestered mountain valley bulwarked on all sides by brilliantly colored vermilion cliffs. Ponderosa, fir, and cedar crowded the road which wound in lazy sweeps for another mile, then broke from the trees into a clearing dotted by several dozen neat and well-kept buildings. A collection of barns, sheds, and cabins was scattered over the meadow, neatly divided by fences and corrals in which livestock moved. Directly opposite and facing them, set somewhat apart from the other structures and hard against the timbered perimeter, was a larger two-story house with a railed verandah as wide as the house itself, extending across the entire front and down one side. Two men stood on the verandah, awaiting their approach.

"That will be my father and brother," said the girl softly, her expression one of uncertainty. The stiff independence she had demonstrated on the trail had left her. "I'll have to explain what happened."

Allard drove the wagon over to the house and pulled in at the verandah steps. He tied off the reins and settled back on the seat, having his first look at Ben and Chester Lenifee. The two, although father and son, were totally dissimilar. Ben Lenifee was a tall, commanding shape, staring down at them, angular in body, stiff-necked and bony, clad in bib overalls, a woolen shirt, and a short coat. A great tangle of black beard, squarely cut like a shovel, hid the lower half of his face and hung to his breastbone. His hawkish features were long and severe, his closely pinched mouth a lipless slit under a high-bridged and melancholy nose. Clamped on his head and blocked low over the bushy eyebrows was a wide-brimmed black hat with a tall peak and a round crown. Chester, who stood quietly at his father's elbow, was a full head shorter, fair skinned and hatless with a wide, full-lipped mouth on a bland and rather grave face. He was stouter than his father and wore dark woolen trousers supported by suspenders tucked into black boots, a loose flannel shirt, and a buckskin vest open down the front. Defying custom, and in sharp contrast to the general habit of a society that went heavily bearded, he was clean-shaven.

With anxious eyes the girl slid a timorous glance at Allard and, dropping from her seat on the wagon, crossed to the house, standing at the foot of the steps. "Father, my horse went lame about five miles from here. This man was on the road and helped me. He put his horse in the traces and drove us here." She paused, not at ease under his stern gaze. "He was very kind."

Ben Lenifee maintained a distant aloofness without any change of expression. When he finally spoke, his voice boomed out with clipped authority. "Go inside, Jo. Chester and I will talk to the stranger. You will have to give an account of this to Wade when he returns."

His words were an order. The girl dipped her head in meek acquiescence, mounted the steps with a straight-backed grace, and disappeared through the doorway.

Now he spoke to Allard. "We do not allow

outsiders in our valley. Who are you, and what is your business in this country?"

"Name's Frank Allard. I met your daughter by accident a couple miles up the road. One of her horses pulled up lame, so we hooked mine to the wagon and drove here."

The older man's tone remained crusty and suspicious. "You running from the law?"

"No, I'm heading for the West Coast and figgered I might find a meal and a bunk. My pony is about played out."

Chester Lenifee, listening closely, put forth his own question. "Where do you come from?"

"Missouri." Then Allard slyly added something he had been waiting to mention ever since learning of it from Amos Burns. "We moved there when I was a kid. My family originally came from Tennessee."

His words were like a spark suddenly struck, and he saw a new and sudden interest in the eyes of both men. Ben's face lost some of its hostility, and Chester Lenifee immediately said: "Your family from Tennessee? Whereabouts?"

"Waynesboro," replied Allard.

"That's right down the road from Clifton," said Chester, agreeably surprised. He turned to his father. "Ain't we still got kin back there?"

Ben did not answer, but, breaking with practice and strangely contrary to his past refusal to do so, he impulsively decided to honor the universally observed Western convention of offering food and shelter to solitary travelers. He lifted a hand to pull his beard aside, revealing trap-tight red lips above a hard-pointed chin and swept one arm in a wide circle, delivering his words in a flat, sermon-like monologue. "The name of this valley is Winona Basin. We found it, cleared the land, and built what you see. We have never accepted strangers into our midst, and it has remained a peaceful place for our families. However" — here he paused as if at war with his own scruples and added in a somewhat changed tone — "you showed my daughter Christian good will, and for that we offer you our hospitality and a brief rest. You will be our guest for a day or two, but then you must depart." His eyes fell on Allard's booted Winchester. "You must leave your rifle with me during your stay. Do you have another weapon?"

"In my roll," said Allard. "A revolver."

"Give it to me," he ordered. "I will keep both and return them when you leave." He dropped his reserve sufficiently to introduce himself. "I'm Ben Lenifee, and this is my son, Chester. You've already met my daughter, Joyce. We're indebted to you for helpin' her. Our roots, like yours, are in Tennessee." He pointed to a low building nearby. "That's the bunkhouse where you will sleep. Just beyond is the dining room and kitchen. Leave the wagon there and put your horse in the corral."

He gave Allard a flinty stare, turned his back, and withdrew indoors, whereupon Chester descended the steps and accepted Allard's rifle and holstered gun. His manner was not unfriendly, and he tried to put Allard at ease with an affable, half-smiling glance. "My father had a bad experience not long ago with others who brought firearms into the basin. You can have these back on your way out."

He wheeled without further conversation, remounted the steps, and passed from sight into the gloomy interior.

Allard drove the wagon to the kitchen, left it there, and unhitched the team, turning both horses into the corral. He removed his belongings from the wagon bed and tramped over to the bunkhouse, suddenly aware he was under close inspection from three figures, lounging in the building's shade. Two were less than imposing men beyond their twenties, dark and obscure, squatting on their heels against the wall, their eyes nothing more than mere slits beneath the shadow of low-drawn hat brims. Both scrutinized Allard with open suspicion from pinched and humorless features deeply puckered by signs of dissipation and hard living. Standing next to them, the point of one shoulder balanced against the bunkhouse wall, was a red-haired kid in his late teens, lank and gangly with an open and friendly countenance. When Allard looked at him, he bobbed his head and seemed on the point of saying something, but after a cautious glance at his companions he had second thoughts and pulled his lips together. Allard returned his nod and laid a bleak stare on the other two men, noticing that both wore guns, although the boy did not. He stored this fact, then turned his back on them, lugging his gear into the bunkhouse.

A row of double bunks, each with a straw tick, lined the opposite wall, three of them obviously occupied with bedrolls and clothing strewn on top. The place had a plank floor and several packing boxes nailed to one wall served as shelves, each containing a man's accumulation of junk. A stove and a half dozen chairs made up the furniture along with a round table covered by a collection of dog-eared mail order catalogues and a grimy deck of cards.

Allard dropped his roll and saddlebags next to an empty lower bunk and sat on the edge to pull off his boots, conscious of an immense weariness. He was bone-tired and rolled back on the bed to lie flat, his body sagging deeply into the straw mattress. From outside he could hear the murmur of voices that lifted and fell and knew the three hands were discussing him, but he was too worn out to care. The tension and pressures of the past week had caught up with him and effectively dulled the thoughts that grew fainter as he drifted into sleep.

The supper triangle began to bang, sending its metallic ringing through the early evening drowse and dragging Allard out of his dull slumber. Full consciousness arrived slowly, and he opened his eyes to view the unfamiliar walls around him. The room was deserted, the outside door closed, and a lamp smoldered low on the nearby table, rendering the air close and fetid. Muffled sounds of movement drifted in from the yard, and he rose, pulled on his boots, and went outside, observing a general movement of people toward the low-shaped dining building. He joined the procession, mounted the split-log puncheon that served as a doorstep, and entered a rectangular hall already partly filled by twenty or thirty adults and a sprinkling of children. They were seated on benches at long tables covered with striped oil cloth. A short bench at the foot of one of the tables was unoccupied, and Allard seated himself there alone.

The savory aroma of hot food reminded him of how long he had gone without a prepared meal. Sourdough biscuits, a plate of beef, and a bowl of boiled carrots had been placed on the table in front of him, along with a pot of coffee and half of a red bean pie. His entrance had drawn an inquisitive inspection from other diners, and he felt their general scrutiny but ignored them and began to eat his meal, consuming the food with a hearty appetite.

His appreciation of the home-cooked meal was clearly apparent, and he had a second helping of everything, then wiped his dinner plate with a slice of bread and ferried over a generous wedge of pie. When he had polished that off, he poured himself water from a pitcher and leaned back in his chair, conducting his own inspection of the room and its occupants. Only those dining at the front table sat on chairs, and at the center point of the head table, enthroned in his usual station like a regal monarch, Ben Lenifee presided over the assemblage, flanked on either side by his son and daughter. He was hatless, and a great black mane covered his head except for a shiny bald disk at the very crown. Occasionally his powerful eyes rummaged around the room, once fastening on Allard, pausing momentarily, then moving on. The rest of Winona Basin's residents sat on benches and ate silently. As he studied these people, Allard saw an unmistakable common cast stamped on every individual, strangely similar characteristics of trait and feature, suggesting a form of racial poverty. They shared a lack of individuality, stemming from generations of intimate social contact and close inbreeding inherent in a closed society that denied the vibrant infusion of new blood. There was ancestral decay here. They lived in a twilight without any driving emotions to carry them along. No burning ambition to improve their lives stirred their souls, for long ago they had surrendered their independence to out-dated and antiquated rites that robbed them of any opportunity for personal identity or achievement.

The food was served by several women indifferently working the tables from the adjoining kitchen out of which rose the usual clatter of pots and dishware. Most were middle-aged or beyond, drably dressed, dull-featured, and impassive. To Allard they seemed apathetic, moving listlessly about the room in an unsmiling, mechanical way. It was apparent that the rigid, time-worn rituals the Lenifee clan had brought from Tennessee weighed heavily upon them all. Imprisoned within the geographical confines of a remote basin and destined to a mode of living bordering on bondage, the women particularly seemed impressed into a position of virtual servitude. There wasn't any human warmth in the room. None of the diners engaged one another in easy conversation; there was no spontaneous laughter, no casual chatter. Except for a muttered word as the platters of food were passed, nobody spoke. Even the children ate quietly with their heads bowed over their plates.

Allard switched his gaze to the head table and to the serene composure of Joyce Lenifee. Her perfectly positioned combination of features and vivid freshness were in marked contrast to the collective sameness of all the other women. He had his own moment to marvel that she could be the product of this lineage, for she was stamped with a singular distinction all her own and bore no resemblance to the others. Some combination of predominant blood lines, perhaps on her mother's side, had fashioned all the fine and clear lines of her face and form, and he had a depressing picture of her prospects among these deficient people, secluded from the outer world and hobbled by their backward traditions.

The two men he had earlier seen in the yard sat with the kid at the foot of the opposite table, their backs to the wall and noticeably apart from the other diners. The wall lamps threw out a bright glow of light and gave Allard a better view of them than he had earlier when they crouched in the bunkhouse shadow. One was short and swarthy, his face deeply pitted by boyhood smallpox, with a black, curling mustache hiding his upper lip. There was nothing uncommon about him except a large, ominous scar extending from above his right eye into his dark hair. His slope-shouldered companion was lank and cadaverous with a thin, reedy neck and a prominent, bony nose. The skin of both men was almost the same weathered shade of copper, but, whereas the thin one's looked desert dry, his companion's hide had an oily gloss. The red-headed kid ate alongside them, but he was not part of their circle for the two men shared their own few, private words as they tackled their food and snubbed him completely. The boy spent a good deal of his mealtime watching Allard.

Another diner, wearing a flat Spanish sombrero which he did not bother to remove, now entered the room and moved along the wall to take his place alongside the two yard men. He was of medium size, closely built, and tightly wound with a crooked nose and high cheekbones on a sun-blackened face. Allard judged him to be in his middle thirties, but intemperance and a latent brutality had prematurely aged him, leaving their telltale marks of dissipation. Several days' growth of rough whiskers darkened his jaw, and unkempt strings of hair, black as a crow's wing, dangled shoulder length down the back of his neck. A revolver with mother-of-pearl handle protruded from the holster on his gun belt.

His entrance caused a stir in the room and drew the sharp attention from some of the men. Several threw discreet glances in his direction, then hastily averted their attention and returned to their meal. One man, some way up the table, leaned across to whisper in his fellow diner's ear, and Allard heard him say: "Cat's back."

The kid stirred himself and said something to the yard man sitting next to him. The man brushed his words aside. He shook his head and grunted: "Shut up, Wiley," after which he leaned across to the newcomer and murmured something under his breath, jerking his head in Allard's direction. Cat Lenifee, until now unaware of Allard's presence, laid on him a pair of muddy eyes, boldly arrogant and completely devoid of expression. Something cruel and depraved behind the face gleamed out of those fixed pools of black liquid, unblinking like a bird of prey and partially concealed by the droop of his lids.

Allard caught and held the dead eyes and their baleful stare. Lenifee continued to glower at him malevolently, then abruptly swung his eyes away, and paid Allard no further attention. He fell to his meal and made a quick job of eating, not carrying on any conversation with his companions. When he rose to leave, both yard men got up and followed him out.

One by one the other diners rose and left. Allard dawdled over his coffee, soberly considering Cat Lenifee and his two partners. They were obviously not original or permanent members of the community but rather reckless products of a roistering nether world of saloons, dance halls, and brothels, one step ahead of a law that had not kept pace with the wave of settlers pouring into the West. According to Burns, one or more of the three men was the drygulcher he was after.

The scraping of chair legs pulled his attention back to Ben Lenifee who had completed his meal. When he pushed his plate away and stood up, both his children rose in unison and moved to the door where they dutifully stood aside, allowing him first passage. Joyce Lenifee hesitated there, her eyes touching Allard for a moment, holding his attention. The glow from the lamps was kind to her, delicately tinting her cheeks and setting up a rich, bronze shining in her hair. She rewarded him with a light half smile, seen by some of the others, and turned out of the building.

Allard hoisted himself to his feet. He moved to the exit and went outside. The sun had slipped behind the western horizon, painting the slice of sky immediately above with horizontal layers of crimson and orange, and suddenly the definite edges of the surrounding landscape were no longer sharp. A pungent coolness of a light wind played against his skin, and other outbound diners tramped by without comment, their footsteps running ahead as evening's peace magnified the sounds.

He liked to stroll as he thought, and moved about the clearing. He idly observed several men standing about alongside one building who had taken off their coats and were pitching horseshoes. The pointless chatter of the settlement children ran through the growing twilight, echoing distinctly in the drowsy quiet. The red-haired kid stirred somewhere in the yard, but Allard was preoccupied with his sharp images of the girl. He realized how little he really knew about her, and how little she knew of him, but together they seemed to be caught in a kind of magnetism that stirred up privately held dreams and long suppressed hunger.

He strolled over to the corral and took station there, easing his body against the bars and hooking a bootheel over the bottom rail. As the sky lost its gun-metal sheen and dusk strengthened upon the land, a kind of dreaming stillness held the valley. The settlement itself was neatly kept, all the low-lying log structures clean and in good repair. An occasional pole fence sectioned the basin into rectangular plots, and horses, his among them, churned up a dust in the corral. A small creek broke into the clearing on the far side and meandered through the compound in lazy curves, spanned at two locations by wagon bridges, at other spots by a single plank. Behind the corral the land dropped away to a stock pond beyond which was an orchard of fruit trees. Water had been channeled there from the creek by an irrigation ditch and thence piped to the corral; over his shoulder he could hear its lazy dripping into the trough. The dense forest described a charcoal border around the compound, and purple dusk continued to thicken. Cabin lights winked on and cut their glowing yellow loopholes in the shadows, and on the far side of the compound the larger two-storied building where he had first encountered Ben Lenifee was losing its precise lines. His horse, drawn by his presence, came over to the rails, drank from the trough, and shoved a wet nose into the back of Allard's neck.

At that moment Chester Lenifee and a second man emerged from the main house, descended the steps, and bore down on him at a heavy pace. Lenifee had laid a hand on the man's arm and seemed to be remonstrating with him, but the other thrust his hand aside and continued his measured tread across the open area, halting a yard short of Allard. He was some years younger than Allard but six inches taller and fifty pounds heavier with a great shock of blond hair, growing low on the forehead of a broad, half-handsome face. His features at the moment were angry and bunched in an enormous scowl, his bloodshot eyes rimmed with temper. At his neckline tufts of hair showed through the opening of a somewhat soiled woolen shirt, dampened by heavy sweat at the armpits. His sleeves were rolled up as far as the swell of his biceps would allow, and thick and hairy forearms led to wrists as broad as his palms. He had a massiveness about him, but he was not in the best of condition for a young man, as an apron of fat girdled his midsection and paunched over his belt.

"I'm Wade Bowley," he announced. "Ain't you the newcomer that brought Jo in on the wagon?"

"Yeah," Allard answered dryly, "reckon I am. One of Miss Lenifee's horses went lame on the road east of here, and we drove in together on the wagon. That's all there was to it."

His smooth reply did nothing to lessen the other's suspicious anger. "God damn you," he bawled, sudden fury raking his voice. "*That* ain't all. Joyce Lenifee is my woman. You stay away from her. Understand? Open yore mouth and answer me, or I'll bust you up!"

The overbearance of the man crowded Allard. He had never failed to respond to another man's hostile invitation and could feel himself reacting in his old explosive way. Only the dim flickering of a remote caution prevented him from immediately engaging Bowley, and he wrestled with his own black temper, pushing it down and away. He had to remain inconspicuous and unobtrusive in the basin, steering clear of any encounter, forever mindful of his dubious status. If he were involved in any kind of trouble, it would come to the ears of Ben who would banish him immediately. He smiled thinly and retreated a full step, backing away from the pressure.

"Listen, my friend," he said in a low tone, "your thinking is crooked. You're imagining things. Don't push it any further."

This was obviously the wrong thing to have said and his sharp rejoinder further irked Bowley who took his backward step as a sign of cowardice. It showed in the sudden, sardonic lines that formed on the big man's cheeks and by the smirk that twisted his mouth. Bowley's nostrils widened. "You son of a bitch," he bellowed. "You could've come in and got another horse. I heard durin' dinner you kept flirtin' with her, tryin' to push your luck. You got no business in the basin. Ben should've run you out while you could walk. Now I'm goin' to bust you up so you crawl out."

His loud raving had been heard by others, and the sudden stir of quickly gathering men diverted Allard's attention. He momentarily turned to observe a ring of faces emerging from the shadows, hungrily drawn to the scene by the expectancy of brutal combat. Somebody called: "Hey, Cat, over here," and he saw, out of the corner of his eye, Cat Lenifee and the two yard men approaching from the bunkhouse, trailed by the kid, Wiley.

Too late he realized that Bowley, poised to jump, would wait no longer. When Allard presented him with the opportunity by turning aside, he moved. His right arm had been swinging at his side. When he leaped forward, he launched one ham-like fist in a great looping punch, confident that no man could stand against the blow. Allard spotted the flicker of motion in time to sag at the knees, spin to one side, and drop his head, a canny move that saved him from ruin. Had Bowley's haymaker landed fully against his jaw, the fight would have ended before it began. The sneak punch glanced wickedly along the side of his head but still carried sufficient force to knock him backward, landing flush on his shoulder blades against the corral. When he crashed back, his head struck the topmost rail with a violence that sent a roaring explosion through his brain. Having recently eaten, his undigested food rose to clot his throat, and he writhed at the threshold of consciousness. He felt paralyzed, his legs refusing to work, and Bowley advanced to stand before him, his ruddy face flushed with the expectancy of another quick victory. He thought the fight was over.

So did the gathered crowd of onlookers. Bowley's physical dominance and matching egotism had earned him few friends in the basin, but this was a society that looked upon all strangers as enemies, and, however much the locals might hate him, the circle of men was on his side.

One bystander spoke with a touch of admiration. "By Judas, you're a powerful man, Wade. Nobody can stand against you."

Another individual in the assemblage, sorely disappointed by the shortness of the fight, said: "Where's the fun, Wade? You've finished him too quick. Should've made it last a little longer."

Cat Lenifee stood among the spectators. A brightness shone oddly on the black surfaces of his eyes, and he looked at Allard contemptuously. "Finish the job, big boy," he growled. "Knock him down and put the boots to him. Kick his damn' ribs in."

Lights were flashing in Allard's head and danced in a shower of sparks behind his eyeballs. His heart pounded against his chest with hammer-like wallops. When he tried to flex his arms, his brain refused the discipline, short-circuited by the flinch of pain. His muscle strength had temporarily left him, but he had an uncommon reserve of recuperative power and an inconspicuous vitality that could shake off a great deal of punishment. He felt the slow restoration of feeling in his limbs, and the revival of his normal senses as the pulsing pump of his heart shot adrenaline into his bloodstream, dilating the pupils of his eyes and instantly raising his energy level. He heard Lenifee's sneering remark and lifted one eyelid. The world around him was a gray haze through which Bowley was a blurred shape. Bowley drew back a fist and hit Allard solidly in the face, releasing a new burst of pure agony, but the shock further cleared Allard's head. This blow dropped him to the ground, but he rolled sideways, thereby avoiding a kick. He crawled in the dirt alongside the corral, buying limited time to ride out the storm.

The sheets of pain pounded without letup, but comprehension was slowly returning. Things were back in focus. The dizziness was gone, and he was rocked with a freezing rage that left him without reason or mercy. It was an old wild instinct that, once aroused, he had never been able to control. In time of trouble it was always there to support him and came to him now. When Bowley's legs stopped next to him, he reached out and seized one boot, twisting it savagely and jerking the big man off his feet. Bowley's legs shot out from under him, and he fell heavily, landing on a shoulder and emitting a great yell. He lunged to his feet immediately, but the short period of time had been time enough for Allard to regain his feet, collect himself, and move away from the corral into the open.

Bowley, who had expected no further resistance and was surprised to see his adversary on his feet, now rushed forward like a great beast, raining club-like blows in a thunderous flurry of roundhouse swings. Allard had no chance to return any punches of his own, so he covered up, fending off Bowley's attack with his arms and elbows. He had sufficient room around him to maneuver, so he backed out of reach and side-stepped, shuffling left and right, dodging Bowley's haymakers, content to let the big man tire himself out. As the fight whirled them around, Allard continued to bob and weave. The audience grew jeeringly impatient and urged Bowley on with cries of encouragement.

"Quit foolin', Wade," someone yelled. "Knock him down again and bust him up."

"Cripple the fancy dancer," cried another.

Their shouts incited Bowley to wilder swings at his moving target. Bowley was not clumsy, and his blows had a crushing, oaken power that sledged against Allard's protecting arms and shoulders like great clubs, each deflected impact delivering a shuddering jolt of punishment that ran down his spine. One of Bowley's smashes bounced off Allard's guarding elbows and struck him full in the face, driving his lips against his teeth. He could taste his own blood.

Bowley however, was tiring. He had great short strength for quick triumphs but without much staying power, and his panting breath was coming in quick and shallow gasps as he searched with an open mouth for wind. Allard could hear each convulsive gulp of air coming from the very bottom of his lungs. All his overweening bluster had left him, and he muttered strange things to himself, a bully boy riding largely on his size and reputation.

Suddenly, aware of what was happening

to him, Bowley grew sly and all at once quit punching. He jumped forward and reached for Allard's waist, seizing him, drawing him into close quarters. He applied pressure and squeezed Allard's torso in a bear-like embrace that cracked his bones and held him momentarily helpless. His long arms wrapped around Allard's ribs in a lethal embrace, compressed them, raking up fire-like ribbons of pure agony. Bowley's labored breathing was a hot blast, burning Allard's skin, and he kept tightening his hoop of steel until Allard's lungs sent up a tortured shout. Some ancient intuition told Allard to raise his arms, forcing them upward against Bowley's chest to ease the suffocating pressure. He did so, using all his strength against the big man, and was able to raise a forearm and drive it viciously against Bowley's windpipe. He held it there with his remaining power, ramming it repeatedly into Bowley's Adam's apple. It bent Bowley's head back and broke his hold. He cried out, and his arms snapped apart, allowing Allard to pull free.

For just a moment Bowley's arms temporarily left him unguarded as one hand dropped to his side and the other grasped his throat. Allard had his opportunity then and went at him savagely, driving solid punches into Bowley's face, against his jaw, and into his eyes. All thought of preserving some anonymity in the basin and looking after his own safety left Allard, and he kept relentlessly slugging the great shape before him with both hands, each smash sending back a flat and pulpy sound.

This relentless attack had a telling effect on Bowley. Weariness was written in the slowness of his reflexes. The power had left his fists, and he began to retreat a step at a time, unable effectively to protect himself. Allard grimly followed, his knuckles grinding into Bowley's face and head. Bowley lost his equilibrium and brought his arms up to protect his face. When he did so, Allard saw his opening. Bending his legs at the knees for better balance, he rose on the balls of his feet and used the last of his dwindling strength to bury his fist deeply into the wide pit of Bowley's soft stomach. Bowley's mouth dropped open, and he swayed backward, a hoarse gagging sound welling up from out of his throat. A sick look washed across his face, and he sank to one knee and was in that position when Allard mercilessly hammered home his final punch to the big man's unprotected chin. A look of surprise crossed Bowley's face, and he fell on his side where he lay semi-conscious, making no effort to rise. The fight was finished.

A hush fell over the scene, and the knot of spectators stood about in shocked silence. They had expected another easy conquest for Bowley and were stunned by the defeat of a man they considered unbeatable. Cat Lenifee's small eyes, black and full of hate, fastened on Allard with a fierce attention, the outcome not at all to his liking. His right palm hung just above the butt of his revolver, and he seemed to be considering drawing the weapon when one of his partners pulled him away. Some men broke from the group and moved off into the shadows, but nobody helped Bowley who slowly dragged himself to his feet and stumbled away in the darkness. The rest of the crowd simply melted into the evening, their low conversations drifting back.

Allard stood with his feet wide apart to maintain a swaying balance. He teetered back and forth, gulping, for his lungs found little nourishment in the sweet air and labored for oxygen. He managed to drag himself to the corral and draped both elbows over the top rail, hanging by his arms. He listened to the thumping of his heart and tasted the salt left by his own sweat and blood. When he moved any part of his body, it was with a lead-like stiffness, but he slid sideways, holding to the rails as far as the watering trough, bent and plunged his head into its coolness. The shock brought him back a little, and he slowly removed his torn shirt, immersed it in the trough, and scrubbed his face, then wrung it out and put it on, at once feeling its cooling effect. He had absolutely no vigor. His limbs were made of cement, and he had no will to move.

Standing all this while in the background, Chester Lenifee's full attention throughout the fight had been on Allard, and it clung to him for long minutes afterward with a growing curiosity. When it was over, he swung on his heels and headed back to the big house. But he was not the last to leave. The kid, Wiley, who had followed the action with breathless fascination, lingered in the deep shadows, drinking it all in. Younger than Bowley by a few years but only half his size, he had long endured the latter's contemptuous arrogance. When Allard began to gain the upper hand, he rocked back and forth as each blow landed, exhaling a great sigh when Bowley finally dropped. When he swung away and returned to the bunkhouse, he swelled his chest and felt himself a larger man than he had been before.

The wind's greedy fingers, coldly striking

against Allard's skin, produced a stinging sensation on his perspiring body, and he shivered from its raw bite. His body parts were locking up, and he forced himself to flex his joints. His breathing was returning to normal, and he began to limp around in a tight circle. After a bit he strolled away from the corral toward the closely standing trees whose denser shadows reached out to thicken the night's ordinary darkness. He felt no surge of elation or satisfaction from the fight, only a sour let-down. He was convinced he had destroyed whatever chance he had of remaining in the basin.

The yard was deserted, and full darkness had descended, completely destroying the twilight. He thought himself quite alone and turned, preparing to return to the bunkhouse, when a low voice, close at hand and hidden by the trees, brought him to a standstill. A girl's voice rubbed the night air softly.

"Wait, please."

He turned, and a slim figure materialized from behind a pine.

Joyce Lenifee stood before him, a misty silhouette. A loose shawl covered her shoulders, and she had a finger against her lips. Her low undertone was touched by the breath of fear. It sounded distant and unreal. "Be quiet," she whispered, her words momentarily snatched away by the wind. "If anyone knew I was here, it would mean bad trouble for me . . . and for you."

Her unexpected appearance instantly lifted Allard to a new height of emotion. He caught a delicate fragrance from her hair, and her low voice was a soft melody in his ears. Her features were obscured by the darkness, and he was unable to see her expression. All he could do was murmur: "Miss Lenifee, what are you doing here?"

"I don't know," she replied softly. "I often walk alone at night and saw the end of your terrible fight. You went out of your way to help me and didn't deserve what happened. I scarcely know you, but I had to see if you were hurt. Wade is so awfully strong, and I was afraid he would beat you horribly. Nobody has ever stood against him."

"He's a bull," admitted Allard, "but the fight was not my idea."

"Yes," agreed the girl in a faint tone. "I know. That's why I'm here. To apologize for my family. You did nothing wrong. You only helped me."

"I'm sorry," said Allard, "for what happened to your man, but he was bound to have a fight."

"Please don't call him that," she whispered quickly, an odd note of despair in her voice.

Something in that despondency triggered a fragile hope Allard had carried from their first meeting. "It is not my business," he said, "and I have no wish to pry, but those were Bowley's words."

Something like a sob escaped her lips. Her answer, when it came, was a thin rustle that barely reached him. "It was an agreement made a long time ago by my father. He told Wade we would be married when I reached twenty-one. That's only two weeks away." Her voice caught in her throat, and Allard suspected she was close to tears. "It's a clan custom," she continued, "and the way our family has lived for generations. I am supposed to marry Wade and be content here the rest of my life."

Allard stepped forward and laid a hand on her arm. She let it remain there and stood quite still. He said: "I must confess that I have never been acquainted with anyone quite like you. You have no reason to trust me or believe anything I say, but, no matter what happens, I shall never forget you. My life has been a lonely one, and you have brought me something I will always remember."

His words affected her tremendously. One hand flew to her throat. "Please, don't say such things."

The seeming innocence of this girl, so full of faith and trust, stirred him deeply. He turned suddenly cold, as if someone were walking over his grave — his future, suddenly, becoming his memory. "Do you want to be Bowley's wife?"

Continuing to fight tears, she bit her lip and lowered her head, putting the backs of her hands against her cheeks. "No," she cried softly, her throat working. "No! But it's too late. There is nothing I can do about it."

On an impulse he stepped forward and reached out toward her, touching her shoulders. "Joyce," he said, "no one can force you to do anything you don't want to do."

She raised her head to stare intently at his dim outline, poised above her, and, although the night made it impossible to read what was on his face, she listened to his words. They were words she was hearing from another for the first time, privately guarded words from a secret part of her soul that she had thought was hers alone. "Frank," she murmured shyly, using his name for the first time. "Somehow you seem to understand."

Unable to see her eyes, he nevertheless felt the weight of her gaze, and her soft breath brushed his cheek. She bent toward him and whispered her question. "Can I believe you? Will you always be truthful with me?"

She was so close then that Allard's restraint melted away. He inclined his head and kissed her, drinking in all her sweet richness. A great tide of warmth enveloped him, and his bruised mouth was forgotten, for her lips were soft and ready. Then she pulled away and laid her head on his chest, holding him without shame.

Overhead the pine boughs stirred uneasily in the wind. When she spoke, her words were barely discernible. "I'm sorry," she whispered. "I've never behaved this way. I'm not myself right now." She stepped far enough back from him to raise one hand and lay a silken finger against his lips. "Your poor mouth. It's swollen and probably hurt when you kissed me." Then she withdrew her hand. "Please don't read too much into what has happened."

Astonished at himself for the liberty he had taken, Allard looked down, seeing the outline of her face, shadowed and soft in the darkness. He spoke very slowly, very quietly. "Joyce," he said, "that was something I do not regret and will never forget. I'm sure neither of us makes a habit of kissing someone we just met, but I couldn't help myself. I have never known much about women, but I never expect to meet anyone like you again, and it appears to me that you are unhappy. Forgive me if I'm wrong, but you deserve more from life than you'll find here." When she made no reply, he continued. "Living is never a simple thing, and it has no sure answers. I don't know the feeling a man ought to have when he falls in love, but I have never felt this way."

She put out a hand which he took in one of his own. "Frank," she breathed, "how can you be so sure? We hardly know each other." Then she withdrew her hand and retreated a step, lifting her fingertips to her temples. She shook her head, holding herself together. "I'm not very fashionable and know little of the world, but I have to believe in something, or someone. It would be nice to have the love of a man like you."

Trailing voices from one of the cabins rose on the night air, reaching them and alerting them, diverting their attention. The girl looked around, suddenly aware of the potential danger.

"I must go back. Tomorrow my father will probably want to see you. He may order you to leave, but my brother knows who started the fight and might help. Chester doesn't like Wade very much." She thought of something else. "Be very careful. Wade will be thinking of ways to harm you. He never forgets."

She moved back into the deep shadows where he could no longer see her, and Allard thought she had gone. He stood rooted in his tracks, his thoughts as high and turbulent as the icy wind that whirled its raw bite against him. The girl had faded from sight, but suddenly she reappeared. Her face reached up, and her soft lips touched his cheek. She murmured: "Good night," and once again melted into the trees.

For a time he remained there, feeling unreal and slightly bewildered at the wildness that had swayed them both for a long and dangerous moment. A sickle moon, edging over the east rim, threw off a pale shining, bathing the landscape in soft silver. He felt the frigid air of the night, and dog-tired and weary he limped over to the bunkhouse and went inside. The lamp had been extinguished, and he groped his way in the dark to his bunk, sat on the edge, and pulled off his boots. He sank into the straw tick, and a towering let-down from all he had been through swept over him. He was too tired to sort out dreams from thoughts, incapable of any appetite other than a desperate craving for rest. He felt the leaden approach of total fatigue, and sleep descended on him like a great curtain.

Chapter Seven

A brilliant shaft of sunlight, angling downward through the window and striking obliquely against his face, roused Allard. He was still dulled with sleep, and his awakening required more than recapturing consciousness. There was the physical demand of raising heavy eyelids and moving cramped muscles. When he lifted his head and widened his eyes, the bright light sent a stab of pain into his skull, and he quickly pressed his lids together and fell back on the mattress, flatly spread-eagled on the bunk. He rested there for a few minutes in a lethargic drowse. When he reopened his eyes, his vision had cleared enough for him to see in the silver haze of a slanting sunbeam the agitated dance of dust motes.

Directly above him the warped slats of an upper bunk sagged dangerously close, bowed by time and the weight of assorted bodies, offering perilous support for the flimsy mattress that sloped inwardly from all directions. An acute hunger gnawed acidly at his stomach, and he hauled himself to a sitting position, perching unsteadily on the edge of the bunk, cradling his head in his hands. A lump over his temple gave him a pounding headache, and all his body joints were gritty in their sockets. The torment assaulted him in throbbing waves, and the simple task of pulling on his boots turned into an ordeal. When he stood up and put his weight on his legs, one threatened to buckle under him, and he needed the bunkpost for support, rising to his full height by degrees. He rubbed his stiffened limbs before limping across the room to stare dispassionately at himself in a polished tin mirror, hanging by a nail.

"I look like hell," he croaked, and ran the pad of a thumb along his jaw line, feeling the sandy growth of beard. The tissues around his eyes were taut and painful, and he tenderly probed a swelling on one cheek.

From his bedroll he dug out his razor, took up a cake of soap, and plodded to the door, going outside and mounting a low platform, finding there a hand pump, a tin basin, and a soiled towel on a roller. His cold water shave was a stinging ritual. Afterward he dried his face with a corner of the towel, donned his jacket, and raked his hair out of his eyes with his fingers. Food was foremost on his mind, and he proceeded at a patient walk to the kitchen where a scattering of other diners still lingered. None of the men he had seen at the bunkhouse was there, and the Lenifee family had evidently finished and departed. A dour woman, one of several who moved about the room, silently placed eggs and bacon in front of him. He drank two cups of black coffee before touching his meal. When he was finished, he saw a basket of apples at the end of the table. He put one in his pocket and turned out into the yard.

The meal invigorated him greatly. He strolled idly about, enjoying the purity of the morning and seeking some form for the restless run of his thoughts. The sharply rising parapets that boxed in the basin soared aloft against a cloudless sky that contained only a hint of blue. The rest had been washed out by the intensity of the sun, pouring its brightness everywhere. His grateful body soaked up its warmth, and he began trudging a small circle, breathing deeply and flexing the muscles of his back and shoulders.

He cruised over to the corral and eased himself against the bars. The timber's green foliage fanned out to all points of the compass and stopped only at the very foot of the sandstone cliffs, isolating the valley from the outside world. His horse whinnied from within the corral and drifted over, thrusting a wet nose through the rails, reaching for him. Allard took the apple from his pocket, placed it flat on his palm, and extended his arm full-length between the rails. Wash breathed once on the apple, then seized it, and munched in contentment, while Allard scrubbed the horse's neck with a piece of burlap sacking he had found lying nearby.

An ancient habit engaged in after every meal, the need of a smoke was on him, and absent-mindedly he dug his pipe from a coat pocket and searched elsewhere for his tobacco. Then he caught himself, realizing he had none, and remembered where he had left his pouch. He shoved the cold pipe back. "Damn," he said irritably. "Dumb as a mule. Mebbe I can find a pipe smoker around somewhere."

His musings were interrupted by a horse that careened into the yard and foamed to a halt at the corral, the rider springing off with a grand flourish. It was the red-headed kid who had earlier been in the yard. He saw Allard by the corral, and his glance hung there a moment, then he went into the bunkhouse and reappeared almost immediately, carrying a rough towel and a rifle. He led his pony to the watering trough where he unsaddled and turned the animal into the corral. He lifted his saddle to the top rail, balanced it there with the bridle, and sauntered over in a deliberately loose and casual way.

"We ain't met," he said hospitably, thrusting his hand forward. "My name's Wiley." His eyes were deep and startling green, and on his head was a straw ranch hat with a crushed crown, pushed back from a scramble of untidy red hair. He had bent both sides of the brim upward at a rakish angle, and his worn bib overalls were patched at both knees.

Allard grasped his hand firmly. "Howdy, Wiley. I'm Frank Allard. Looks like you been workin'."

"Cuttin' firewood in a clearing up yonder," Wiley said, waving an arm behind him in a vague gesture. "It's hot, so I came down for a swim in the creek."

Allard saw the boy's features were fresh and clearly defined, unlike the dull sameness stamped on the other inhabitants. "You part of the Lenifee family?"

"Naw. I'm no relation. Last name's Underwood."

"If you're not kin, how is it you're here in the basin?"

"My old man knew Ben back in Tennessee. We was friends with the Lenifees.

When they hit out for Oregon, we went along." Wiley paused a moment, then added: "There was just two of us. My maw died when I was born." He looked curiously at Allard. "You're name ain't Lenifee, either. How'd you get here if you ain't a relative?" When Allard told him, the boy whistled in surprise. "You're lucky," he said. "The old man's dead set against outsiders."

"What about your father. He here with you?"

"Died a year ago. Ain't no Underwoods left but me."

Allard was prepared to offer words of condolence, but Wiley caught his forming thoughts and headed them off with a noncommittal shrug. "I'm gettin' along fine. Doin' a man's work every day."

"Three men live with you in the bunkhouse?"

"Only two. Emmett Hanks and Pinto Daly. Cat Lenifee's got his own cabin on a knob up in the trees, past the meadow. Him and Jack Slade lived there until Jack got nabbed down at Mountain Pass. Where did you learn to scrap? Nobody ever licked Wade Bowley in a fist fight. Even Cat won't tackle him without a gun." Then he added pensively: "I wish I was good with my fists, but there's nobody around here my age to fight with."

"That your rifle?"

Wiley nodded vigorously. "Sure is. There's lots of ground squirrels down by the creek." He grasped the rifle by the stock and offered it to Allard.

Taking the weapon, Allard looked at it closely, running his fingers along the octagonal barrel. "Why," he said with some surprise, "I had the same kind of rifle when I was a kid . . . a .22 Remington. You a good shot?"

"Yeah," answered Wiley a little sheepishly. "Pretty good, I guess." Perhaps a boyish effort to advance himself in Allard's esteem prompted him to take the rifle back and cradle it in his elbow. "Wade's powerful jealous if anybody looks at Joyce," he continued. "That's why he was sore. He's plannin' on marryin' her. Everybody saw you eyin' her in the dining room."

Allard thought about that. The boy's casual observation made it clear that any notion he fostered of going unnoticed was hopeless. The basin had already marked him. "Is Bowley a relation to the Lenifees?"

"Somebody in Wade's family was related somewhere. I think he's Joyce's third or fourth cousin."

"The other two men eating with you in the dining room? That Hanks and Daly?"

"Yep. I was sittin' next to Emmett." Then he sank his voice low. "The one that came in late was Cat Lenifee, one of Ben's cousins. He was in New Mexico and some place in Texas before he come here. When Cat showed up, he brought Emmett and Pinto and Jack Slade with him. Everybody knows they're gunfighters. Ben tried, but he couldn't get any of 'em to give up their guns. Cat and him had a big argument. Cat won, and Ben backed off. I think he's afraid of Cat." Wiley remembered the towel he carried over his shoulder and used it to scrub sweat from his face. "Wade and everybody else is, too."

"That so. This Cat *hombre* must be a tough one."

Wiley nodded. "Mean when he's sober and poison when he's drinkin'."

"Cat?" mused Allard with a smile. "Where'd he get that moniker? Seems to me his name ought to be Tiger."

Wiley grinned slyly. "Pinto told me Cat spent a lot of time in a cathouse when they was in Santa Fé, and Clay Allison hung the nickname on him. Then Jack Slade picked it up. Pinto says Allison and Slade are the only men Cat's scared of, so the name stuck.

156

Them two could say anything they wanted 'cause they're faster than Cat, and he knows it."

Allard's mind was already moving elsewhere. "What about this fellow Slade?"

"Jack Slade? One of Cat's ridin' partners from Texas. They been travelin' together. When Cat brought him here, nobody knew he was wanted for murder."

Allard clucked in surprise. "Murder you say. What happened?"

"Way I heard it, Jack pulled a robbery in Sweetwater, and two men was killed. The sheriff in Mountain Pass, name of Burns, had a warrant for him, but Jack didn't know it. He hit for town one night to get whiskey, got drunk, and a deputy arrested him. Pinto told me they never would have got Jack 'cept he was juiced up." He watched Allard solemnly for some response. Receiving none, he added: "They took him to Saint George, had a quick trial, and strung him up before Cat could break him out."

"Kinda tough on Jack."

"You should've seen Cat when he heard about it," Wiley declared ominously. "He went loco. I'm glad I wasn't the deputy that arrested Jack."

"Why not? What did Lenifee do?"

"Couldn't say for sure. I wasn't around.

157

But Pinto told me he never saw Cat so crazy mad. He rode out and didn't come back for two days."

"I thought the old man was the law in the basin."

"He is, for most of us. But not for Jack, or Cat and Emmett and Pinto. They been doin' as they please. When Jack was thrown in jail, Ben told 'em again to get out of the basin." He grinned at Allard. "They're still here, and the old man don't know what to do." A sudden prudence overtook him and brought him to a stop. He looked around, realizing he may have talked more than he intended, so he said, in an earnest voice: "You ain't gonna tell anybody what I been sayin', are you?"

Allard dropped some of his reserve. He smiled. "Wiley, you think like a man. We're friends, and what we talked about is just between us."

"I don't know how long Ben will let you stay after your fight with Wade. He don't like trouble, and he's got his hands full with Cat and the others." Wiley permitted himself a sigh of relief. "I been thinkin' of leavin' the basin myself. Like to travel further west to Nevada or maybe California. Which way you headin' when you leave?"

"Haven't decided for sure. Probably the same direction."

"How about some company? I'm a good cook."

Allard looked at him seriously. "You'd make a good ridin' partner. Might work out."

Wiley swelled perceptibly. "Shucks, if you'll take me, I'll go in any direction. I'm tired of this place. I think it's ready to blow up."

Allard pushed his legs against the earth, feeling the give of his muscles and testing his reflexes. He smiled again. "If I wasn't a bag of sore bones, I'd go swimming with you, but Bowley left me some aches and pains. You better go cool off."

"Sure," said Wiley, "reckon I will," catching up his rifle and moving off in the direction of the creek.

Chapter Eight

There was little activity in the immediate vicinity of the yard at this time of the day. The men were off working somewhere, and the various women of the settlement could be seen crossing from one building to another, busy with their daily tasks, some carrying laundry or household goods, others on private errands of their own. Occasionally children ran about, their small voices shrill and quickly calling across the compound. As the morning dragged on, Allard found himself growing more and more frustrated with his situation. He couldn't bear inactivity in any form for long and saw his opportunities fading with the passing hours. Somewhere here in this basin was the murderer he sought. How did he find him? Where did he start?

Killing time around the yard accomplished nothing, and he drifted over to the corral, got his saddle, and threw it on the chestnut. His muscles responded slowly with considerable discomfort. When he lifted the leather skirt and hauled up on the latigo, he could feel the stretch in every sinew of his arms. He mounted with all his muscles in protest, squared himself in the saddle, and rode directly into the trees, aiming in the general direction of the meadow Wiley had mentioned.

As soon as he entered the timber, daylight's brightness vanished, and he traveled in perpetual shade on a spongy cushion of pine needles. A hundred feet above his head the stiff tips of the forest giants spread in a lacework of branches that trapped the morning's crispness and pleasantly cooled his skin. He came to an ill-defined path and followed it on a slight upgrade through a stillness broken only by the rhythmic fall of his pony's hoofs. A transparent shade hung beneath the trees, diffusing the sunlight, and from somewhere in the underbrush a quail sent its liquid call. It was a lazy atmosphere that induced lethargy, and he abandoned his accustomed caution to drift along.

He was preoccupied by daydreams of Joyce Lenifee and little else when he heard the sharp swell of sounds ahead. The trees thinned out, and it grew lighter. He pulled up in a clump of saplings and scanned a small, stumpy clearing in which two men from the basin were cutting wood. They were some distance away, and the rhythmic rise and fall of their axes sent flat echoes through the trees. Neither man saw him, and he had no wish to be seen, so he reversed in his tracks for a short distance and circled the meadow, resuming his original path. The trail carried him on a gentle upward slant for a long half mile and terminated at the base of a round, largely bald knob. A log shack with lime-chinked walls and a shake roof squatted in the center. A single door and window faced him, and beyond the cabin he observed a shed and a corral in which horses stirred.

This was probably Cat Lenifee's cabin. Allard studied the place with interest, aware of no sounds other than his own breathing and the occasional stamp of his horse. Somewhere off to his left the staccato hammering of a woodpecker began, then abruptly ceased, and he heard the sound of the bird's wings as it flapped off in agitated flight. Had he been less deep in his reverie, he might have thought something unusual about this sudden departure, but he felt himself secluded and was about to turn back the way he had come, when he was frozen in the saddle by a raspy challenge.

"Sit right there, or I'll put a bullet through you!"

A horse and rider slid out of the pines behind him, and Cat Lenifee circled slowly, coming to a standstill facing him. He was astride a black pony with white spots. He had drawn his revolver and laid the raw muzzle squarely on Allard. His face was an odd mix of cunning and cruelty.

"You damned spy," he grated. "I had a hunch you might be snoopin' around. What the hell you doin' up here?"

Allard knew Lenifee had him alone and away from the settlement. He was completely at the mercy of a volatile personality. The smell of blood was all about him, and a growing notion to use his gun was apparent on his wedge-shaped face as he swayed on the delicate edge of firing.

Allard's thoughts were precise and swift. The gun was pointed straight at him, and it took a special effort to hold himself motionless. "Just looking over the place. Didn't know there was a law against it." He inclined his head at Lenifee's revolver and said with a wicked calm: "You always pull down on an unarmed man? I've got no gun."

His words drew Lenifee's aroused stare, and his eyes dropped to Allard's beltless waistline and remained there. "How come you ain't heeled?" Then understanding came to him, and his lips thinned in a mocking smile. "I know what happened. The old man took your guns when you came in."

The knowledge amused him and he seemed to be enjoying himself. Then his mood changed. The man was delicately balanced, a single step from violent action, and the realization raised a thin sweat on the surface of Allard's skin. He never removed his eyes from Lenifee's face and maintained an unruffled calm. "Put up your gun," he said, "and go about your business."

"Where you from?"

Allard, who had never been east of Utah, was tempted to invent a fictitious location, but, unsure of Lenifee's past travels, he was reluctant to concoct a story that might trap him. He considered Lenifee bleakly, and, as he did so, a sudden flame of temper flared out of control. "None of your damned business," he said, his words blazing. "Now get the hell out of my way."

His defiant words instantly inflamed the dark, cold man. "You son of a bitch. I'll make it my business."

Without warning, Lenifee spurred forward, crowding his horse against Allard's. He lifted his gun so rapidly that Allard had no time to put up his arms to shield himself and in one sweeping, back-handed motion raked the barrel across Allard's cheek, slicing a ragged furrow deeply through the flesh. The impact knocked Allard sideways. He nearly fell from the saddle but hooked the pommel with one hand and hung on, the warm wetness of fresh blood streaming down his cheek. He was stunned and half groggy. Everything was swimming out of focus, and his dazed eyes turned aimlessly from side to side. He blindly slapped his right hip with the palm of his hand, automatically searching for his gun. When his hand came away empty, his dulled senses remembered that he had no weapon. His hand searched for his hip pocket, and he pulled out his neckerchief to mop his cheek and his neck, meanwhile staring at Lenifee.

The sight of blood had a strange effect on Cat Lenifee. It aroused some primal impulse, and he watched Allard narrowly while in the depths of his strange eyes a queer glow got brighter and brighter. Lenifee began to taunt him. "Not so tough now. You knocked Bowley down, but the big boy's slow and soft, and he's dumb. I'm goin' to finish what he started and make you crawl. You'll leave the basin in a wagon bed . . . or a coffin."

With that he touched his boots to his horse and spurred forward to deliver another blow but was arrested by a sharp hail.

"Cat! Hold up there!"

Ben and Chester Lenifee rode from the trees, coming to a halt ten feet away. Neither man wore a gun or had a rifle in his saddle boot. Ben rode his horse ahead of his son. Cat Lenifee swung around to meet the newcomers, his body tense and poised for trouble, his hand still holding his revolver at the ready, covering all three men.

Ben Lenifee's expression was masked except the fixed, severe stare of his powerful eyes. His voice rumbled out of his chest. "Cat, what goes on here?"

"This damn' newcomer is a spy, Ben," Cat snapped. "He's got no business pokin' around up here. I aim to work him over and run him out."

Ben's tall, cadaverous shape was sharply defined in his saddle, like a carved figure. "Since when do you make the laws in the basin? This stranger" — he waved an arm in Allard's direction — "is here by my invitation." He swung his attention back to Allard, and his voice jumped at him. "What were you doing up here by the knob? Are you a lawman?"

Cat broke in angrily. "What you askin' him for? Ain't my word good enough? He sneaked up here lookin' for somethin'."

Ben Lenifee ignored him, his formidable

166

eyes still on Allard, waiting for an answer. "Does he speak the truth? Did you enter our valley for a dishonest purpose?"

Allard sat on his horse daubing at his slashed cheek which burned like a ridge of fire. Rage and bitterness pulled his cheeks together and his hot eyes stared at Ben Lenifee. "I came into your damned valley as a peaceful man," he said, "and you took my guns. Since then, one bruiser picked a fight with me for helping your daughter, and now this *hombre* pistol-whipped me for no good reason. That's a hell of a welcome from a God-fearin' man like yourself."

From atop his horse Ben Lenifee swung his gaze back to Cat. The two men were like strange dogs, stiffened against each other and waiting. The older man's slow-moving wrath rose from the depths of his character. "The stranger was on the east road when Jo's horse went lame. He showed her courtesy, used his horse to pull the wagon, and brought her home. For that I offered him our hospitality. He is without weapons, and you know that gun play has no place here. I will tolerate nothing further from you. Do you understand?"

His forceful words only served to infuriate Cat Lennifee. "You'll play hell with such talk, Ben. I've had a bellyful of you and your damn' laws. Ever since me and the boys got here, you been tryin' to get rid of us. Maybe the women and kids and the rest of your spineless sodbusters will let you play God in the basin, but back off from me or I'll kill you."

He swung his gun around and laid it directly on the older man who watched its motion with his stern mouth tightly shut and stiffened himself in the saddle, rigidly indignant. His authority had never been subject to question and never opposed. Cat's defiance and contempt were things he could not endure. A monumental outrage displayed itself openly on his face. Cat Lenifee reacted immediately.

"Don't get any ideas, you old bastard, or I'll drop you where you sit. We may be distant kin, but you mean nothin' to me."

"Cat," Ben intoned, "it is not the blood of our relatives that runs in your veins, but the blood of the devil himself. I could not deny you entrance because you are kin, but we have had no peace since you and your partners arrived. I did not know Slade was a fugitive, wanted by the law for murder, and it is my further belief that you yourself have taken other lives." He lifted and pointed a long finger. "You have blasphemed me and disobeyed my orders again, leaving me no choice. For the last time I order you to leave!"

Cat Lenifee found wry humor in the older man's ultimatum. He leaned forward in his saddle, and light danced oddly on the surfaces of his eyes. "Don't talk tough to me, Ben." His hard, sardonic stare bracketed both father and son. "Neither you nor your pup here can run us out, so quit tryin'. There ain't any heroes ready to die in the basin." He paused to let his words sink in, then jerked his head in Allard's direction. "And if you don't send this *hombre* packin', I'll kill him."

No one challenged him, and he settled back against the cantle, cast a scornful glance at all three, and rode off along the base of the knob, soon disappearing.

Ben Lenifee's stony and dignified posture showed no outward signs of change, but Allard, who was watching him closely, thought he saw a shadow of doubt in his eyes. With a loss of certainty the older man seemed to shrink a little in his saddle. Chester Lenifee, beneath his mild manner, exhibited a troubled countenance. This was a new game to him, and he was anxiously concerned over the outcome.

Ben said to Allard: "Ride back with me," and reined his horse about. Allard fell in beside him, and they traveled back down the trail. Chester rode behind them.

When they arrived at the bunkhouse, Ben continued on toward the ranch house, while Chester drew up, turning about in his saddle. "Allard, my father and I came looking for you this morning and trailed you to Cat's cabin. Seems we arrived at the right time." He was slow and easy with his words but was not wholly comfortable, and his mild face showed lines of strain. "You have had your share of problems here, and for that I express regret. Our habits may seem odd to you, but they have served us for generations. We are grateful for the help you gave my sister. Within a few days you will be rested and ready to travel. Beyond that time you cannot remain here. If you stay close to the yard and keep off the trails, nobody will bother you. As you saw, we have some difficulties of our own to take care of. My sister thanks you for helping her and says good bye, as she will not be seeing you again."

These last words caused Allard to stare at Chester intently, searching for some further explanation, but none was forthcoming. He saw no guile in the man's eyes. The practical face showed only a slight shame and embarrassment. His rôle was simply that of a conduit, an unassuming and obedient messenger, delivering his father's instructions. When Allard volunteered nothing additional, Chester gave him a final, impersonal glance and cantered off across the yard.

Mounting the steps to the verandah of the ranch house, Chester found his father there, sunk in his favorite rocker, brooding. Ben threw up a hand, beckoning him over. The sun's rays angled in under the eaves and shown squarely on his father's weathered face, laying bare the creases down each side of his nose, the dark smudges under his eyes, and exposing a network of spider veins on his spare cheeks. Chester was mildly surprised at himself for not having noticed how his father seemed to have aged suddenly, and his dryly compressed lips, always a reflection of his rigid self-discipline, now betrayed a thin uncertainty at their corners.

As far back as Chester could remember, his father had been a pseudo-religious crusader, priding himself on his ascetic and stern dedication to unswerving principles, one of which was the conviction that all human life was an eternal struggle between virtue and sin. Ben made all the important decisions for the community, directing his followers' daily lives and relieving them of the burdens of uncertainty. Blunt to the point of brusqueness, requiring strict loyalty and obedience from his flock of adherents, they nevertheless deemed him an inspired leader. He thought of himself as a saintly visionary, divinely endowed, and made it an exact practice to dispense justice according to his own lights.

"My son," he said gravely, "I have been blind and misled by Cousin Cat. He and his partners are outlaws of the worst sort, and I cannot allow them to remain in our midst."

His words marked the first time he had ever taken his son into his confidence or, for that matter, shared his thoughts with him. It was also the first time Chester had noticed a frailty in his father who seemed downcast and unsure of himself. "What are you going to do?" he asked.

"Got to run him out. I'm convinced the man is capable of murder. I saw it in his eyes today."

"You can't go up against him with your rifle," Chester said immediately. "Nobody around here can. How you gonna get him to leave?"

"Ah," Ben said in his dogged, obstinate way, "I will prevail by following the path of righteousness. Outlawry and violence are a wickedness that I cannot let flourish in this valley." He shook his head and dropped his shoulders, festering anger controlling his voice. "Cat is a distant relation of mine. You may remember that his mother married my second cousin. Although our laws permit any kinfolk to live among us, Cat has defied me on several occasions. Today he threatened me with a gun, and those same laws give me the right to expel him."

"You know that you can't use a gun against him," Chester repeated. "You have preached against violence. Think of some other way and remember that Cat would have shot you down today if you had bucked him further."

The old man was now staring into space. If he heard his son, he paid no attention. Speaking piously, as if to himself, Ben delivered up his soul. "In this valley I have tried to lead our people in living God-fearing lives, as we did in Tennessee. It is no longer possible, so long as Cat and his companions are among us. They are sinful men, and with God's help I will put them out, using any means necessary." With that declaration he pushed himself heavily out of his chair and went inside the house.

Joyce had been in her bedroom while her father was on the verandah. She was about to descend to the first floor when he came through the front door and climbed the staircase to his own room, passing in front of her.

When he saw Joyce, he paused and asked: "When do you go to town next?"

"Tomorrow," she answered.

"I need some shells for my Henry. Pick up a box at Tinker's."

As soon as he disappeared, Joyce sought out her brother on the verandah. She repeated what Ben had said.

"That's why he wants ammunition," Chester said, after relating the events earlier that afternoon. "His mind is on Cat and how to get rid of him. It's pretty obvious what he intends to do, but he's a fool if he tries."

He moved toward the door, but Joyce ran after him and pulled him around. "Chester," she exhorted in an impassioned voice, "you can't let him do this."

"I will try to stop him, but he's never taken advice from anyone, especially from you or me."

The girl's eyes reflected her fear. Better than anyone she knew her father's implacable beliefs. Once his mind was set, nothing could change it. In her brother, however, she thought she detected a newly found independence and felt a sudden affinity with him. "What I don't understand is that he has never tolerated gun play. Nobody up here uses hand guns. What's happened to him?"

Her brother sighed deeply. "This was the second or third argument he's had with Cat, and I saw something snap in his head today when Cat threatened to shoot him."

"If there's a next time, do you think Cat will kill him?"

Chester nodded. "No doubt about it. But he considers himself above harm."

Joyce stood quite still, then laid a hand on her brother's arm. "Can he be that blind?"

"You know how seriously he takes his religion. He told me once his time on earth was preordained. He really doesn't think a bullet can reach him."

"What can we do," she implored? "I know we haven't been close since Mother died, but he is still our father, and we can't simply let him die."

"I'll do what I can, but I'm no gunfighter. Neither of us would stand a chance against Cat or . . . Emmett or Pinto, either."

They ran out of things to say and stood dismally regarding each other. Chester felt as if he had opened the cover of a new book, recognizing in his sister emotions deeper than he had realized. An immense admiration for her suddenly rolled through him.

"Jo," he said, peering down at her intently, "you happy to be marryin' Wade?"

This personal question, so unlike her brother and asked in the midst of their other immediate concerns, caught Joyce by surprise. She looked at him, her glance inquiring and warm. "I wasn't aware you cared much about my feelings. Maybe something good will come out of all this. It may bring us closer."

"You didn't answer me," he said, prodding her gently. "It appears to me you have taken a fancy to this new gent."

"Has it been that obvious?" she murmured, a delicate pink tinting her cheeks. Then her voice hit him with a fervency that shocked him. "Oh Chet, something wonderful has happened to me, and changed me. I will *never* marry Wade. If that means leaving the basin, I'll do it."

Chapter Nine

Early in the bright morning Henry Tinker walked down an alley in Mountain Pass. He was a tall, spare man with a craggy, hawk-like face framed by a magnificent set of mutton-chop whiskers. Born and bred in Boston, he possessed a shrewd New Englander's mind and had come to the western frontier for the chances it offered. He was one of the original citizens of Mountain Pass, and the town's leading merchant. He banged the flat of his hand on the side of the broken-down wagon in which Verne Posey was sleeping off his previous night's excess.

"Posey," he called loudly. "Wake up!"

No response was forthcoming, so Tinker delivered several stout kicks against the box. Verne Posey's head appeared above the top board, his unshaven face crumpled into a wrinkled map still heavy with sleep.

Tinker pushed a thumb behind him with morning grouchiness. "Get yourself cleaned up and go see Gus at the restaurant. He'll give you breakfast. Then come over to the store. I've got a load of supplies for you to take to Amos."

The unkind sunlight streamed down and struck Posey fully in the face. He cupped a hand over his forehead, blinking the fogginess out of his eyes, and squinted dully at Tinker.

"You hear me," said the latter impatiently. "Get out of there and be over to the store in an hour." He tweaked his nostrils at the putrid alley odors, scowled at Posey, and wheeled about, tramping back to the street.

An hour later, his stomach full and his face half wiped from a quick wash, Posey presented himself at the back door of Tinker's store. Coffee and breakfast had steadied him somewhat, but he looked drawn and peaked. His eyeballs were red-shot, and his hands had a slight tremble. He stank of stale sweat, whiskey, and slept-in clothes, and stood obediently and silently in the doorway. Tinker pointed to a muslin sack nearby, stuffed with provisions.

"Take this out to Burns's place like you've done before. Use my sorrel mare. She's down at Conroy's. Don't waste time. If you're back by sundown, I'll stake you to supper and a bottle."

Posey was hung over and only half awake. He nodded without speaking and bent over to test the sack, lifting it a few inches off the floor, then letting it drop. It was heavier than he expected, so he got down on all fours and worried the sack around until he got a shoulder underneath it. Hoisting the sack on his back, he lurched unsteadily to his feet and staggered out the door under the skeptical scrutiny of Tinker. Posey wove his way down the street to the livery stable where he dropped his burden to the ground.

Hank Ennis, who worked there, saddled Tinker's horse and gave Posey a hand lifting the sack aboard and lashing it with saddle strings behind the cantle. Posey rode out of Mountain Pass on the north trail. Once out of town the trail ran northward through velvet sweeps of timber, and Posey cruised blissfully along in a dreamy stillness broken only by the sharp chattering of darting jays and the familiar creak of the saddle. Tinker's words stuck in his mind and filled it with fanciful thoughts about the coming evening.

Posey covered the three miles to Burns's cabin in an hour and hauled up short of the porch. He sent a shouted: "Hello, there!" before sliding from the saddle and tying the horse to a corner post. He lugged the gunny sack up the steps and dragged it across the planks where he banged loudly on the door.

"Sheriff! It's me, Posey, with a sack of food."

Burns's voice met him. "Bring it in. Door's unlocked."

Posey pushed the door open and found Burns out of bed and seated in a chair by the window, his hat on his head. The sheriff was only a suggestion of what he had been a few short months before. He had thrown an old overcoat over his night shirt, and his naked legs, thin and white and whiskered, protruded from beneath the bottom of his coat. He was thin and pale but appeared broadly pleased to have company and greeted Posey with genuine warmth.

"Been expectin' somebody. Ain't had a visitor lately and was startin' to run low on supplies. I'm even glad to see you, Posey. Bring any onions?"

"Don't know what's in the sack, Amos. When I picked it up, Henry had it tied and ready."

"Bring it over here in the light, and we'll have a look."

Posey skidded the sack next to Burns's chair, and the sheriff leaned over, rummaging through the contents.

"Ah," he announced, withdrawing several red onions. "Henry read my mind. Had a hankerin' for some of these."

The last time Posey had brought supplies Burns had been bed-ridden. To see the sheriff up and sitting in a chair caused him to say: "Glad you're feelin' better."

"Gainin' a little more every day," said Burns, "but still weak as a kitten. You tell Tinker I might try a trip to town in two more weeks." He put his hands on the arms of the chair and rose slowly, maintaining a delicate balance. "Get stiff, sittin' all day." He looked out the open door, spotting the horse tied there.

"Whose sorrel is that?"

"Henry's."

"Ain't seen it before. Didn't know Tinker owned a sorrel. Mighty pretty animal."

"Shore is, but not like a palomino. They got better coloring."

"How would you know? No palominos in the Sage Hen or the Gilt Edge. When was the last time you saw one?"

"Not long past," said Posey, strangely recalling the horse. "In the alley one night when I was in bed. Prettiest horse I ever seen."

"You see a lot in that alley. What night was this?"

Posey found the whole conversation bothersome. He had plans for the evening and was anxious to be on his way. He didn't answer Burns who didn't repeat his question. Posey said: "So long, Amos, take care of yourself," and backed his way across the room, going outside to the horse.

Burns trailed behind him, walking slowly to the edge of the porch where he stopped, gripping the rail with a pale hand so thin that white bone showed under the skin. He was lonesome and longed for company. Even Posey's was better than none, and he watched the little man scramble up on the sorrel and claw at the reins, his soft body flaccid and loose, resembling an overflowing sack of wheat.

"It is a strange thing, Amos," Posey said, now mounted, scrubbing a hand over his cheeks, "why I should remember that night. It was when your deputy got shot. A fella was in my alley with the prettiest palomino I ever seen."

The sheriff's jaw dropped, and his eyes, lately disinterested and sleepy, flamed with a flare of his old vitality. "What man? What palomino?"

Posey was startled and dismayed by the abrupt change in the sheriff. He sat speechless. When he failed to answer, Burns lost his patience.

"Posey," he roared, coughing as he did so, his breath sawing up from his lungs, "climb off and come down here!"

His manner was so threatening that Posey reined away in alarm, a move that further provoked Burns.

"God damn you, Posey! I mean it! Climb down, or I'll get my rifle and shoot you out of the saddle."

Posey dismounted warily and approached Burns with leaden footsteps, openly apprehensive. The sheriff displayed a surprising vigor for a sick man. A scarlet flush of excitement had replaced the pallor on his cheeks, and, when he laid his suddenly bright eyes on Posey, Burns saw him cringe.

"Posey, this is damned serious. Tell me everything you can remember about that night."

Posey shook his head. "Amos, that was a while ago, and it was one of those foggy nights. I couldn't see anything. I don't know who he was."

Burns was not to be put off. "By God, you saw a palomino, and somebody had to be ridin' it. Why the hell didn't you say anything about it before? You sure you ain't imaginin' all this?"

"I'm sure," wailed Posey. "I'll never forget that horse, long as I live." Then, slowly comprehending, he asked: "Amos, you think that might have been the feller shot your deputy?"

"Hell, yes, I do. It's the only thing I got to go on. Nobody else saw anything that night."

The stress of the moment and his exertions cost the sheriff dearly, for he fell into a succession of hacking coughs, each inhalation bringing forth its own wheezing hollow of sound. A tremor shook him, and he backed to the porch where he hooked an arm around the corner post and placed his weight there. He said in a milder tone: "Verne, this may be the most important thing you've ever done. I want you to tell me each detail about that night. Take it slow and try to remember everything."

Posey felt better, safer. He pulled his ruined features together in heavy thought. "I was goin' to sleep and heard somethin' outside. The wind was blowin' the fog around, makin' it tough to see, but, when it opened a little, I saw this horse and rider."

"Keep thinkin'. Tell me some more."

"Well, like I said, this palomino was standin' right near my wagon. When the moon broke through, I could see his gold hide shinin' with a white mane and tail." His rheumy eyes blinked at Burns as he remembered something else. "Had ivory

184

stockings and a white blaze face, too. You ever seen markings like that?"

"No," said Burns impatiently, "but the man! What did he look like? What was he wearin'?"

Posey was losing his concentration. He needed a drink badly.

Burns saw him drifting off and moved to stop it. "Verne, think hard now. Do you remember anything more?"

Posey shook his head sorrowfully. "He came runnin' down the alley right after the shots and lit out in a hurry. All I saw was a shadow. Honest, Amos, that's all I remember." He looked pleadingly at Burns. "Henry told me to have this bronc' back by sundown. I better go."

The high excitement was beginning to tell on Burns. The coughing fit had used up his temporary vitality and reaction was setting in. His cheeks were losing their flush, turning waxen and bloodless. Fever laid its layer of fine perspiration on his brow. "You can go, but take a message to Tinker. Tell him to come see me right away." A spark of fire flared again for an instant in his eyes, and he looked at Posey intently. "Damn it, do you hear what I'm sayin? Talk to Henry before you have a drink!"

Burns was beginning to frighten Posey

again. "Sure, Amos, sure," he said, mounting and reining around the sorrel. "You take good care of yourself. I'll do it soon as I hit town."

He wore no spurs on his worn, grimy boots and banged his worn-down heels against the horse's belly. When the animal, used to the bite of steel, didn't move fast enough to suit him, he pulled off his hat and batted it across the pony's ears, frightening the beast into a headlong rush down the trail.

It was early twilight when Posey turned the sorrel over to Ennis at the livery stable. Burns's instructions had stayed with him all the way to town, and he asked Ennis: "Is Henry still at the store? I got somethin' to tell him."

"He went home," said Ennis shortly. "Got tired of waitin' for you."

"He promised me a meal and a bottle," protested Posey.

"Keep your shirt on. Henry said for you to go over to the Staghorn and tell 'em he sent you. They'll give you supper."

He purposely offered nothing more, intentionally baiting Posey who immediately said: "What about my bottle?"

"I was expectin' your question," said Ennis with a foxy grin. "There's one waitin' for you in the Gilt Edge." He turned and led the sorrel into a stall, handing Posey a final bit of advice over his shoulder. "Better get a meal under your belt before you start on the whiskey."

Posey left the stable in high spirits. *I'll eat first, then drop by Tinker's house and give him the message.* He marched up the street with a precise straightness, headed for the hotel. His route took him past the Gilt Edge, and, when he came to the entrance, he stopped short, squinting into the opening from which streamed the pleasurable rankness of freely flowing whiskey. The pungency pulled him like a magnet. *Maybe a short one before I eat. After supper I'll go see Henry and then come back.*

Impressed with this logic, Posey turned with quickening steps into the saloon and worked his way directly to the bar. There he was confronted at once by Ed Burrows who moved down the bar to face him, wiping his hands on a dirty apron. He stood with palms flattened on the bar's surface.

"This is your lucky day, Posey," the bartender said. "You won't have to mooch off anybody tonight." He reached under the bar for a full bottle of bourbon which he placed before Posey. "Henry Tinker paid for this, and it's yours, but you better polish it off someplace else. If you try to sleep in here, I'll throw you out in the street."

"Just a moment, sir!" exclaimed Posey in high dudgeon. He pulled himself up to his full height with a show of dignity. He wrapped his fingers around the neck of the bottle and pulled out the cork. "Put two glasses on the bar, Mister Burrows. I should like to buy you a drink."

"Don't mind if I do," said Burrows, immediately more amiable. He poured a generous drink for himself and downed it in a swallow. He gave Posey a gap-toothed grin.

The hearty feeling of camaraderie widened beyond the bartender. Posey hosted drinks for many newly found friends, and toasts were raised to various causes until the bottle was empty, and one by one his erstwhile comrades drifted away until he stood alone at the bar. By this time he was soddenly drunk, and Amos Burns's message for Henry Tinker had been wiped from his mind.

Chapter Ten

Long after Posey rode off, Amos Burns lay hopelessly awake, turning from side to side on his blankets and rearranging the quilts beneath him. Posey's confession had reopened channels of hope and anticipation he had all but abandoned. It furnished the starting point for Frank Allard, but he had no means of communicating with Allard who was somewhere in the mountains, traveling blind. He cursed the physical restraint forced on him by his injury and tossed about, too weak to rise and too disturbed for sleep.

His only link with town was the message he had given Verne Posey, but he was apprehensive about its delivery. He knew the little man thoroughly and had small faith in him, but it was a gamble he had had to take.

Presently he grew hungry, so he crawled off the bed and dug into the sack of provisions, unearthing a can of beans, a potato, and an onion. When he stood up, he grew dizzy and was conscious of the fever's heat on his skin. He took a few minutes to gather himself and muster sufficient strength to plod into the kitchen where, over a considerable period of time, he prepared and ate his meal, afterwards returning to bed.

He lay listening to the wind swirling around the cabin in rising and falling howls of sound. The food in his belly had a sedative effect, and, in spite of his best efforts to reactivate his thoughts, exhaustion struck him like a great maul, and he fell into a shallow sleep.

Sometime later, when he opened his eyes, the window's rectangle revealed the blackness of the outer world, and he knew he had slept for several hours. During sleep he had thrown aside his blankets and perspired heavily. The cabin was cold, and the bedclothes sticky and clinging. Shivering in the grip of a fever that left him alternately burning or freezing, he punched his pillows into a mound against the headboard and fell back on top of them, pulled up his covers, and lay thinking. If Posey had followed instructions, Henry Tinker would have arrived from town by now. Therefore, his hunch was correct. Posey had run true to form, and Tinker had not received his message and never would. Nobody was coming out from town. He might not have a visitor for days, and he couldn't wait that long.

At four o'clock in the morning the sheriff

finally threw off his coverlet and sat bolt up-right in a sodden nightshirt. A sourness lay in his stomach and fever from the infection in his blood burned through his body with a heat he could definitely feel. He wasn't rested at all, dead-beat and weakened by the combination of his illness and the inertia of advanced age. His night-long grappling with a problem that had netted him nothing did not help. Frank Allard's precarious ex-posure in Winona Basin and his own mis-judgment by entrusting Posey with a vital errand made further rest impossible.

From its place on the table the coal-oil lamp guttered weakly, throwing off a slack soot that collected on the ceiling in a suffo-cating cloud. He stared dully at the flame, his spirits much like the feeble light, flicker-ing ever downward. His wandering eyes roamed the room and fell on the half-used pouch of Kentucky Burley tobacco still ly-ing on the table where Frank Allard had for-gotten it. Sight of the pouch sparked an idea. He found the stub of a pencil on the bedside table and pulled an old reward dodger from a pile of papers. Turning it over, he tediously wrote:

A palomino with white mane and tail was in the alley the night of the shooting.

191

The horse had white stockings and blaze forehead. Owner could be our man.

A. B.

He folded the paper into a small square, tucked it deeply in the loose tobacco at the bottom of the pouch, and pulled the draw strings tight. Through the window an increasing grayness signaled approaching dawn, and with leaden movements he moved into the kitchen with a dragging gait where he boiled up some coffee and fried two eggs. Recurrent chills shook him, and from time to time he suffered a loss of equilibrium, making it necessary to stabilize himself against the wall or grip the edge of the table. His wound had reopened. It seeped blood and began to send out higher waves of pain.

He coughed into his handkerchief, noticing blood in the sputum. From the contents of a bottle on the shelf he spiked his coffee with a generous jolt of whiskey and drank two cups straight down. The liquor's kick gave him enough short-term strength to shoulder into his coat, pull on his boots, and clap on his hat. He slid the pouch into a pocket of the coat, left the cabin, and moved sluggishly away from the porch. He picked up a stick leaning there and used it as a cane, slogging across the clearing.

Halfway to the stable he felt light-headed and had to stop. It looked a half mile distant, but the nausea eventually left him, and he resumed his slow progress, reaching and entering the shed. When he came alongside his horse and made one faltering attempt to lift his saddle from the rack, he knew he would have to ride bareback for he lacked the strength to hoist it on the horse. He took the harness from its familiar hook and worked the bit between the pony's teeth, slipping the bridle into place. After knotting the reins, he led the horse out of the shed. He went back inside and poked around in the dark until he found two lug boxes which he piled one on top of the other, next to the horse.

Waves of faintness continued to sweep him, swelling and waning, and he heard the slugging rhythm of his heart close beneath his ribs. He leaned against the horse, listening to his own weakness. Sweat already lined his clothing with a clammy film. He dug out his bandanna, mopped his brow, and crawled laboriously atop the boxes, maintaining his precarious balance by keeping one hand against the horse's haunch. He said: "Easy, Belle," and with great effort heaved himself up on the animal's back, his slack body draped crosswise.

The exertion had worn him out, and for a time he limply hung face down, lacking the strength to sit up. The distress in his shoulder was a trip-hammer pounding that broke through every ordered thought, and his body was heavy and lead-like. He knew he had to stick on the horse's back, for, if he fell off, he could never remount. When the misery eased somewhat, he raised himself, took a handful of the horse's mane, and swung one leg across to right himself, finally astride. When he sensed the onset of another dizzy spell and felt himself reeling, he entwined his fingers through the horse's mane and hung on, beating back the nausea to keep from fainting. When it passed and some stability returned, he took hold of the looped reins and pulled them toward him.

He rode into the sullen mist of early morning and struck out at once for Mountain Pass. The approaching dawn raised a pink glow in the eastern sky, but the sharp edges of each jagged peak were barely visible through the haze. Dew lay wetly everywhere. The grass underfoot was sodden, and steady moisture dripped from the trees, but Burns saw none of this. Pain from his wound took on the rhythm of his pulse, and he rode with his eyes closed, steeling himself before the onset of each wave. Every ordered faculty he could summon was concentrated on a single purpose — to stay on the horse's back. If the horse trotted or cantered, he knew he would fall, so he held the animal to a moderate walk in the center of the trail.

The measured cadence of Belle's gait and the gentle *chock-chock* of each hoof fall set up a soothing sound that floated to him from a great distance, and he fell into a troubled half doze, drifting in and out of consciousness. Strange images rose in his mind and died there, and he lost touch with reality, aware only of his tightly locked fingers through the horse's mane.

Without any guidance Belle was in no particular hurry and stopped frequently to graze at the roadside. Each time, when the familiar rocking motion ceased, Burns would rouse himself and restart the animal by squeezing both his legs against her sides. The beast responded slowly, and he croaked: "Hup, Belle, hup. Move, girl."

In this aimless fashion horse and rider converged on Mountain Pass, arriving there in the late morning. Burns was in sorry shape, unaware of his surroundings and burning up with fever. His upper body had fallen sharply forward from the waist, and he was slumped so low that his chest lay flat on the animal's withers. His arms were clamped around the beast's neck in a death grip, and his eyes were tightly closed. During the ride his wound had bled steadily, and escaping blood seeped from under the dressing and ran beneath one side of his coat, leaking into his boot. The blood loss together with his fever had whipped him down until he had nothing left.

When the horse halted of its own accord at the livery stable's watering trough, Hank Ennis, emerging from the gloom of the interior, found him. "What the hell, Amos. You ain't supposed to be ridin'." He leaned closer and saw fresh blood on one leg. "You're bleedin'. You all right?"

Burns didn't hear him. He lay like a dead man, half on the horse's back and half on the animal's neck. He was barely breathing. When Ennis reached up and tugged at his sleeve, the sheriff's body was an unresponding lump of coal. Ennis pried the old man's fingers apart and pulled his arms from around the horse's neck. When he did this, Burns let go all at once and fell heavily into his arms.

Other townsmen, who had observed the arrival, now gathered. They crowded around Ennis whose supporting arms kept

Burns from sinking to the ground. One man, closely searching the sheriff's ashen face, said: "He don't look like he's alive. Why'd he ride into town?"

"We better get Doc Webber here fast," said Ennis. He looked around. "Anybody know where he is?"

"Yeah," said a man who had just pushed into the circle. "He's in his office. Saw him go in there."

Another bystander said: "I'll get him," and swung away at once.

"Gimme a hand," Ennis said.

With help from two others the hosteler lifted Burns and carried him into the stable office. The dingy room was a cluttered mess of assorted tack-room gear, broken harness, and dirty men's habits. Ennis kicked his way through the jumble, swept aside a pile of garments from a low cot, and they laid Burns there, covering him with a horse blanket.

Ennis seized a water bucket and lifted Burns's head, holding the tin dipper to his lips. The sheriff's eyes were still closed, but he sucked greedily, much of the water spilling down his chin and onto his chest. He coughed up some blood and pinched open a pair of fever-glazed eyes, looking confused by his whereabouts. He recognized Ennis standing over him. "Hank," he breathed, "where the hell am I?"

"In the stable office. Shut up and lie still till Doc Webber gets here."

Instead of dropping his head to the pillow, Burns raised himself on an elbow and clutched Ennis's shirt with bony fingers. "Get Henry Tinker over here, and fast."

"You need Doc Webber," said Ennis. "Whut you want Henry for?"

Burns didn't answer, and one of the bystanders said: "Henry's probably at his store. I'll find him." He left the room.

Burns's head dropped forward until his chin rested on his chest. Ennis turned to the cluster of onlookers, jammed into his small quarters. He was the central figure in the drama and extremely conscious of his heavy mantle of authority. "Everybody get the hell out of here. Give the sheriff some air." When nobody moved, he lifted his voice higher. "Damn it! Everybody out."

Somebody from the rear said: "Who the hell you think you are, Hank, Gawd Almighty?" — but there was nothing more to see, and the group stirred, moving away with reluctance. The last man to leave stepped aside at the doorway as the townsman arrived with the doctor.

Sam Webber was a short, peppery man

beyond middle age who had practiced buck-shot medicine in Mountain Pass for the past ten years. During his tenure he had witnessed the results of enough mayhem in life's unexpected whimsies not to disturb the dryness and the skepticism of his character. He had come away without his hat. When he squatted next to the cot and laid a hand on Burns's forehead, his bald pate, encircled by a ring of gray fuzz, shone as a polished ball in the room's fitful light. He opened his satchel, withdrew a wooden stethoscope, and placed it against the sheriff's chest. He listened for a moment, muttering to himself, then unbuttoned Burns's shirt and cut away the soiled wrapping for a view of his shoulder.

"Amos," he said at last, "you're in bad shape. Riding in here was a damn' fool thing to do. We've got to take you over to my office, *pronto.*" Evoking no reaction, the medical man lifted each of the sheriff's eyelids with a fingertip, then took out a wooden depressor, peered into his throat, after which he rose to his feet with his diagnosis. "The sheriff's a mighty sick man. I believe he has pneumonia. He was in no shape to ride. Why did he come to town?"

Ennis shook his head. "He ain't sayin', Doc. He wants to talk to Tinker."

"I don't care what he wants," said Webber sharply. "He'll do as I say." He narrowly considered his patient and wagged his head from side to side. "Otherwise, he could go out on us."

Voices rose from the street, and Henry Tinker stepped into the room. The locals respected him, and, when he strode through the doorway, they moved aside. He nodded at Webber and crossed at once to the cot, stooping and looking down at Burns, obviously shocked by the old man's appearance. "Amos," he said. "What are you doing here? You should be home in bed. Didn't Posey deliver your supplies yesterday?"

The sound of his voice roused Burns. His eyes blinked open, and he peered up at Tinker, his face gray with the knowledge of his own dying. "Henry," he croaked, "I got somethin' to tell you. Get these people out of here."

Doc Webber broke in, addressing himself to Tinker in a purely professional attitude. "Henry, Amos has pneumonia and will die if I don't treat him immediately. We have to carry him to my office without delay."

Burns heard his words. "Doc," he whispered, "I got to have three minutes alone with Henry . . . whether I die or not."

Tinker turned and made a pushing motion with his hand to the others standing about. He was by nature an easy-going man, but he could act decisively. The few lingering townsmen withdrew at once. The merchant turned to Webber. "Step outside a minute, Doc. I don't know what he has on his mind, but he's got to get it off his chest. Then you can have him."

Webber moved to the door, grumbling irritably. He slammed the office door behind him.

As soon as they were alone, Burns weakly grasped Tinker's sleeve. "Did Posey give you my message? Why didn't you come out yesterday?"

"I got no message. Haven't seen Posey since yesterday morning."

"God damn him. I thought as much. Knew I had to come in myself." He slid one hand into a pocket of his coat and pulled out Allard's worn tobacco pouch. "When do you expect the Lenifee girl in town again for supplies?"

"Probably in the next day or two." Burns's unexpected question startled him. "What do you want with her?"

"Henry," said Burns, his labored breathing fast and shallow, "ask me no questions. There ain't time. What I'm tellin' you is important." Tinker inclined his head without speaking, and Burns continued. "Take this pouch of tobacco." He pressed it into Tinker's hand. "Don't throw it out. Get a new pouch from your shelves and see that Miss Lenifee takes both of 'em with her when she leaves. Tell her to give 'em to a man named Frank Allard who should be in the basin."

Tinker thought Burns delirious and hallucinating. "You crazy? You're damn' near dead and worrying about somebody's tobacco. Who's this Allard?"

Burns swept the question aside. Fever flushed his cheeks and put an unnatural brilliance behind his eyes. His shaky voice kept ebbing, but a stubborn determination drove him on. "Never mind. I ain't crazy. I know what I'm doin'. Here's the rest of it." His eyes burned up at Tinker with a dying glow. "When you give the girl both pouches, you got to tell her a little story, but keep me out of it entirely. If my name is mentioned at all, this man Allard will die. Understand?"

Tinker nodded. "What kind of story?"

Burns's gray face had taken on a more distinct pallor. When he spoke now, Tinker could barely hear his words. "This is what you tell her. A couple weeks ago a stranger came through here. Stopped in your store. You got talkin'. His name was Frank Allard. He bought pipe tobacco. He went off and

202

left it. Along with his old pouch. Give her both pouches. Tell her they belong to him. If she runs into him, she should return them." He stopped speaking. His eyes closed.

Tinker, as he stared down at the frail body on the cot, could see what this had cost him. Burns's thin body now lay so still that Tinker could not even see his chest move with faint breathing. He rushed across the room and opened the door, beckoning to Webber who waited just outside. The doctor reëntered at once and bent over Burns. He said vehemently: "It's probably cost him his life. He's a damn' fool."

"Doc . . . ?" Tinker said softly, putting a hand on Webber's shoulder, "he just may be a better man than any of us."

Chapter Eleven

When Joyce Lenifee arose on the morning following her discussion with her brother, she inspected herself in the mirror on her dresser and beheld an unfamiliar person in that catoptric image. Particularly of late she had been making an effort to examine the growing current of unrest that plagued her. Her life had ceased to be the same, and she gave it a lot of thought. When she failed to recognize in her mirrored appearance the timid and unsophisticated girl of the past, her imagination supplied a ready answer. Something miraculous had turned her life around and given it new substance. One bothersome riddle which would not leave her, however, was the nagging question whether it was possible to lose her heart completely in such a short space of time, and to a veritable stranger. She couldn't explain that and didn't try, but her world had grown suddenly larger, and the rich riot in her own soul told her to seize her present happiness because misfortune was sure to follow.

Wade Bowley had been erased from her mind as completely as if he had never existed. There was no emptiness in the space he had once occupied, and looking back, comparing him now with Frank Allard, she was amazed at how complete had been her self-deception and how indifferently she had once accepted their predestined relationship. It was a hard thing to admit. She had failed to recognize his unstable character, and had her own quick fear over what he might do when she broke with tradition and refused to honor her father's pledge.

From the day of their mother's death at Fort Bridger, any rapport she and her brother had previously enjoyed with Ben had disappeared. She was sure Chester had his own plans, and, presumably, one day would head the Lenifee clan, but she could conceive no possibility of release for herself unless she left the basin. It also seemed implacably to be her destiny that, since Frank Allard was but a drifter and bound in his own direction, anything she might do for herself she would have to do alone.

She gathered up a few last-minute articles for her run to Mountain Pass and was about to go downstairs when a new and long-forgotten fancy detained her. It was an unaccustomed whim and caused her to pause and consider the clothes she wore, faded men's denims and a long-sleeved shirt.

Oddly swayed by something deep and very feminine, she opened her closet and chose another outfit into which she swiftly changed, and left the house. Not wishing to encounter either her father or Wade Bowley, she slipped out the back door and crossed to the dining hall kitchen where she prepared herself a quick breakfast. Through the doorway she caught a brief glimpse of Frank Allard, seated alone at a far table, but he had his head down. Moments later, when she looked again, he was gone. Afterwards she crossed to the barn, there meeting Wiley who helped her to harness two ponies to the wagon.

She brought the rig around to the big house and went inside to pick up her list and a jug of water, then climbed back on to the wagon seat, and turned into the westward road for town. The ponies were full of repressed energy and hit the traces with vigor, jerking the protesting buggy along at a lively clip. For the first mile Joyce let the animals have their morning run, then she pulled them to settle into a comfortable trot. To either side of her the vertical parapets confining Winona Basin vaulted heavenward, gradually decreasing in height as she neared the western gateway. One of her father's guards was posted there on an outcropping above the road and waved a greeting as she passed below.

The morning was one of those shining days when sunlight has a golden quality, beautifying and giving a special splendor to familiar, common objects. On such a day Joyce normally would have been in a light mood, for her trips to town were always a welcome break from the basin's dull routine. But on this day she was only distantly aware of the landscape's radiance. It failed to gratify her in the usual way for she was struggling through her own dilemma and above it all, hanging like a suspended blade, was her haunting sense of impending disaster.

It was midday when she reached Mountain Pass and halted the rig in front of Tinker's. Having had nothing to eat since breakfast, she crossed to the hotel and lunched alone at a corner table. Other diners observed her, their glances appreciative and full of interest, for she was a striking girl and something of a puzzle to the town. She had a reserve that was beyond the reach of their curiosity, and, over the period of years during which she had made many trips to Mountain Pass, no one had been able to develop a rapport with her. Modest and courteous to all with whom she came in contact, she made no effort to cultivate friends, remaining in town only long enough to complete her business.

When her lunch was over, she left the restaurant and immediately set about her shopping, making a brief stop at the blacksmith's, then the dressmaker's, and then at Gleason's, depositing her purchases in the wagon after each errand. She was crossing the street to Tinker's when a group of townsmen emerged from Dr. Webber's office and made their way up the street in her direction. They were engaged in heavy discussion, and talk flowed freely among them. They saw her approaching and broke aside to let her pass, their talk swiftly dying. She was conscious of their thinly disguised admiration and dropped her eyes as she went by, quickening her pace and entering Tinker's store for the balance of her supplies.

Fred Pond, Tinker's clerk, moved out of the dim interior to wait on her, pleasant and solicitous. They were working on her list when Henry Tinker entered from the street, a cigar burning between his lips and the inevitable trail of smoke drifting past his face. He saw her at once and advanced to greet her with obvious pleasure.

"A very good mornin', Joyce." He removed his hat. "This is a welcome surprise. Haven't seen you for a spell. How are things in the basin?"

"Fine, thank you," she answered, and watched his shrewd eyes fall upon the boxes of rifle shells stacked among her other items on the counter.

"Don't sell much of that caliber any more," he observed, watching her narrowly. "Your father's about my only customer. No trouble at home, I hope."

"No." Her guard was up. She met his sidelong glance with her own direct one. "No trouble at all." Her words threw up a screen, and Tinker removed his cigar, rolled it back and forth between his fingers, and devoted his attention to it. He said in a wholly conversational voice: "When you have finished your business with Pond here, please come back to my office. My wife sent along a couple more books for you. I have them back there."

Once Joyce had finished her shopping and Pond had carried everything outside to the wagon, he helped her tie down the load. They both reëntered the store. She settled her account and ventured back through the dusky interior into a stuffy puddle of store-room smells. She ducked around rows of piled sacks, containing grain and flour, sugar and potatoes, and skirted cases of canned goods, finally coming to Tinker's small office at the very rear of the building. She found him comfortably stretched in his desk chair under a rolling cloud of tobacco smoke. When he saw her wrinkle her nose, he leaped to his feet, violently waving away the fumes he had created and crushing the burning end of his cigar into a clay ashtray on the desk. He crossed to a window and shoved it open, ineffectually fanning the smoke in an attempt to sweep it outside.

"Please sit down," he said affably, with the solicitous behavior of a cultured man who finds himself alone with an attractive woman. He indicated a single chair facing the desk and observed the graceful manner in which she moved across the room. He remained standing, until she was seated, then retreated behind his desk and established himself in his own chair.

"There's the books Martha sent along," he said, indicating two volumes on his desk. "She's finished with both, so you may keep them."

"Please thank her for me."

Tinker rested the points of his elbows on the desk and put the tips of his fingers together, measuring her with a speculative glance. "I've been bothered by a slight problem, and you might possibly help."

"If I can."

He leveled a finger at two tobacco pouches on the desk, one new, the other folded and worn. "See those?"

The girl nodded.

"Not long ago a stranger came through town and stopped for a drink in the Gilt Edge. I happened to be there at the time and engaged him in conversation. He was a pleasant young gent, and we hit it off rather well. The following morning, before he left town, he dropped in here for some purchases, and we talked some more. For a fact he sat right there in your chair. When he left, he forgot his pipe tobacco. Those two pouches belong to him."

"Really Mister Tinker," said the girl, completely mystified, "what has this to do with me?"

"Only that any pipe smoker would miss his tobacco, and I believe this gent was headed in your direction. You might have run into him already. If not, you may see him when you return. Nice straightforward young fellow named Allard."

Tinker had caught her off guard. A small excitement lifted Joyce's heart. Her eyes widened just for an instant, and a little crease of doubt broke the smoothness of her forehead. "Why, no," she said as indifferently as she could, "I haven't seen him. You probably know my father doesn't allow strangers into the basin."

"I'm familiar with your laws," said Tinker dryly, "but this tobacco belongs to that young fellow. Since he will not be returning here, please take it with you on the slim chance that he may pass through your valley. You will be doing him and me a great service. If you don't see him anytime soon, throw them away or give them to someone else." He picked up the pouches and leaned across the desk, pressing them toward the startled girl's hand. Before she had time to refuse, he added: "I'll have Pond throw an extra sack of flour in your wagon for your trouble," and got out of his chair hurriedly and turned from the office, calling loudly into the store for his clerk, leaving her with the tobacco pouches.

Her initial thought was of her first meeting with Allard on the east road into the basin. He had not mentioned being in Mountain Pass. In fact he had been on the other side of the divide, and the idea that she might have been misled bothered her. She placed this uneasiness into the back of her mind, kept the pouches, picked up the books, and went back through the store, emerging finally into the street. Tinker had vanished, and Pond was at that moment hoisting the sack of flour into the wagon. When she climbed to the seat, he untied the horses and handed up the reins. She swung the team smartly around in a tight circle, waved her hand to Pond, and drove off at a fast trot.

Chapter Twelve

With the afternoon sun behind her and sinking swiftly toward the western rim, Joyce now urged the team into a light run. Ahead of her the chiseled cliffs soared skyward in extravagant shapes and ever-changing colors, gradually converging down to the pinched aperture that marked the western entrance. The road ran before her like a furrow through the hills, a confined alley between evergreen fences of pine and aspen, entirely deserted by other travelers.

Her head was bursting with many things. In her pocket were the tobacco pouches. In her mind was a troubling thought that wouldn't leave. In books she had read of men who could make a lie out of their silence, or a truth, whichever suited them best, but she would not allow herself to believe the worst of Frank Allard. She speculated again if it was the opportunity he presented for her to escape life in the basin that drew her to him, but her heart spoke up and said: *no, it was much more than that.*

Midday's heat had faded, and the afternoon wound down as she covered the final miles, arriving at the narrow defile where a different guard acknowledged her passage. When she entered the compound, she drove directly to the dining building where, in response to her call, several women came forth and carried the bundles inside, after which she made various other stops, unloading something at each.

When her deliveries were completed, she pulled up in front of the barn doorway and saw Wiley working inside. He looked up at her approach and smiled, stepping outside to approach her. "Help me unhitch the horses, will you, Wiley?" she asked, and then reined the horses forward around the barn to the wagon yard in back.

Together they unhitched the team. Wiley took the horses inside, hung up the harness, and forked hay into the feed bins. When he emerged from the barn, the girl was waiting for him in front.

She gave him a precise, searching look. "Wiley," she said in that deeply personal way she had, "the stranger, Frank Allard is a friend of yours, isn't he?"

"Sure is."

The girl held out two tobacco pouches. "Give these to him," she said. "He left them at the store in Mountain Pass. Mister Tinker asked me to bring them." She studied him carefully and then added: "Say nothing about this to anyone." She erased her businesslike expression with a smile, and then crossed to the big house with the last of the bundles and the books.

Her father was in the living room, deeply sunk in his favorite chair. He had pulled it in front of the window and sat, staring over the landscape. He had nothing to say except to inquire if Joyce had brought the ammunition he had asked her to fetch from Tinker's and had her put it down on a nearby table. She did so, cast a second look at his stern, bitter features, and went into the kitchen.

The balance of the previous day and today Frank Allard's life had been a humdrum monotony. As Chester Lenifee had admonished him, he stayed off the trails and took no rides into the timber. He was an alien in this valley, and, whenever he was outdoors, he noticed a man loitering nearby, confirming his suspicions that Ben Lenifee had assigned somebody to keep an eye on him. Sometimes he took short strolls about the settlement, but otherwise he spent his time in the area around the compound, taking his meals in the dining room, squatting in the sun, or currying his horse. The aftereffects of the fight with Bowley were fading, but he still had a nagging ache on the left side of his face where a badly swollen cheek reminded him of the pistol-whipping he had received from Cat Lenifee. When he studied his lop-sided features in the bunkhouse mirror, he saw a crusty scab forming beneath one eye and knew he would carry a scar there for the rest of his life.

He had seen nothing more of Cat Lenifee, and, in the bunkhouse, the two beds previously occupied by Cat's partners, Hanks and Daly, were now empty. Not only had they moved out, but they no longer dined with the others. His fruitless brooding this afternoon came to an abrupt halt with the arrival of Joyce Lenifee, her wagon whirling in from the west road and clattering into the yard. When she swung into view, he turned to watch her, for the girl never failed to capture his complete attention. Her appearance introduced a welcome diversion into an otherwise wasted day, and Allard followed her movements as she guided the team across the clearing.

He immediately noticed that she was dressed in something other than men's clothing, accentuating the graceful symmetry of her body. The sight of her, poised and cool, had the effect to buoy him up and stir the ashes of a very private vision he had sheltered since their first meeting.

The girl had spotted him when she first drove into the compound. Their eyes briefly met, not accidentally, but, as if she had been expecting it, and in the moment of locked glances she seemed invisibly to warn him of others who might be watching. His glance seemed to have its own effect on her, and he sensed again the alchemy that floated between them and wondered if it were merely his imagination at work. She gave no further sign but drove from building to building, completing her deliveries. She steered the wagon to the barn where Wiley, having heard her approach, appeared at the entrance. They had a brief conversation, after which they both disappeared into the wagon yard. Sometime later the girl spoke again briefly to Wiley, handed him something, and then crossed the yard to the big house.

A man stepped from the kitchen door, seized a bar of iron, and banged it inside the dinner triangle suspended there, sending a strident call over the area. People moved toward the dining hall, and Wiley trotted over from the barn. He was holding in leash an inner excitement for his cheeks were flushed and his eyes bright. He looked around, to assure himself that no one was within earshot, then said in a confiding voice: "Joyce told me to give these to you." He handed over the two tobacco pouches. "She brought them out from town."

Allard was hard put to conceal his surprise. He recognized his own tobacco pouch at once and saw that an unopened one had been added. Immediate questions sprang into his mind, but he had been weaned in the frontier practice of masking any shades of feeling, and he kept all expression off his face. His passage through Mountain Pass was supposed to have been a secret shared only with Amos Burns. Who else knew he was in the basin, and who else could have given his tobacco pouch to Joyce Lenifee?

Wiley unwittingly supplied a partial answer by adding: "She said the storekeeper in Mountain Pass, name of Tinker, gave these to her. Said you must have forgot 'em when you was there a while ago."

Allard made it a point to show no particular surprise and thrust the pouches into his pocket. "I been wonderin' what happened to these," he said carelessly. "Now I remember."

"Does the cheek still hurt some?"

"I won't win any beauty prizes," Allard conceded, lifting a hand to touch the forming scar. "You heard about my run-in with Cat then?"

"Surely did. Ran into Pinto this mornin'. Cat told him all about it. Lucky thing Ben and Chester showed up, otherwise Cat was goin' to work you over good. He told Pinto he was mad enough to shoot you."

"He may get his chance to try." Allard's long lips clamped together, and his eyes darkened. He studied Wiley's face. "I see Hanks and Daly cleared out of the bunkhouse, and they don't eat in the dining room any more. They leave these parts?"

"Naw, they're batchin' it with Cat. After the last argument with Ben, they cleared out of the bunkhouse and moved up to the cabin. Cat's got his own grub and a cookstove there . . . and whiskey. They get drunk 'most every night." The boy's mind was concentrated on Lenifee. "Ain't nobody around here fast enough with a gun to match Cat. I think he'll shoot Ben if the old man pushes him any further. When you leave the basin, I want to go with you."

"So you've said."

"This place's gotten bad. There's trouble comin', an' I want no part of it."

Allard laid a hand on Wiley's shoulder and said: "Let's eat."

Together they entered the dining room, finding space at the foot of one of the side tables. The room was rapidly filling, and at the head table Joyce Lenifee was already eating, flanked by her father on one side and by Bowley's great shape which spilled over a chair on the other. Allard felt Bowley's steady, beetling stare and the smoldering animosity behind it. The man had not forgiven his beating and never would. His reputation in the basin had suffered irreparably, and the memory must be gnawing bitterly at his damaged pride.

Everybody at the head table seemed ill at ease. Ben Lenifee especially was not his usual imperious self, apparently oblivious to anyone in the room and immersed in his own problems. Chester's bland cheeks revealed nothing, but his head remained bowed over his plate of food. He ate rapidly and finished before anyone else, got up immediately, and departed. Throughout supper Allard was careful to keep his eyes from the girl, but on the single occasion, when he did glance her way, he found her eyes on him. She seemed to be imploring him for something he did not understand and revealing it by way of a silent signal. Then she dropped her eyes, and he wondered if he could have been mistaken, or if it was merely his own fancy that had made it seem so plain.

When his meal was complete, Allard

caught up his usual apple and moved outside, Wiley tagging along as far as the compound where he left Allard to pack his things so he would be ready to pull out with him when the time came. Allard, alone in the dusk, became quite conscious of the new pressure of the pouches in his pocket. He went over to the corral and fed the apple to his horse, then pulled his pipe from one pocket, and withdrew his half-filled pouch from another.

He thumbed the pouch open and used a forefinger to loosen the packed grains inside. His finger struck something besides tobacco at the bottom, but he was keenly anticipating his first smoke in a long time and paid it scant attention. He got some tobacco in his palm, blew through the stem of his pipe, and began to fill the bowl, packing the grains with a loose firmness born of long experience. He scratched a match, swept it forward and backward over the bowl, and drew the long-awaited smoke into his mouth and lungs, afterwards carefully creasing the poke and sliding it back into his pocket.

The sun had set some time earlier, and night's velvet cloak covered the basin. High above his head, the encircling cliffs of the cañon walls inscribed their irregular black slash against the sky, and a light wind had begun to pick up. People moved as shadowy figures about the compound, their low murmurs reaching him over the distance in soft waves of sound. Allard smoked in silence, carefully nursing his pipeful, and it was not until the pipe was smoked out that he remembered feeling something besides tobacco at the bottom of the pouch. Idly curious, he withdrew it, loosened the draw string, and dug two fingers deeply into the grains, touching the sharp corners of a small object at the bottom.

He pulled out a crimped square of paper, unfolded it, and struck a light, at once recognizing Burns's printing, identical in form to his earlier letter. The brief words struck him with a powerful flood of expectation. He scratched a second match to life and touched the flame to a corner of the paper, watching it char and drop to the ground. He ground the fragments beneath his boot. The break he had been waiting for was now his. Somehow Burns had discovered the first tangible lead to identify the assassin. It was up to him to locate the horse, if indeed the animal still remained in the basin.

It was now full night, and the slowly appearing stars hung brilliantly remote. Solitude settled over the compound as foot traffic ceased and cabin doors closed. Rubbed by a fresh enthusiasm that impelled him into movement, Allard began to circle the corral. Wiley reappeared from the bunkhouse and fell into step with him.

"I've got all my stuff together," he declared. "Hope you got California in mind for us. Always wanted to see San Francisco."

Allard pulled up at one end of the corral and laid a big-boned hand over the corner post. He looked carefully at the boy. "I been thinking. We should take along an extra bronc'. You think we could get one around here?"

"Don't know of any for sale. Cat's got his own string up at his cabin, and Pinto has two or three in his remuda, but you ain't goin' to get a horse from them." He started to grin at the idea, then thought better of it.

"Always had a hankering to own a palomino," Allard said. "Ever see one in the basin?"

"Not around here. I don't know what's in the cavvy at Cat's place. Ain't been up there since he moved in."

Allard lowered his voice, speaking confidentially. "Before we pull stakes, I'd like to ride around and see something of the basin. I think somebody's keeping an eye on me to make sure I stay around the yard. If I used my own horse, they'd spot it sure. Since we're going to be travelin' partners, maybe you'd lend me your horse tomorrow for a couple of hours?"

"Sure, he's easy ridin'. When you want him?"

"In the morning. A little before daylight. When I wake you, go out and throw my saddle on your bronc', then bring him around to the door."

Chapter Thirteen

At five Allard rose and shook Wiley awake. The first fingers of the new day were touching the eastern horizon, and every escarpment began to define its edges against the dawn. The fire had gone out in the bunkhouse stove, and the room held a dank chill as the kid, still fogged with sleep, stumbled from his bunk and went outside. Allard pulled on his boots and shrugged into his heavy coat. From long habit he looked around for his gun, had no success, and the grim realization again came to mind. He was at the door when Wiley appeared, leading his horse.

"Kid," he said, "I'm just goin' to mosey around here and there. Might be back before they know I'm gone. But, if somebody comes looking for me, you don't know anything."

He swung up and deliberately headed into the trees on the opposite side of the clearing from the trail he had previously followed to Cat Lenifee's cabin. If Wiley was later pressed for information as to his whereabouts and caved in, he didn't want his primary destination known.

The thin tinges of morning's first light failed to penetrate far into the trees, and it was still dark and gloomy on the forest floor. With no clearly defined trail Allard found it slow going at first through the undergrowth of saplings and vines. The light gradually increased, and his vision improved. He circled the compound and dropped into the same rutted path he had previously traveled, leading to the knob.

When he came to the stumpy meadow, he rode directly across and continued up the gradual incline. His previous encounter with Cat Lenifee had demonstrated the man's superb wariness. As an unwelcome and unarmed trespasser he knew that, if discovered again near the cabin, Lenifee would kill him without hesitation. He abandoned the trail, preferring to work cautiously through the stands of pine and skirt the clusters of undergrowth that grew in profusion beneath the trees.

When the timber began to thin, he dismounted and pulled the horse into a thick-growing stand of quaking aspen, pushing through to the center where the foliage was deepest. He tied his mount at that point and continued on foot among younger trees, arriving at the foot of the knob. He worked around it, picking his path with utmost care and keeping covered all the way.

In the eastern sky, above the sharpening horizon, a broad band of pink was developing, and details of his environs took on distinct form and shape. Through the trees and directly before him Cat Lenifee's unpainted clapboard shanty came into view, sitting squalidly on the rounded crest, a single-room, jerry-built shack of pine logs in a low state of repair. One end of the cabin, with a partly opened door and a window with the glass pane broken, faced him. Another window, presumably, was on the rear wall, out of his sight. A corner of the tar-paper roof sagged precariously, and the roof itself was punched full of holes, the result of some hail storm. A pyramid of discarded cans and bottles stood beneath the fractured window, and the whole place looked like it had been battered by a grimy fist.

Morning's sunlight was fast running down the cañon walls, and, momentarily, the occupants would be stirring. Somebody in the cabin groaned, and behind Allard a diving jay shattered the silence with its squawking racket. Somewhat higher and halfway up the rise was a bright green patch of thick-growing bushes with the rails of a pole corral immediately beyond. Keeping the clump between himself and the cabin, Allard bent low and ran to the thicket, pawing his way into the center of this dense cover. He brushed aside some small boughs and from this observation post had his clear view of the cabin's door. A man's asthmatic snoring rasped the stillness, and thirty yards away, directly above him, was the near side of the corral.

There were a half dozen animals in restless motion at the far end of the enclosure, tightly bunched and fidgety. As he observed their high-spirited milling, three animals broke from the others and bolted across the corral, plunging to an abrupt standstill at the rails directly above him, their eyes widely rolling and their flared nostrils exhaling blasts of steamy vapor. Allard stiffened. The middle horse, standing above the others and scenting the air, was a flaxen palomino with long-flowing silver mane and tail, streaming in the wind. Somebody in the cabin rode the palomino. Once a man threw a saddle on that horse, the final chapter in a strange and wild sequence of events would begin.

The sun came into view above the east rim and began its steady climb in a still sky, swiftly dissolving the remaining shadows that hugged the ground. Allard knew that he had arrived undetected, but he still harbored concern over his place of concealment. It was quite close to the cabin, and he would be in a dubious position, if discovered, for he was afoot and unable to escape.

The sound of snoring quit, and a man's wheezy coughing carried down to him from the cabin. Somebody's boots struck the floor. The door swung farther inward, and a pair of hands threw out a bucket of water. Men's voices rose, grumbling and cranky, their talk reaching him in low murmurs. Presently the chimney began to belch intermittent puffs of grayish-black smoke, and a pot's metallic rattle split the morning hush.

Allard also picked up the sound of an approaching rider. He spread the foliage with his hands and saw Ben Lenifee's horse emerge from the trees to his left and come grunting up the slope. The tall old man made a formidable figure, squarely seated and towering large in his saddle. A knee-length buffalo coat hung loosely on his gaunt frame, and under his black, broad-brimmed hat his stern features, chiseled and seamed by the years, were darkly fixed on the cabin. He had his rifle with him and carried it across his lap, resting on his thighs. He rode straight up the rise into the open and sent his halloo forward in a strident voice that struck hard against the cabin walls.

"Cat," he called. "Come out here. I want to see you."

Sounds of immediate movement arose from within. Chair legs squeaked, followed by footsteps, and Emmett Hanks, sallow, lanky, and cadaverous, appeared in the doorway. He stared briefly at Ben who sat like an old soldier, ramrod straight on his horse. When he spoke, his words caused his Adam's apple to move convulsively under the loose folds of skin on his long neck. "Well, well," he said, "look who's here," and swung his head around to speak over his shoulder: "Cat, we got company. Mister Ben Lenifee's come to pay us a visit." He turned back with a sharper attention, saw the rifle, and added: "Looks like he's been eatin' raw meat."

A second man moved up from within, shouldered him aside, and Cat Lenifee stepped across the threshold, unshaven and squinting through red eyes into the morning's brightness. He had come directly from his bunk without his boots and was clad only in his undershirt and trousers. His disposition, invariably bad-tempered and moody, was made worse by a night's drinking, and his black, disheveled hair dangled over his forehead in a stringy mass. From a face still dulled for want of sleep his dark and muddy eyes regarded the old man with irritable hostility.

"What the hell you doin' here at sunup, Ben? You're off your track. What's on your mind?"

"Cat," Ben intoned, spacing his words with biting precision, "since your arrival here you have upset the peace. I have made allowances because you are kin, but you continue to defy me. There is no goodness in your soul. The three of you must leave the basin today."

His pronouncement stirred up scornful amusement in the other man who retorted with a blast of angry language. Cat cursed the old man roundly. "That so? I warned you about botherin' us. We ain't leavin' until I'm damned good and ready, and it ain't today. Get the hell back to your place and say a prayer of thanksgiving you made it alive. If you come up this way again, I'll plug you!"

Cat's reaction was not unexpected. Ben had foreseen such a response and was ready for it. His frosty eyes burned over the space between them. "I have given this matter much thought," he said slowly, his words dropping like heavy weights in the strained silence, "and it occurred to me you might resist. Therefore, I came prepared to do what I must." He tightened his grip on the old Henry in his lap.

Cat Lenifee's glance dropped to the rifle and Ben's palm lying broadly across the breech. He was no longer wooden from sleep but wide-awake and watchful. The darkened skin over his cheekbones looked like a leather mask. "Maybe you're right, Ben. The basin is too small for both of us. Why don't we do somethin' about it."

He dodged back into the cabin with a swiftness that caught the other by surprise. Ben brought the rifle up to his shoulder and steadied it there, ready to fire, but there was no one visible. For an instant the faintest stain of uncertainty crossed his features, but he was committed to a single purpose and seemed to be unaware of his peril. The signal of coming death was lost on him. He spurred forward, holding the weapon in one hand and grasping his reins in the other, waiting for Cat to reappear.

A hollow bloom of ragged light leaped from the black rectangle of the doorway, and a bullet tore into his body. The rifle fell from his grasp. His hat flew off and rolled across the grass. He grabbed for the horn to keep from tipping. His head fell to one side, and his eyeballs rolled upward in their sockets. Then his body began to sag at an increasing angle, and all his muscles gave way at once. He tumbled from the horse like a great loose scarecrow, striking the ground in a series of collapsing folds.

Cat emerged from the doorway with a smoking revolver in his hand, followed closely by Hanks and Daly. His features were distorted into a cold mask, lips thinly stretched over teeth. He walked across to Ben who lay twisting on the ground. Cat looked down without expression, watching him die, and then, impatiently, pumped two more shots into the fallen body, the impact from each slug causing a spasmatic reflex in the old man's slack muscles. After a time the strange glow in Cat Lenifee's eyes receded, and his breathing returned to normal. He swung back to his companions. "The crazy old son of a bitch thought his prayin' could stop a bullet. He was wrong, and he ain't the king around here any more."

Before either man could respond, a flicker of motion in the bordering pines caught the eyes of all three, and they swung their attention that way. Chester Lenifee, who had quietly trailed his father from the house and arrived in time to see him gunned down, now raced away in headlong fashion, screened in part by the protecting trees. A small break in the foliage exposed him to view for a moment, and Cat sent several bullets after the receding figure.

Hanks blurted: "We got to go after him. He'll get his rifle and come back . . . maybe with help."

"Wake up, you damn' fool," said Cat angrily, his wedge-shaped face dark and contorted. "We can't get him now. He's gone hellbent, and we're on foot. You think we can saddle up and catch him before he gets home?"

"He'll get help and come back," insisted Hanks.

"Like hell he will," said Cat in his surly monotone. "Chester won't do anything. He's weak. The old man had him buffaloed. And those brushpoppers in the settlement with their squirrel guns ain't gonna help him. They're afraid of their own shadows, and with Ben dead they won't know what the hell to do."

Daly broke in: "What about Bowley?"

Cat gave him a sidelong glance. "What *about* Bowley? No sand in his craw, either. You afraid of Wade?"

Daly bristled at his words. "Hell, no, I ain't afraid of him or anybody." He thought a minute, and then said: "What about the stranger?"

Lenifee spat into the dust. "That's

somethin' else I will take care of personally. That bastard smells like a lawman, and I'm goin' to kill him."

"What'll we do with the old man?" asked Hanks, staring now at the dead figure. "His horse run off."

"So what," replied Cat Lenifee. "Leave him lay. We can dump him off at his house later."

Hanks and Daly reëntered the cabin, but Lenifee remained where he was, scanning the timber, straining with attention until he was satisfied they were alone. Finally he walked slowly back toward the cabin.

Allard crept out from his cover and retreated down the slope, keeping in the aspens and circling the knob to his horse. He led the animal beyond earshot before he swung into the saddle and moved out.

Earlier that same morning Joyce Lenifee had been seated in the living room, reading one of Mrs. Tinker's books when her father came from some other quarter of the house, carrying his rifle, and walked out of the front door. He descended the steps and went into the barn. By the grim set to his features she thought she knew what he was going to do and went in search of her brother.

"I believe he's on his way to see Cat. You've got to talk to him, Chet, before he goes there."

"I tried, but he won't listen. If he goes up there and pushes Cat or one of the others, they'll kill him." But his sister's sense of urgency seized him anew. "I'd better try to stop him before he does something crazy."

He wheeled and ran from the house. Joyce heard his horse drum out of the yard, and a helpless terror closed down on her. Greatly disturbed, she roamed from room to room, thinking of Frank Allard. She wandered outside as far as the verandah, her eyes reaching over the yard to the corrals and bunkhouse, vainly hoping for some sign of him. Early sunlight had driven the chill from the air and burnished the treetops with a pale silver light. She observed all the usual morning's activity around the compound but saw no sign of Allard. It left her alone with a desperate loneliness, and she walked back inside, chilled and fearful as the invisible march of calamity crept closer.

She was so absorbed by her thoughts that she failed to observe Wade Bowley, approaching the house. When she heard his heavy footsteps, she turned to meet him. Except for an unsavory growth of beard his bruised face had returned to nearly normal proportions. He gave her no greeting of any kind, and his manner offered little politeness. He had obviously been brooding over something and flung his question at her in a disagreeable tone.

"Your father around?"

She stared at him, and he stared back. They were two people who were unhappy with each other, and the girl, like awakening from an unpleasant dream, was completely unaffected by his nearness. "He's not here. What do you want with him?"

Bowley was pushed by some kind of strain that flushed his face and quickened his breathing. "I been thinkin'," he said in his heavy, driving voice, "that our weddin's overdue. I'm tired of waitin' for the traveling parson. We'll go into Mountain Pass and be married there."

Since receiving her father's promise of future nuptials, he had been agreeable to delay without any great reluctance until she was twenty-one. That date would soon be upon her, and, looking back, she deplored her casual and disinterested acceptance of a situation she had allowed to progress too far. She knew now there would be no wedding. All this was clear to her as she coolly regarded Bowley. He kept studying her with his scowling expression, highly displeased and waiting for her response.

"Wade, this is much too sudden. I need time to prepare. When Father returns, we can discuss it further."

Bowley had a wide face and small eyes, set closely under heavy brows. "I got nothin' to do," he said, walking to the window and looking outside. "I'll stick here till Ben shows up." He turned and eyed her narrowly, a dull suspicion he had been nursing and could no longer suppress rushing out of him. "Are you stallin' because of that stranger?"

She hesitated before answering.

Bowley noticed the pause and grasped her arm with his big fingers. "So that's what's happened," he said, heated by sudden anger. "You've taken a shine to that buzzard! Ain't it so?"

"No! No, it isn't so." Then, lowering her voice, she said more calmly: "You're hurting me, Wade. I don't think you realize your own strength. When Father returns, we'll talk."

She feared for a moment her words might have the opposite effect, but then his face cleared and change came over him swiftly. His grip relaxed, allowing her to pull free. "By God, Joyce, you better not be lyin' to me. That stranger mean anything to you?"

"Of course not. I scarcely know him."

His flushed face relaxed, and some of his assurance returned. His answer had a grudging arrogance in it. "We'll damned well talk about that, too, when your father gets here."

Bowley was on the point of saying more when a horse and rider bolted out of the pines and tore into the yard. They moved together to the edge of the porch in time to see Chester Lenifee rush up and leap from his horse before it had entirely stopped. He was distraught and ran awkwardly forward, halting short of the steps, his face taut with grief, the cords lining his neck tightly drawn and quivering.

"Father's dead!" he cried passionately. "Cat just shot him out of the saddle. It was murder. Cat kept shooting him when he was dying on the ground. I'm goin' back and kill him." Seeing Bowley, he made an effort to compose himself. "Wade," he said, slowly swallowing and holding his voice in check with some effort, "I'm glad you're here. I'll need some help because Hanks and Daly are up there, too. I never thought of killin' a man before, but I'm goin' after Cat."

He ran up the steps and stopped, staring at Bowley who scraped his boots on the boards and delayed his answer. His eyes refused to meet Chester's, and he kept watching the bordering trees. "Are they follerin' you?" he asked in an odd and curious tone.

Chester had lost his hat. He showed the effects of his furious ride. "I don't know . . . or care. Go get your rifle, Wade." He looked helplessly at his sister. "Jo, Cat's gone crazy. For God's sake, he killed his own kin!"

The girl stood with frightened eyes fixed on her brother, too overcome to accept the immediate relief of tears. She had feared an impending disaster, but the sudden actuality wiped out any reserve of courage. She was fighting to hold back the tears, and, when her eyelids fluttered, she put her face in her hands, fearing she might faint. Chester saw her sway and moved to her side at once. For the first time in their lives he put his arms around his sister and drew her against him, continuing to hold her until he felt her tremors subside.

Finally Joyce withdrew from her brother's arms and stood, trying to collect her thoughts. Chester turned his attention to Bowley, who had been hanging back, neither moving nor speaking.

"Damn you, Wade!" he demanded. "Go get your rifle!"

Bowley persisted in hulking silence on the porch. He ran his tongue across his lips, and

241

a peculiar glaze overlaid his eyes. "You better think twice, Chet," he said, apprehension showing clearly on his face. "There's three armed men up there, all faster with a gun than anybody in the basin. We wouldn't stand a chance."

Joyce, watching him closely, saw small fugitive shifts spread over his cheeks. His overbearing strength, dominant in the basin until Allard whipped him, had deserted him, and now his arrogance had disappeared. She had never questioned his physical courage, assuming it to be abundant, but she saw a chink in that façade as he hesitated. Cat Lenifee, physically no match for Bowley, was a seasoned killer, and the girl realized that Bowley would never face him with a gun.

Chester saw the same shrinking collapse of Bowley's nerve. "Wade, you've lived here under the old man's protection, and you ate well. Cat just shot him down like a dog, and I got to do somethin' about it. If you ain't got the stomach to come along, say so." He shifted his glance to his sister, his eyes searching all the way through her, then returned to Bowley. "If I make it back," he said in a harshly censuring tone, "there'll be some changes. I won't have you as a brother-in-law."

Before Bowley could react, Chester ran into the house, reappearing presently with his rifle. When he climbed back into his saddle, Joyce followed him. Her eyes were wide with alarm, and she came alongside, reaching up and laying a hand against his knee.

"Chet," she pleaded, "you must have help. Round up some of the men. Gil or Stuart will go with you. There are three gunmen up there, just waiting for you. Father had no chance by himself and neither will you."

Chester looked down at his sister with a softening expression on his face. No longer was he the silent and timid brother she had known, living in his father's shadow. He had grown purposeful and decisive, but at the moment he was so consumed by a wild passion for revenge that he failed to observe the urgency in her eyes.

"You are now head of the family. Please wait until you get some help."

"Sis, I've got to go back there."

He patted her hand, squared his shoulders, and brought his horse about, ready to depart. At that moment Frank Allard, still riding Wiley's horse, galloped into the yard and hauled to a stop before them, his faintly irregular features black and grim. The girl's breathing quickened, and her eyes immediately clung to him.

Allard's first glance was to the girl, where it remained for a long moment, then he looked away, not quickly, as if embarrassed, but slowly, as if some silent question had been answered. He put his attention on Bowley who had advanced to the edge of the porch and stared back at him with open animosity. Bowley didn't speak, and Allard said to Chester: "Where you headed?"

"I'm goin' up to the knob." Chester's red eyes gave Allard a wild and impassioned stare. "Cat Lenifee just killed our father. You're a stranger here, and it ain't your quarrel."

Joyce's frightened eyes had not left Allard since his arrival and seemed to be appealing to something only he understood. It was to Joyce that he directed his reply. "I was near the knob in some brush when your father rode in. I saw him shot, and then shot again. Without a gun I couldn't do anything." He swung back to Chester. "I'll ride along. You can use some help."

Bowley dragged his boots across the porch. His voice broke in: "What's your interest in this?"

Allard regarded him coldly. "The old man didn't have a chance." Then he said to Joyce: "I need my guns. Not much good without them."

The girl promptly entered the house. Chester was keyed up, eager to depart, and greatly heartened by Allard's offer. He was on the point of speaking again to the silent Bowley when his sister came from the house, bearing Allard's weapons. She handed them up, and Allard strapped the gun belt around his waist and laid the rifle across his knees. He lifted his reins and looked at Bowley. "You comin' or stayin'?"

Chester broke in. "No, he ain't comin'."

But something had changed Bowley's mind. "Count me in. I got my rifle on my horse." He descended the steps and mounted, a dark expression on his face.

Chester shrugged his shoulders and said nothing more, turning his horse to follow Allard who had moved off. Joyce watched them with great concern. The misery in her eyes grew greater and greater, and she had a hard moment of dread as she envisioned the possible aftermath. At the far boundary of the meadow Allard twisted about in his saddle, just before entering the dark belt of timber, and swung his hat, receiving a small lift of her hand in reply. After they had disappeared, she turned into the house, knowing now with dreadful certainty that her world had collapsed around her.

Chapter Fourteen

By no particular design Allard assumed the lead and rode ahead while Chester and Bowley made a pair behind. He pushed the horses in some haste, intent on arriving at the cabin before the occupants finished breakfast and scattered. The three men there were immensely sure of themselves, confident they had nothing to fear from anyone in the settlement, but, if they left the cabin in separate directions, picking up their trails could be time-consuming.

There was scant underbrush here, and their travel through the red-barked pines and aspen-lined corridors was rapid. The day was windless, and a cathedral-like hush lay among the forest giants. Dipping and rising with gentle contours, their route took them through thick timber and under a green canopy of foliage where sunlight seldom penetrated. Allard's mind was astir, reaching forward to what awaited them, and he dropped one hand to his hip to pull his revolver from its holster and spin the cylinder. Chester Lenifee, following closely and buried in his own desolation, observed this and shoved his horse forward until their stirrups touched. He glanced at Allard but said nothing, his mouth tight and his normally mild face grim.

Bowley was behaving strangely. He now dropped some distance behind and angled his hat so that his eyes, already half covered beneath dropped lids, were further hidden by the brim. They kept searching the rough contours and black edges of the undergrowth with keen attention. When Allard turned about and saw how far Bowley had fallen behind, he was unwilling to risk a shout, so he waved his arm until he caught Bowley's attention and signaled for the latter to catch up. Bowley made a half-hearted attempt to close the gap and urged his mount to greater speed, but, once Allard turned his back and squared himself in the saddle, he lagged to his former position.

When the pitch of the slope began to steepen toward the knoll, Allard reined in, Chester after him. They waited for Bowley. When he finally pulled alongside and halted, Allard raked him roughly with a swift command. "Pull out of here and slide around to the other side where you can see the rear of the cabin. Keep in the trees. When we brace the shanty from here, you back us up. Ought to be a window around the other side. If anybody tries to climb out, shoot him."

Bowley appeared resentful and on the edge of open rebellion, but he said nothing and rushed away, rowelling his horse cruelly. Allard and Chester continued their march, rising toward the knob and keeping well within the sheltering screen of pines. When they arrived at a particularly thick stand that afforded an unobstructed view, Allard halted. Before them sat the rough shanty, its door hanging partly open and a rising curl of white smoke issuing from the chimney. There was no sound at all from within. Silence pulsed around him like the beating of his own heart, and behind the building an empty corner of the corral could be seen. All the horses were collected at the far end and out of sight, and Allard was not able to tell how many unsaddled animals were in the corral, a fact that bothered him. Beyond, a fringe of trees made a solid green wall against the cliffs.

Allard remained astride his horse, studying the place with a searching attention. He threw up an arresting hand to hold Chester. It was a useless gesture. Chester had spotted his father's lifeless form in the clearing, lying precisely where he had fallen, his arms flung limply above his head, as if in agonized supplication. A wrenching groan broke from Chester's throat at the sight, and he hauled his Winchester out of the boot in a wild frenzy. "I'm going out there," he shouted in a half-strangled cry and plunged his spurs into the sides of his horse, charging heedlessly into the open. He was only halfway to the cabin when Cat Lenifee, Emmett Hanks, and Pinto Daly, all of whom had been waiting in the trees, moved into view.

Lenifee was in the lead. Hanks and Daly fanned out to either side, brandishing their weapons. Hanks was up on a gray roan, and Daly rushed forward on his sorrel, waving his gun over his head. He yelled at Chester: "We been expectin' you, plow boy. You want some trouble, you can have it!"

Hanks opened up, driving a shot at Chester who was galloping wildly over the ground, one hand clutching his rifle. Chester reeled in the saddle, made a futile grab at the horn to save himself, and fell heavily, shoulder first, to the earth. He raised himself on one knee, which supported him temporarily, then it buckled beneath him, and he keeled over, coming to rest on his stomach. He was still conscious and lifted his head, discovering his Winchester which had fallen close by. He began to drag himself on his belly over to the rifle, but Hanks saw this and galloped toward him, steadying his revolver for a second shot.

Allard immediately raised his rifle, took quick aim, and fired, the smash of his bullet striking with a dull, muffled sound. Hanks threw both palms skyward, uttered a cry, and cartwheeled out of his saddle in a whirl of arms and legs to die beneath his horse, his body tumbling crazily, struck repeatedly by the crazed beast's hoofs as it ran blindly over him.

Lenifee and Daly immediately turned their attention to Allard and poured a hail of fire into the grove. The bole of a great fir offered protection. Allard got behind it, hearing the howl of lead fragments whine past and slap the leaves. He steadied the rifle's stock against the trunk and delivered a volley of his own, spacing his shots carefully. One bullet grazed Daly's horse, causing it to neigh in wild panic and throwing both animals into a bucking, snorting disarray. Lenifee and Daly wheeled at once, two weaving shapes racing for the timber.

Lenifee, who was leading, had reached the first line of trees when a singing bullet tore through the head of Daly's horse. The dying animal reared up on its hind legs and expelled an indescribable sound that only a mortally wounded horse can emit, something uncanny between a scream and a groan. The beast jack-knifed its forelegs under its belly and crashed to earth, pitching Daly from the saddle. Fortunately for Daly the animal capsized sideways, and he was thrown clear, striking on outstretched arms and rolling to his feet, scratched and bruised but otherwise unhurt. Chester Lenifee, prone in the clearing and sorely wounded, had managed to crawl to his rifle. It had been his bullet that had dropped Daly's horse.

Cat Lenifee, safely within the trees, now spurred boldly back into the open. Swinging low in his saddle, he looped an arm under Daly's shoulder, catching him around the chest and holding him against one stirrup. Daly reached up with a clawing hand and locked his fist around the pommel, hanging there by one arm, his legs swinging like limp pendulums. He kept slipping lower and lower until his boots dragged and bounced over the uneven ground. Lenifee charged back into the trees with his burden, somehow escaping the rain of lead that followed.

Echoes of their retreat drifted back to the clearing as subdued eddies of sound, and, in the suspended interval that followed, nothing else moved. Allard automatically slid fresh shells into his rifle, but his eyes remained focused on the spot where Lenifee and Daly had vanished. Cat Lenifee had been astride the brilliant-coated palomino.

Chester lay exposed in the clearing, and his anguished groans reached Allard who shoved his rifle back into the boot and rode from the grove. He had forgotten about Bowley, camped in the timber on the opposite side of the clearing, whose gun had been silent during the fight. A signal in his brain swelled, and his reaction was purely instinctive. He yanked hard on the reins, pulling his grunting horse around in a whirling turn, and sunk his spurs into the animal's ribs. A rifle shot barked from the hidden marksman, and he heard the rustling as a bullet bisected the space he had just occupied. A second echo of the hidden gun, delayed by distance, followed him as he plunged back for the shelter of the trees. He threw up his own revolver to thumb a return shot in Bowley's direction. By the time a third bullet sang past his ear, he was safely in the pines and heard the slug thud into the trunk of a tree somewhere behind him.

The same great fir again offered safety, and, pinned down behind it, he brought his rifle into play and began to pump a steady shower of bullets into the far trees. He reloaded and kept at it, patiently and unhurried, his lead systematically searching the undergrowth. He was unexpectedly rewarded by a wild howl and the sound of Bowley's high-pitched cursing. The man had insufficient bottom to stand the pressure of whining lead, and his nerves had given way. His voice quit all at once, and Allard sensed the shift of a body in the undergrowth. The sounds picked up as Bowley launched his horse through the trees and away in full retreat, protected by a wall of timber so densely ranked that Allard had no opportunity for a shot. He shoved his rifle back into the scabbard and listened to the diminishing hoofbeats of Bowley's horse.

Chester Lenifee was no longer on his knees but had fallen to the earth and lay flat on his back. His features were compressed by pain when Allard dismounted and crouched beside him. His teeth were clenched, and fine sweat greased a face that had lost its definition. "Did you get Cat?" he whispered weakly.

"No," said Allard. "He got away."

"He won't go far," murmured Chester. "He ain't afraid of anybody around here. You dropped Emmett Hanks?"

Allard nodded and slid a hand behind Chester's shoulders, pulling him to a sitting position. He opened the wounded man's coat, unbuttoned his shirt, and had a look at the raw cavity, halfway between the right shoulder and breastbone. The lead had entered his chest, tearing its ragged way clear through, and had left a pulped exit wound. Blood ebbed steadily from both cavities. Allard used his knife to cut away the shirt and slit the flannel into narrow strips. He folded some of these to pack the wounds, then wrapped the other strips around Chester's body, encasing it to hold the wadding in place, able to staunch the bleeding in a small way.

Allard said: "This'll be rough, kid," and reached down to hook Chester beneath his armpits, setting him temporarily upright and bracing him against his own knees. Chester was unable to offer any help, so Allard squatted on his heels and then straightened, using his big leg muscles to hoist the limp body on one shoulder. He carried Chester like this over to his horse and pushed him up into the saddle, supporting him there. He took Chester's hands and placed them around the horn, where his fingers instinctively tightened around the pommel. His boots swung limply out of the stirrups, and he rolled around like a drunken man unable to control his balance. His fevered eyes opened briefly to focus on his father's corpse, lying nearby. "We can't leave him here," he groaned. "Got to take him home."

"Already figured to," said Allard. "He's coming back with us."

Allard crossed to Ben's body and lifted him in his arms, surprised that he wasn't heavier. He carried him over to his own horse, all the while making low, familiar sounds to soothe the beast. He lashed the body face down across the saddle, collected the reins, and swung up behind the cantle on Chester's horse, curling one arm around the man's waist, holding himself steady. Keeping the reins from his own horse, he turned downgrade, propping up his burden with one hand and bunching both sets of reins in the other, heading back to the settlement.

He initially tried pushing the horses to a trot, for he was immensely uncomfortable with their present situation, realizing that his burden with Chester made it impossible to carry on a fight. It was his assumption that Cat Lenifee and Daly, with only one horse between them, would return to the cabin to get another mount. He had sufficient time, handicapped as he was with a wounded man, to get Chester home before they caught up. He knew for a certainty that, if he was cornered in the trees, they would kill him on sight. Even now every clump and thicket threatened danger, for he was unsure of Bowley's whereabouts. The big man could have stopped his headlong rush and concealed himself along the way, waiting for another chance to attack.

The afternoon sun still hovered high in the azure sky and filtered down through the green canopy of foliage in shafts of transparent silver. The pine and fir grew so densely at this point that the lacework of overhead branches diffused the light, and the horses moved from brightness into shadow and back again. The dappling effect created false images in the filmy galleries and played tricks with Allard's vision, making it difficult to catch the outline of a moving shape. He continued to weave his way along as rapidly as he dared. Chester was continually worsening. The one thing keeping him in the saddle were his hands, clamped vise-like around the horn. Tremors shook his body, and blood had soaked through the dressing, trickling down his leg and onto the saddle's skirt. He was a heavy, limp weight on Allard's arm.

Chapter Fifteen

It had been a shattering day for Joyce Lenifee. After her brother and Allard, together with Wade Bowley, left the yard, she was unable to quiet her racing mind. She reëntered the house and paced aimlessly from room to room, depressed by the cold premonition of some calamity. She touched her cheeks with a handkerchief, seated herself in a favorite armchair, and folded her hands in her lap. Leaning back, she tried resting her head against the cushion. Now in the aftermath of her father's death, when she looked down at her folded hands, she observed them trembling uncontrollably and found she had twisted the handkerchief into a sweaty rope.

Rising, she wandered to the living-room window, pulled the curtains aside, and stood behind the glass, slipping her hands into the pockets of her Levi's and gazing abstractedly outside, her solid resolution not to relive the past slipping away. Spread over the meadow, the neatly kept buildings of the settlement were arranged about the compound in systematic fashion, some of the panes of window glass sending back bright flashes of sunlight. She was reminded of how the basin had been when her family first arrived, not so many years before, wild and unmarked. She recalled how her father's heavy presence had been the dominant force in settling the little valley. Although an autocratic leader whose convictions were as implacable as polar ice, he had gathered together a dispirited collection of souls, had set himself up as their leader with the promise of a stress-free life, and had transformed the fledgling settlement into a peaceful and self-sufficient community.

When she was small, back in Tennessee, he had been a hearty and vibrant man, but, after her mother contracted cholera and died at Fort Bridger, he was never the same. He withdrew behind a massive wall of stoicism, sometimes lapsing into fits of brooding that lasted for days, masking his grief by a heavy embrace of religion. He spent many evenings alone with his Bible and developed an intolerant disposition toward those closest to him. From that day forward his inability to overcome that cold aloofness made it impossible for him to express or demonstrate affection. He had been unable, or unwilling, to show any visible warmth for Joyce or her brother, almost forgetting they were his own children. As time had passed and she became increasingly disillusioned, the rift between them widened to exclude sentiment of any kind. She could not remember exactly when she first became aware of her inability to respond with the affection that a daughter should have, but much to her disappointment their relationship had decayed into a state of distant formality. Yet, if long ago she had lost the capacity openly to love him, his violent death left behind an appalling sadness and a wrenching heartache for the many things they had lost along the way.

Perhaps it was simply having no one in the basin to communicate with that affected her life most acutely. Her existence had been a solitary one, totally lacking in companionship, a condition that she had accepted as commonplace, being aware of no other. In spite of repeated efforts she had been unable to strike up any lasting relationship among the limited number of girls her own age, finding them unimaginative and dull, acquiring by inheritance the endemic similarities of their mothers.

Ben, with no formal schooling of his own, had consistently taken a peevish pride in maintaining that his was a mind uncorrupted by books. He was fond of saying —

"Men, not books, deeds not words" — and never encouraged either of his children to read or learn to write. Chester, with few independent thoughts of his own, had been content to follow in his father's footsteps, but Joyce's yearning for higher learning was unflagging. Ben had not prohibited whatever education the clan members could provide for themselves, and therefore some of the children were taught the basic rudiments by a few clan elders possessing those talents. Joyce, with her spirited strength of mind, determined and hungry for intellectual stimulation, had flourished under this freedom. Curiosity was one of her most notable features and, determined to learn more of a world outside the basin, she had become a voracious reader, consuming every book she could locate with an insatiable appetite. She read and reread each of the few tattered volumes brought west in the wagons, for books were rare on the frontier. In recent years she had been systematically enlarging her library through her regular supply trips to Mountain Pass, locating a book here or there, in one store or another, each time steadily adding to her collection. Martha, Henry Tinker's wife, a literate woman herself and aware, through her husband, of Joyce's interest, had taken to saving books as she finished them, leaving them for the girl at the store.

Joyce's notions of chivalry and affairs of the heart were derived solely from her reading. She had never been in love. It was an emotion completely foreign to her, but she often envisaged herself at the center of a rending love affair, setting her imagination on fire. These were things she thought about and, until recently, never believed, for in recent years she had known nothing but unhappiness in the basin. Fresh in her mind was her encounter with Frank Allard and the awakening magnetism of something rare and unusual that had brushed them both. It was like an exciting wind blowing freely through her, offering a sublime opportunity to convert her dreams into reality and alter her life forever.

Within the Spartan society of Winona Basin time-worn practices originating in the Tennessee mountains endured as clan laws that prevailed over individual choice. Joyce knew she was the only inhabitant who identified those age-old habits as demoralizing precedents, surviving in a climate of ignorance, and she had long ago resolved to flout them. They hastened a long-festering rebellion within her soul, a determination to gain her independence from the old-fashioned constraints she had grown to despise. Suddenly, imbued with a fullness in her heart and filled with great expectations, she was willing to stake everything on the impulses that stirred her innermost feelings, and she told herself that, after so long, she had a right to be selfish. As far as she was concerned, her father's death released her completely from any commitments he had made for her. Chester was now titular leader in the basin by right of primogeniture. Although she knew little of Chester's inner convictions, some instinct brought about by his recent behavior inspired her to believe that many of his opinions were not compatible with those of their father. Even so, no matter how Chester felt, Joyce made up her mind to go with Frank Allard when he left the basin.

Wade Bowley no longer occupied any space in her thoughts. It was a hard thing to remember how indifferently she had treated their meaningless relationship which held neither respect nor the slightest degree of ardor, realizing how mistaken she had been. It shamed her and made her lose faith in her own honesty. She had never allowed Bowley to touch her, but his company had been tolerable, and she could see now that it was the result of a lonely desire for simple companionship, because there had never been the slightest emotional exchange between them. Then Frank Allard had intruded into her life, and nothing was the same any more.

The sound of a horse beating into the yard interrupted her, and, on the assumption it was Allard and her brother returning, she laid her musings aside. When she moved to the verandah, she almost collided with Wade Bowley who came bounding up the steps in a feverish haste. Something had shaken him. There was a heavy scowl penciled across his forehead. He was temporarily short of wind and glared at her with a pair of redly formidable eyes, his great chest rising and falling.

"Wade," she cried, grasping his coat, "what happened? Where are the others?"

He was in the grip of some kind of violent turmoil, his nerves wire-tight and jumpy. He seemed not to hear her and turned away, his small eyes combing the adjacent timber. When he shook his great shoulders in an excited gesture, it spread his chest muscles and stretched the tight fabric of his shirt. He kept his head turned away from her, and his eyes refused to meet her demanding stare.

"Answer me. What happened at the cabin?"

Bowley made a half-twist of his body,

coming around to face her with a strange rigor on his cheeks. "Your brother's been shot. Emmett Hanks is dead, but Cat and Pinto Daly are around some place. They could show up any time." He cast another worried glance at the surrounding timber. "We better pull out."

He clamped a massive hand on her arm, drawing her rudely against him, thick fingers closing on her elbow with such pressure that she cried out in pain, but he had misjudged her temper. She wrenched her arm free, consumed now by a greater alarm.

"What are you talking about? We can't leave. How badly is Chester hurt? Is he dead?" Joyce lifted both hands to frame her forehead, pressing the tips of her fingers to her temples. The callous announcement confirmed what she had dreaded would happen. Then a new thought flashed across her mind. "What are you doing back here? How could you leave Chet? Take me to him at once."

"Your brother may be dead. He's got a bullet somewhere in his gut. We're not goin' back there." There was an air of restless urgency, rendering him immune to her feelings. "We got to move out before Cat and Pinto show up."

His big leathery hand closed on her wrist.

He pulled her toward him again and put both arms around her. When she tried to wrench free, he bent slightly and lifted her with no effort, carrying her down the steps. She was half strangled by the pressure of his oak-like limbs but twisted her body around in a blind panic, beating her boots against his legs and ineffectually striking at his face with her head.

"Wade! Let me go. I must help Chet."

She had no chance to work free. When they reached his horse, he set her down and said in a flat, commanding tone: "Climb up, Jo. I'm through foolin'. If you try to run, I'll bat you one." The desire to strike something was upon his face, for his temper had punished him all day. "I'll get your horse, and we'll ride into Mountain Pass and see the parson."

When she heard his words, delivered with uncompromising finality, she tried to present a self-composed countenance in order to reason with him. "I can't possibly go until I see how badly Chet is hurt. How can you think of such things at a time like this?" Then a question slipped from her lips that rose out of a concern she could no longer suppress. "What happened to Frank? Is he also hurt?"

"It's Frank, is it? I thought as much. You

been lyin' to me. By God, I swear I'll kill that son of a bitch if Cat don't get him first." He laid a rude hand on her back, shoving her roughly toward the horse. "Now get up there, god damn you!"

A kind of blind terror seized her again as she made a second, senseless attempt to break free, fighting him desperately and silently, tearing at him with her hands and kicking at his shins. She clenched her fists and struck out blindly, catching him in the throat. At this, he uttered a vile oath, raised one ham-like hand, and clubbed her alongside the head. A stifled cry broke from her lips, and she would have fallen had not Bowley caught her. He spun her and got a thick arm around her waist, one heavy hand clamped on her slenderness. In a single motion he raised her up and flopped her over the saddle of his horse, where she hung openly sobbing, stunned and only half conscious.

Tying her hands and feet together beneath the horse's barrel with a piggin' string, Bowley led the animal over to the corral. There he caught and saddled Joyce's pony, a dainty black mare. When he had finished, he untied Joyce, pulled her from his big gelding, and carried her over to the mare. Boosting her into the saddle, he then tied her feet together beneath the mare, took up her reins, and led both horses.

"Don't give me any trouble," he warned her, "or I'll beat that pretty face of yours to a pulp and break your ribs!"

A handful of local residents stood in their doorways, silently watching. Although two were men, nobody made a move to interfere, for they were the kind who had long ago learned not to mix in another's business, no matter how questionable or offensive. Bowley was mindful of their scrutiny. When he turned his hard stare in their direction, he saw fright in their faces.

His forearms were red with the gouge marks the girl's nails had made, and he paused at the watering trough to sponge them. Removing his hat, he dipped and filled it, then clumsily dashed the cold water over the girl's face. It splashed on her cotton shirt and soaked her hair, but the cold shock did not remove the gray and dazed expression on her face.

It was the big man's plan to proceed directly to the parsonage in Mountain Pass. He knew the preacher would cave in before a show of force. Joyce would marry him, even if he had to beat her bloody in front of the parson, had to beat the words of commitment out of her. He also realized somebody would eventually come after the girl, but an idea struck him and turned him crafty. He raised his voice deliberately and spoke loudly to Joyce, making sure the watching residents heard his words.

"We'll take the east road out and cross into Colorado. We'll get married there and settle in Oklahoma. Got some kinfolk there."

He wasted no more time but mounted his gelding, still holding onto the reins of Joyce's pony. His horse trotted off at a fast clip with him roughly hauling the protesting mare behind him. A sense of urgency was bearing down on him. He crossed the clearing and fell into the eastern wagon road, urging the horses along at an ever faster gait, until the road curved around a low rise, and the settlement faded from sight. When he was certain they were out of earshot, he slowed his ramshackle run and left the road completely, cutting a full half circle around the settlement.

Sometime later they emerged from the pines and came upon the west road, leading to Mountain Pass. Bowley threw the horses into the road at once. His unsettling demand for speed took over then, and he lifted the gelding into a jostling run, instantly putting a strain on the trailing reins and the iron bit which cruelly tore at the mare's mouth. The little animal, unaccustomed to being hauled along by her bridle, put up a constant fuss, snorting and tossing her head, threatening to snarl the reins and jerk them from Bowley's fingers with each jarring hoofbeat. The confusion hampered progress and eventually slowed Bowley's horse. He kept his attention focused on their back trail, scanning it and listening.

Unsatisfied with their progress and growing more frustrated by the minute, Bowley knew he could tow the mare no farther, and presently he drew to a halt. He made a half turn in his saddle and laid a heavy stare on Joyce. The ride had added a flush of color to her cheeks, and she now sat very straight in her saddle, returning his gaze with defiant scorn, openly despising him.

He abandoned any attempt at courtesy or reconciliation. "You ride ahead. I ain't haulin' you any longer. Stay in the middle of the road and head for Mountain Pass. Keep movin'. I'll be right behind you." When she remained passively unresponsive, a fierce flare came into his eyes. "Listen, Jo, you better believe what I say. If you try to run off, I'll shoot your horse. You'll be next! Remember that. Now get goin'."

The girl swung ahead of him, lifting her

horse into a canter with Bowley following closely. The afternoon sun thrust its burning rim above the dark mass of the forest and was immediately before them, its glare squarely in Bowley's eyes, making any close observation of their surroundings more difficult. He saw no signs of life and heard no interruption in the deep silence of the surrounding forest, but the dust cloud they left behind was fresh and thick.

A measure of sanity was slowly returning to Bowley. The enormity of his action had finally dawned on him, and now he was beset with a new fear. The West's unwritten law never forgave a man for holding a woman other than his wife against her will, and he had crossed that inflexible line. The brutal blame was on him and would remain there. It could be he would eventually be hunted down and even hanged without a trial. His story would spread all through the basin and surrounding territory, and every door would be slammed in his face. His only hope lay in an immediate marriage. A man could not be condemned for beating his own wife.

The portion of the road they traveled was arrow-straight, traveling through semi-open land, before tunneling into the pine forest on its run to the west portal. Nobody else was on the road. As they rode along, Bowley maintained a constant surveillance behind them and in the adjacent trees but paid scant attention to what lay ahead. He failed now to notice the ever-widening gap between himself and the girl. It came as a complete surprise when he shook himself out of his solitary brooding and looked up to see that she had already reached the narrow and rocky defile well ahead of him.

Posted there on look-out was a man from the settlement who had observed their approach from afar and recognized them both. He was in his fifties, dressed in work-worn bib overalls, and sent down a friendly hail to the girl. Expecting nothing out of the ordinary, he reclined easily against the overhanging rock shelf, paying them only casual attention. Bowley, with the western-slanting sun fully in his eyes, did not see the man until he heard his voice. The girl, however, had been planning for this moment. She abruptly spurred up to the rock and stood erect in her stirrups.

"Gil," she cried frantically, "help me! Dad's dead. Chet is badly hurt. Wade is forcing me to go with him out of the basin." She turned and pointed at Bowley, now coming up fast. "Don't let him take me!"

Gil seized his rifle and jumped forward.

He knew both of these people and had heard long ago they would someday be married. Their personal affairs were none of his concern. He took his orders from Ben Lenifee who had told him to keep outsiders from entering the basin. The news of the old man's death stunned him. He was not able to grasp the full significance of it, and therefore he hesitated.

Bowley came galloping up in wild anger, his normally florid face smeared with fury. He was so enraged that he failed to recognize he might have bluffed his way through this man who was overwhelmed by what he had heard and was not planning to challenge him, but the recent past had stripped Bowley of the ability to think ahead clearly. He yanked his Winchester from the scabbard under his left leg and raised it to his shoulder.

"Throw your rifle down, Gil! We're goin' out. Don't try to stop us."

Gil, although somewhat dazed, was a redoubtable man himself and not about to be threatened. If the old man was dead, it seemed to Gil, at this moment, most logical to listen to his daughter.

"Hell with you, Wade!" he said and dropped behind the escarpment.

Bowley pumped a shot in his direction

and spurred forward, firing again, both bullets striking against stone and ricocheting with a high-pitched screech into the far distance. Gil's rifle barrel appeared around the ledge, and he leveled a shot, narrowly missing Bowley, who ducked his head and let out a shout, driving his mount forward. He made a wide sweep with his left arm, reaching for the girl's horse, but she saw him coming, pulled her pony back, and cut past him, streaking through the stony corridor and racing pell-mell down the road for Mountain Pass.

Bowley cursed her and wheeled his horse around, plunging his spurs into the animal's sides and sending him rocketing forward in labored jumps, rushing after the girl. Gil Tyner's final shots whistled past, near enough for Bowley to feel the wind of their passage.

Chapter Sixteen

It was with tremendous relief to Frank Allard when he and Chester Lenifee broke from the trees and pulled up at the big house. The place looked deserted except for Wiley, his .22 rifle cradled in his elbow. He saw Chester slumped in his saddle, and he saw Ben Lenifee's dead body on the second horse, but his mind was surmounted by another matter. He ran up to Allard at once. "Joyce's gone. Wade Bowley took her away with him. He roughed her up some."

He was unprepared for the tide of black wrath that rushed over Allard's features. He flung his next question at the boy, "When did this happen?"

"Maybe a half hour ago. She didn't want to go with him, but Wade hit her. Then he got her horse, and they lit out."

"Which direction?" asked Allard bleakly.

"Yonder," said Wiley, pointing to the east road. "I heard Wade say he's takin' her out of the basin to marry her."

Chester Lenifee, temporarily forgotten, now emitted a moan of pure anguish and began a see-saw motion, threatening to topple from the saddle. Bathed in heavy sweat, he continued to shudder with violent chills, and Allard saw bloody froth bubble from his lips. "Wiley, this man needs a doctor. There one hereabouts?"

Wiley shook his head. "None closer than Mountain Pass. When somebody's hurt in the basin, Maude Crandall takes care of 'em." He pointed to a nearby log shanty. "That's her place."

"You stick here," said Allard, "and watch the trees. If you see Cat or Pinto Daly, fire your rifle. I'll be back to take care of Ben."

Wiley nodded a nervous affirmative and accepted the reins of the horse bearing Ben's body. Allard rode with Chester to the low building where a large and very plain woman stood in the doorway. She had seen him coming and regarded him impassively.

"You Maude Crandall?"

She nodded, reserved and unemotional, and had a question of her own. "Chester hurt bad?"

Allard said: "Not good. A bullet hole through his ribs. Can I leave him here?"

The woman remained unperturbed. She shrugged, her bold features almost masculine. "Everybody else comes to me when they're hurt, but this will be the first time for Chester." She stepped aside. "Bring him in."

Allard dismounted and pulled Lenifee off his saddle. The man was heavy and solid, wet with his own blood. It had soaked through his clothing and turned his body damp. Allard carried him into a room that was starkly unadorned but neat and orderly. The woman indicated a bunk against the wall, and Allard laid Chester there. He removed the man's coat and pulled off his boots and trousers, covering him with a quilt.

He turned to the woman. "He's lost considerable blood. You've got to stop it quickly, or he'll bleed to death."

"I'm no miracle worker," the woman retorted, "but I'll do what I can." She placed a pot of water on the stove and laid out some cotton strips. "We don't have much of this kind of thing in the basin. Who shot him?"

"His cousin. Cat Lenifee."

"Not surprised," said the woman. "He's an evil man." She dropped her glance to Chester and shook her head. "All these killings. I saw Ben dead, tied face down on his horse, and now his son lyin' here, hurt bad. I don't know what will happen to us."

A young girl entered the room, thin and unattractive, with a dull set of features bearing the common resemblance of the basin women. When she saw Allard and Chester's body on the cot, she wheeled to go, but Maude Crandall's words stayed her. She stopped at the door and stood dutifully quiet.

"Jenny. I need you to help me," said the woman. She turned to Allard. "You can go. We'll do our best . . . with the Lord's help."

Chester was unconscious and sweating heavily. There was no motion to him other than the quick rise and fall of his breathing, coming through an open mouth and frothing the flecks of red foam on his lips. Allard dropped a hand to his shoulder, held it there a silent moment, then turned, and left the cabin.

Wiley was keyed up. It was now past mid-afternoon, and in the bowl, deep below the lofty crags, shadows were already forming. "I been watchin' the trees," he said. "No sign of anybody. If you're ridin' after Wade and Joyce, I'm goin' along. What happened up at Cat's cabin?"

Allard gave him a brief account, concluding: "Somebody has to stay here. You're the only one left I can trust." He moved to Wiley's horse and lifted down Ben Lenifee's body, meanwhile continuing to talk. "Swap saddles while I'm inside. You got a good bronc' there, but I better take my own horse."

He carried the old man's body into the deserted living room and laid him on a couch, folding his arms across his chest. He draped a blanket over the still form but left Ben's face exposed. Allard stood over him, briefly thinking of his own father and of long-past events once so crowded with meaning. When he emerged from the house, he found that Wiley had exchanged saddles. He was sitting in his saddle with his old hat on, ready to travel.

"I ain't doin' any good here," he said. "Take me with you."

Allard mounted. Wiley's eyes clung to him patiently. Allard laid both palms on his saddle horn, one atop the other. "Wiley," he said, "all hell's breakin' loose around here. Cat Lenifee and Daly are bound to get my scalp. If you string with me, they'll be after you, too. You're just a kid with no close kin hereabouts. If you're smart, you'll pack your things and head out of the basin. Go west and start out fresh."

The boy was stubborn, and his hope was hard to kill. He met Allard's eyes unflinchingly and didn't answer for a moment. Then he said doggedly: "We're partners. You told me so. I ain't leavin' these parts until you do."

"All right," Allard said in a milder tone,

"but I still want you to stick right here and stay out of sight. Lenifee and Daly probably stopped for another horse. Then they'll be along." He held himself rigidly in the saddle but had a last bit of advice for the boy. "Keep in the trees. If they ride through and then go on, follow, if you can. Those boys are my next piece of business, and I want to know where they're headed. Can you trail 'em without bein' seen?"

Wiley accepted his new responsibility with eagerness. "I'll do it," he said. "I'm a good tracker."

"Partner," Allard said with a tight smile, "it's a deal." He leaned over and gripped the boy's hand. "If you tag after them, watch yourself. Good trackers don't run into an ambush. Those are two smart and dangerous men."

"They won't see me," he said.

His assurance satisfied Allard who lifted his reins, dropped his spurs, and galloped across the compound where he fell into the east trail. As he rushed eastward on the same road by which he had first entered the valley, he leaned down to check his Winchester and closed his hand around the solid butt of his revolver. When he arrived at the narrow defile, marking the eastern point of entry, the guard placed there sat smoking on a rock above the road. It was not the same man as when Allard had first entered Winona Basin, but, being under instructions to prevent only unauthorized entrances into the basin, he offered no protest to persons on their way out. Although Allard was a stranger to him, he remained seated and lifted a casual hand in greeting, but Allard rode straight up to him, halted, and threw up his question.

"Joyce Lenifee been this way recently?"

"Nope," said the man. "Been nobody gone in or out since I got here this mornin'. What's the news? Seems I heard some shootin' earlier."

"The news," said Allard, "is all bad. Ben Lenifee is dead, and Chester's been shot."

"My God," exclaimed the man, thoroughly shaken. "What happened?" He jumped to his feet, staring at Allard in disbelief. Then the barrel of his rifle lifted and swung around to cover Allard, a slow suspicion growing on his face. "Ain't you the stranger that whipped Wade Bowley? Why are you in such a big hurry to leave?"

Allard looked steadily at the man. "Don't be a fool. If I'd done that shooting, I'd have put a bullet through you and be on my way out. Cat Lenifee killed Ben, and his partner, Hanks, shot Chester. I took Chester over to

Maude Crandall's."

"Maude's my wife," said the man. "Chester hurt bad?"

"He's got a bullet through his chest. Hope it missed his lungs." He swung his horse around, facing back the way he had come. "I'm on Bowley's trail. He's gone loco and is trying to take Joyce Lenifee out of the basin against her will. I'll back track. If he shows up here, stop him, even if you have to use your rifle."

Confused by what he heard, the man paused, still swayed by distrust. Finally he lowered his rifle, and Allard took advantage of his hesitancy, wheeled about, and rushed his horse down the road in the direction he had come.

By not traveling in the eastward direction he had stated, Bowley had delayed pursuit. Allard realized that the lack of dust smell on the road ahead should have alerted him, and he was disgusted with himself. He tried to guess Bowley's moves. The big man was not apt to remain in the valley or anywhere in the vicinity. All doors would be sealed and local sentiment flatly against him. His only escape would be to abandon the basin immediately and lose himself with the girl in distant parts. There were only two avenues out. Since he had not come this way, he had taken the Mountain Pass road.

Allard pounded back over his own tracks, heading for the west portal. He raced straight through the compound, settling into a rhythmic three-beat canter that Wash could sustain for some time. A scattering of inhabitants watched him from their doorways, and, from a further distance in the timber by the big house, he saw Wiley step from behind a pine, wave a hand, then fade from sight. Allard never paused, holding the chestnut to a steady run.

Once it left the openness of the meadow, the road ran into the forest and funneled through the trees in sweeping contours. Allard was deep in the shadowed reaches when he first heard the crack of a shot, closely followed by a second ragged volley, the echoes bouncing through the hills. The firing, he judged, to be dead ahead in the vicinity of the west entrance. In grim haste he kept his horse toward the sounds in a headlong run.

The road abruptly left the trees and pointed squarely into the setting sun which hung just above the looming western ramparts, causing Allard to draw his hat brim lower to shield his eyes. An instant later the sun and its glare plunged below the rim to be instantly replaced by a cool and pine-scented shade, and, just as quickly, the haze of early twilight descended, faintly dimming objects which, until a moment before, had been sharply etched. The acrid tang of recently disturbed dust hung above the road, indicating someone's recent passage and reassuring Allard of recent travel. When he rounded a shoulder-high barrier of rock and came upon the stony cleft marking the west gateway, he drew his revolver, expecting a challenge from the guard. But none was forthcoming. Searching the surrounding rocks, he saw no sign of a guard.

Above him was an outcropping, a likely spot overlooking the road where a man might post himself. He dropped off his horse and climbed up through loose shale to the small shelf, some twenty feet above the road. Someone had spent time here, for matches and discarded cigarettes were strewn about. The pungent trace of powder was still strong in his nostrils, and he saw scattered shell casings. The guard had evidently been here only moments ago and had fired his gun.

He clambered back down the slope, remounted, and turned into the wagon road toward Mountain Pass, convinced that Bowley and the girl were in front of him. The dust in the air was fresher here, and

Allard rode on, racing toward town as the chill of the evening's first wind ruffled the treetops and began to nudge him with its pressure.

Chapter Seventeen

Somehow escaping the hail of gunfire that whipped around him, Cat Lenifee, dragging Pinto Daly alongside, made a run for the trees and reached the protection of the dense growth that surrounded the knob. Daly's flailing boots bounced loosely on the uneven ground and kept striking the palomino's hocks, spooking the animal into pitching and fighting the reins. As soon as he was in the timber, Lenifee released his grip on Daly who struck heavily, bouncing and rolling through the dry brush.

Daly had lost his hat. Blood ran from his nose, and his long hair hung in a disheveled tangle over his scarred face. When he lurched to his feet in a fit of strangled cursing, Cat Lenifee, who sat unruffled in his saddle, watched him with a slanting scorn.

"So, tough guy Chester killed your bronc'. Ain't that a shame. You goin' to let him get away with it?"

Daly was furious. "I'll lay that son of a bitch out beside his old man!" He pointed a finger at Lenifee. "The god damned stranger just shot Emmett. What you goin' to do about *that?*"

A look overlaid Lenifee's dark cheeks that increased the cold-blooded glitter in his eyes. "Frank Allard's as good as dead. I'll take care of him. Far as Emmett's concerned, he took his chances, same as we did. His luck just ran out." He spurred alongside and pulled a boot from one stirrup, offering it to Daly. "Climb up behind, and we'll get you a fresh bronc'."

They were interrupted by the sudden burst of Bowley's three shots from across the meadow. It caught them by surprise, and Daly, who had one foot in the stirrup, stopped in mid-air. "Who the hell's shootin' from that angle?" he rasped. "Them shots came from the trees on the far side."

His words were no sooner out than the rattle of Allard's return fire snarled up from another quarter, and they heard Bowley's frenzied shouts, followed by the retreating sounds of his horse as it raced away. Soon thereafter they picked up the hoofbeats of Allard and Chester Lenifee's departure, and a temporary peace settled in.

Daly's temper still blazed with a white passion. "I think they came up here with Bowley, and he's double-crossed 'em. He may get to the stranger before you do."

Cat Lenifee's face was inscrutable.

"Won't happen that way." His eyes narrowed down at the corners, and his lips showed a vague change beneath the screen of his scraggy mustache. "Allard's tougher than Bowley. The big boy ain't smart, and he's no hand with a gun. If they tangle, he'll die. Bowley's gone soft. The woman's on his mind. That's where he's headed now." He touched his empty stirrup with the point of his boot and repeated his earlier command. "Git on up here, or I'll leave you walk."

Lenifee waited for Daly to swing behind the cantle. Then he spurred the horse into a run, rode from the trees, and crossed the knob to the cabin where he pulled up short and gave the surrounding area a stiff survey before dismounting. By now it was late afternoon with half the valley already in shadow. The sun perched precisely on the western rim, and the forest was already ushering in coffee-colored smudges of semi-darkness. Lenifee briefly studied those spots in his watchful way, waiting and listening until he was satisfied nobody lurked there, then he dismounted, and went inside.

Daly entered the corral and roped himself another horse, stripped his gear from the dead animal, and cinched it in place on his new mount. When he returned to the cabin, he found Lenifee seated at the table with his feet sprawled in front of him, scowling at nothing in particular. The lamp had been turned up, and an empty bottle of whiskey stood at his elbow. He had split the remaining contents between two glasses, each containing only a single swallow. His muddy eyes, normally heavy-lidded and expressionless, threw out an odd gleaming, a signal of some new rashness crowding him hard. He had his mind on something, and a mental picture was taking shape in his head. His fingers, long and supple as a woman's, pushed his glass around and around in a slow circle, his eyes following the track it made on the table top.

"Help yourself to a drink, Pinto. Damn' bottle's empty, and we ain't got another." He picked up the glass he had been fingering and poured the few drops that were left down his throat.

Daly settled down in the opposite chair and put his whiskey away in a single gulp. "This ain't like you, Cat," he said. "What the hell we waitin' for? It's goin' to be dark soon. Let's finish this job before the stranger lights out."

The lamp threw its yellow shine directly against Lenifee's face, accentuating the strange glow of his eyes. "Hell, he won't go nowhere. He's sweet on the girl, same as Bowley. Didn't you know that?"

The jolt of liquor hit bottom in Daly's empty stomach and brought a pink flush to his face. "Never seen you back off like this before. First Jack and then Emmett. Chester and this Allard bastard will be down at the yard by now. We're wastin' time here. I want to see 'em both dead."

Lenifee shifted in his chair, but he didn't rise. "Pinto, slow down. You never did have any brains. Emmett plugged Chester, and, if he ain't dead already, you'll get your chance to finish him off in bed." He grinned, then his expression changed. "We go battin' down there now, and Allard will be forted-up, waitin' for us. Might talk a dozen of the sodbusters into helpin' him. They'll be hidin' in the trees and behind every door, each one with his rifle. Allard and Bowley are goin' to fight over the girl, and Allard will gun him down. Save us the trouble. Then, I'll gut-shoot Allard and watch him die slow. Now, shut up and quit worryin'." The light shown fitfully through the globe's soot, and Lenifee's eyes showed a colder and colder brilliance. "I settled for Jack, and I'll do the same for Emmett. Tomorrow's time enough. Right now, we're goin' to town for whiskey. It won't be the first night ride we've made."

He got up and stood behind his chair. Daly watched him uncertainly, never sure what to expect from the other's mercurial nature.

"I been thinkin'," Lenifee said contemptuously. "With Chester out of the way I'm the only Lenifee left in the basin, 'cept for his sister. That mean anything to you?"

Daly shook his head from side to side, not following.

"After we finish this business, you can have this place all to yourself. I'll be movin' into the big house with somebody who's a damned sight better cook than you are."

Daly looked with sharp surprise at the wolfish smile spreading over his partner's face and suddenly saw Lenifee's lustful ambition plainly written there. "Hell, Cat, you can't marry Jo. She's your kinfolk."

"Who the hell cares? She's a female, ain't she? And who said anything about marryin'?" He seized the liquor bottle by its neck and threw it savagely across the room where it struck the stove and shattered in an explosion of glass fragments. "What the hell! Bowley's a closer cousin to her than me, and he was fixin' to marry her. I ain't marryin' nobody, but I need a woman, and nobody in this place can stop me from takin' her." He looked sideways at Daly. "You got any objections?"

"Not me," said Daly immediately. He knew how unpredictable Cat's temper could be when aroused.

Lenifee got to his feet and moved across the room to a wooden peg driven into the wall. He lifted down a second gun belt and holstered revolver, identical and opposite-hand to the one he wore, and cinched it on his left hip. He pulled out the six-shooter, thumbed fresh shells into the piece, and dropped it back into its holster. Lenifee caught Daly's inquisitive stare.

"This might come in handy. Right now, we're goin' to Mountain Pass. Tomorrow we'll come back and see who's left. Then I'll make a call on the little lady."

"Ben's horse is gone, and so's his body," Daly said. "They must have taken him down. We better bury Emmett before we go."

"We ain't got time. Gettin' dark. We'll dig a hole for him tomorrow."

"Plant him deep," commented Daly, "and put some rocks in the hole. Wolves up here and coyotes. Coyotes will dig him up."

Daly trailed along outside, and they went over to where Hanks lay. They wasted no sentiment, picked him up by his arms and legs, and carried the gangling corpse back to the cabin where they dumped it unceremoniously on a bunk. Lenifee was bereft of any feeling. It was a distasteful chore, and he swung away immediately, going outside. Daly remained by the bunk, stayed for a moment by brief recollections. He had known Emmett Hanks for a long time. They had ridden down many dark trails together, rustled cattle, held up a stage or two, and gunned down other men. When Lenifee's impatient yell reached him from outside, he whipped a hand across the lamp's chimney, quit the cabin, and climbed on his horse.

The sun had by now disappeared, and twilight's first violent eddies were creeping up the ramparts. The basin and its western entrance lay behind Bowley and the girl, and the pale road stretched ahead through an evergreen alleyway of fir and pine. The gleam of a little creek ran alongside, then veered sharply north, and faded from sight. The evening wind had picked up, and within the trees deep shadows piled up, layer on layer, offering concealment and safety. To Joyce, who had made this trip many times, each bend of the road was familiar. The densely ranked pines formed a solid wall, boxing in the road on both sides, closely confining the pounding drum of Bowley's oncoming horse, rushing up now behind her. Although the little mare was flying at top speed, she knew Bowley would overtake her momentarily and had no doubt that, if he could stop her no other way, he *would* shoot her horse.

Bowley's horse was almost abreast when suddenly, without warning, she sharply swung her pony with a long, graceful dip of her body and shot off to the right in a spinning turn, plunging into one of the dark avenues among the trees. Bowley was so close behind that the gelding's momentum carried him a distance beyond before he hauled his mount around in a feverish, whirling turn.

Once in the sheltering forest Joyce was immediately enveloped in a condensed gloom, the giant pines closely gathered, thick-bodied and protecting. They afforded a temporary screen, and the black hush of evening dropped its soft mantle over her. Running blind and half-paralyzed with fright, she deliberately tried to blank her mind because her hands were trembling so violently she could not trust them. She slacked the reins and gave the mare its head, allowing the little animal to dash along the forest corridors without caution, ever conscious of the grunting sounds of Bowley's clamorous pursuit, close behind. At times he was so near she could hear his labored breathing as he smashed through the brush, and his heavy voice drove forward in streaks of sound as he cursed the blanket of darkness covering them.

Abruptly all sound from Bowley's direction ceased. In the quiet that followed, Joyce understood that Bowley, having temporarily lost her, was frozen in his tracks and intently listening. She immediately reined in and brought the mare to a standstill, sitting motionless in the strained silence. She was fearful her pony would whicker or grind its teeth on the iron bit. Either sound would carry clearly on the night air, but the little horse stood rock-still, and presently she heard Bowley resume his pursuit.

He began beating through the trees in a circling pattern that would eventually bring him close to her hiding place. Knowing this, she decided to move on and lifted the reins, lightly touching the mare with her heels. She held the horse to a precise walk, attempting to travel without noise, but she failed to heed some low-growing bushes in her path. When the pony pushed through this underbrush, the wet boughs snapped against her, discharging a shower of water.

It was a sound immediately picked up by Bowley. Night's heavy shadows and the solid wall of timber made distant viewing impossible, but upon hearing her and, without warning, he fired a shot in her general direction. The stray lead came so near she winced. Somewhere behind her she heard the slug strike a tree.

Bowley yelled: "Pull up, damn you, Joyce. That was a warnin'. I'll shoot again."

The wild yelling and Bowley's chance shot raised the possibility that he had really lost her and that it had been a futile act of desperation on his part. It sent a surge of confidence through her, and she was determined not to lose her sense of direction, circling blindly back the way she had come. Sounds of his pursuit reached her ears but were fading, and the distance between them seemed to widen. She allowed herself a short pause and drew a folding knife from her pocket, reached down to one boot, and cut the piggin' strings, freeing her feet. The new ease of movement served to steady her nerves, and a measure of confidence crept into her.

Even if he had lost her trail temporarily, he would deliberately place himself between her and the west gateway, effectively blocking her return home. Her only chance to elude him lay ahead to the west, to Mountain Pass. This was a part of the country through which she had passed always on the road and during daylight hours. Now it was up to her to find the town by a rugged, cross-country route under cover of darkness.

It was pitch-black in the hills, absolutely no distinction between the sky and the surrounding mountains, effectively preventing her from detailed identification of any landmarks. The horizon simply wasn't there, but she knew a full moon was due to rise later in the evening and prayed she could keep her bearings until then. She tried to remember from which direction the horse had brought her as she was not sure that her recollection of the general terrain was sufficiently fresh to guide her to Mountain Pass without more light. She thought to herself — *I can't stay here all night!* — and plugged on, riding blindly.

The dark heavens were cloudless, and a faint lemon glow began to amass on the rim of the eastern crest, announcing a later arrival of the moon. It brought with it a lighter toned background of sky, and, as the flush of light increased, the girl's self-assurance grew with it. She was able to see the earth underfoot and, with the imminent moon about to rise behind her, felt confident her westerly progress would eventually lead her to the village.

She began the more arduous ascent of a rock-littered hogback. When halfway up she rode into an open swath of ground, scant of timber, from where she could see the entire night sky. She identified a single bright star that always lay low in the west and from it took her bearings. She made out the profile of low hills ahead and recalled that two ridges, divided by a creek, separated her from Mountain Pass. The incline she scaled was the first ridge.

When she achieved the crest, she pulled up and sat quite still, listening in the silence of the night. There were few trees at this spot, and all at once the gleaming silver globe of the full moon rose behind her to shed its phosphorescence over the uneven terrain that sloped away in rolling surfaces toward a lower valley somewhere ahead. Greatly heartened by its light, she tarried a final minute, listening for any discordant sounds. She heard nothing and saw nothing, leading her to believe that Bowley may have given up for the night and returned as far as the west entrance, intending to intercept her when she returned home.

She jiggled the reins and began a careful

descent down a stiff, shale-strewn grade, eventually reaching the creek bed where bubbles of foam from a swiftly moving rivulet murmured whitely at her feet. If she had judged correctly, only one more hill, rising raggedly ahead, stood between her and town.

She waded the mare through the shallows and began her final climb, this one somewhat steeper than the first. It was, like the other, thinly timbered and overlaid with crumbling stones that put her pony to great labor. The little mare was nearly spent. She could feel it giving out. Therefore, she plugged methodically up the slope at a more unhurried pace, pausing frequently to let the jaded animal rest. Her eyes had long before adjusted themselves to the night, and with the aid of the moon she guided the little horse over the treacherous surface, skirting bushes and a lacework of randomly growing vines.

Except for the continual sighing of the wind in the dark and somber mountains, all sound of pursuit had died away. She resumed her climb and was greatly cheered when the little mare grunted up the last few yards to gain the brow of the ridge. The distant glitter of lights from Mountain Pass twinkled into view as a handful of tiny diamonds flung against the black line of the forest. Still vaguely uncertain as to Bowley's whereabouts, she began an angling descent toward the town. Her nervous fingers tightened on the reins with a vise-like grip, as much from her doubt of what lay in front of her as from reaction to her ordeal.

When she reached the last of the timber and came upon the town itself, she caught the glimpse of a low roof behind a picket fence and the spire of a bell tower. Her eyes identified the triangular shape, and she immediately recognized the little chapel. In automatic recoil she jerked her pony away and rode through the timber for another hundred yards south, to a part of town that lay dark and noiseless, reining in at the foot of a dingy alley.

There was a little wind running its cold breath around her, carrying sharp-scented moisture that accumulated in a thin, wet vapor on her cheeks. Thirty feet from where she sat, faint illumination sifted down from a low-burning light in an upstairs, unshuttered window of the hotel, and sparks from an inside fire whipped out of the high chimney to flee in the wind. Through the thin wall she heard the rustle of a woman's voice, and from a distance the guttural growl of talk, issuing from the two saloons, reached her, rising and falling with the incipient breeze.

On her many trips for supplies Joyce had always appreciated the Tinkers' courtesy and kindness. What she needed now was protection and shelter where she could hide, and it occurred to her that the store-keeper might provide both. She had been to their house on a couple of occasions and now drifted within the shadows that held fast to the backsides of buildings until she encountered the cross street she was seeking. Ragged bursts of noise from the lower part of town continued to roll up the street, and she was conscious of movement and voices within some of the nearby structures. The lightless front of Tinker's store was immediately opposite her, and down a side street, behind the store, somebody was home, for dim light filtered through the drawn curtains of a window.

She heard boots trot through the night, and from the darkness she watched two men emerge from a doorway, stroll down the board sidewalk and enter the Sage Hen. After their passage she rode quickly across the street and dismounted before Tinker's home. A cedar hitching post had been driven into the ground next to the entrance, and she tied her horse to the ring. The thin glow from within framed the outline of the doorway, and she caught the odor of recently cooked food and heard the low vibration of a woman's voice.

Her soft knock was followed by the scraping of a chair's legs, a door slammed, and she heard the sound of a lock being unfastened. In a moment Henry Tinker stood before her, holding a kerosene lamp above his head.

"Why," he said with a good deal of surprise, "this is most unexpected. Please come in." He stepped aside and called over his shoulder: "Martha, we have a visitor. Miss Joyce Lenifee."

The low-lit room Joyce entered had some pretentions of comfortable elegance with stained wooden walls and calico curtains bordering the shaded windows. An open fire of resinous pine logs crackled in the hearth, and an armchair stood facing the fire with its back to the window. Martha Tinker, a white-haired woman of middle age and ample girth, laid aside her knitting needles, threw off a lap robe, and rose from the chair. She wore a faded wrap-around and slippers and came forward, both hands extended in front of her, a quiet pleasure on her face.

"My dear," she said, seizing Joyce's hands

with her own, "you look upset. Please, come in and sit down."

Joyce took the proffered chair, close by the fireplace, and sat tensely uncomfortable with her hands in her lap. She was self-conscious and somewhat embarrassed, but both Tinkers were quietly regarding her with soft smiles, and some of her nervousness disappeared. She looked down at her folded hands, not knowing how to begin, and Henry Tinker, sensing her discomfort, made it easier for her by speaking first.

"I've grown accustomed to your supply runs during daylight hours, and always look forward to them. But what brings you to our door at this hour?"

His cordial words and his wife's gracious manner relieved some of her uneasiness. Her recent tragedy, the confusion that followed, and the ordeal of her flight from Bowley had left their marks. Nervous strain and fatigue showed on her face, impressing dark half circles under her eyes. Emotional let-down was a delayed reaction that pushed her close to tears, and she drew a handkerchief from her pocket, lifting it to daub at her eyes. A stiff pride insisted that she contain her emotions and not cry openly.

"I'm sorry," she apologized in a low voice.

"We've had terrible trouble in the basin. My father's dead, and my brother's been shot." Her eyes, honest and direct, lifted to them for a brief moment and then slid away. She tried to hold her feelings away from them, but Tinker could see how near she was to breaking. "I can't return home tonight," she murmured barely above a whisper. "I don't know anyone else in town very well, so I came here."

Martha Tinker's moist, bright eyes widened. Upon hearing the girl's words, she asked in dismay: "What happened to Ben?"

"His cousin, Cat, killed him," Joyce replied. "He's gone mad. One of Cat's partners shot my brother."

The Tinkers were shocked by this news. "Is your brother dead?" Henry queried.

"No, not dead, but I think he's badly hurt. I should be with him, but I can't go back to the basin tonight."

Tinker asked: "Is this cousin of yours after you? Where is he?"

Joyce shook her head. "I don't know. I have been running from another man, Wade Bowley, who is after me. I can't return to the basin while he's loose."

"Good God," exclaimed Tinker, "has everybody up there gone insane?" Then the sharp edge of something else cut across his

303

mind and aroused it. "Is Bowley a huge, blond man who has come to town on occasion?"

The girl nodded. "He's been hunting for me since sundown and is trying to force me to marry him. With my father dead and my brother wounded, there is no one in charge. Wade has a gun, and he's already used it. If he finds me, I don't know what he'll do."

"My heavens," Martha Tinker broke in. She threw a look of alarm at her husband before turning back to Joyce. "Did this man, Bowley, follow you here."

"I don't think so," the girl replied. "I believe I lost him in the dark, just outside the basin. He doesn't know I'm here."

Tinker had long admired this girl and his protective instincts welled up inside him. "You have had a catastrophe," he said reassuringly. "We'll assist you in every way we can."

"Thank you," murmured the girl, "you are both kind." She straightened her body in the chair and eyed each of them in turn. Her glance, particularly toward Martha Tinker, was touched with a look of appeal as she said quietly: "The one person who might help me is Frank Allard. He has not been in the basin long, but he fought for father and for Chet, and I think he's gone after Cat."

Martha Tinker was a warm-hearted woman in spite of a surface crustiness and was stoutly determined when aroused. "My dear," she said, smiling away all the girl's embarrassment, "you will stay right here for as long as you wish. Where are your things?"

Joyce's shoulders shrugged the question away. "I was running from Wade Bowley and brought nothing with me. I have only my horse."

Tinker's mind had gone back to the strange instructions Amos Burns had given him. The sheriff had had a purpose, and Allard must have been part of it. When he thought about the girl's predicament and imagined her recent hours of terror, alone in the hills with Bowley on her trail, he admired her spirit. He found reason to smile, looking with approval at his wife and then back at the girl. "You will be safe with us, and we are delighted to have you as our guest. You must remember that I have met this fellow, Allard, and once gave you his tobacco pouches."

Martha Tinker rose and came forward. She raised Joyce to her feet. "You have been through a great deal," she clucked. "That's enough talk for tonight. Come and try to rest."

Sensing the girl's concern, Tinker moved

to the door, lifting his coat from the rack on the way. "I'll take care of your horse," he said and left the house, catching up the mare's bridle and heading for the livery stable.

Chapter Eighteen

Wade Bowley's fruitless beatings through the forest long after darkness had fallen finally convinced him that he had lost the girl's trail. It was his strong belief that she would attempt to return to the basin. She would want to see her brother and to find Frank Allard. Bowley now was certain that Allard had somehow become the man in her life. He was responsible for her change of heart and her rejection of him. He was determined to kill Allard and, if necessary, Joyce Lenifee to prevent their union.

He knew her general location was somewhere west of him in the direction of Mountain Pass. Therefore, he retraced his way back to the rocky aperture, knowing Joyce eventually had to pass this point. He approached cautiously, expecting to find Tyner still in position on the ledge, but there were no sounds at all, and he concluded that the guard had departed. He tethered his horse and climbed up to the shelf where he sat on a rock, waiting and watching. It was the same spot vacated by Frank Allard not a half hour before.

An enlarging thirst propelled Cat Lenifee and Pinto Daly toward Mountain Pass, both in a wicked temper. Neither man felt any remorse for gunning down Ben and Chester Lenifee. Except for Daly's brief display of concern, neither particularly mourned Emmett Hanks who had been a drinking partner and riding companion, sharing a lawless existence with them for a fleeting period of time. There had been others before him and more would follow, for most alliances between roving gunmen on the frontier were short-lived, usually ending in a blast of gunfire with lawmen or among themselves. Such transitory combinations rarely become enduring bonds of friendship.

Night had cast its opaque blanket over the valley, and the moon's reflected light turned the westward road into an indistinct, silvered ribbon. Totally secure within the aegis of their fearsome reputations, Lenifee and Daly saw no need for caution and raced through the settlement in full view of the inhabitants. Cabin lights winked out of the blackness, and vague, silent shapes rose in doorways, but no call breached the night, and no hand was raised against them. Still pounding westward, they vanished in the darkness.

From his look-out on the porch of the big house, Wiley watched their dark outlines rush by. Although the two horsemen were only shadowy blurs in the night, he was quite sure that the riders were Cat Lenifee and Pinto Daly. They had come from the direction of Lenifee's cabin, and nobody had left the settlement. Turning, Wiley seized his rifle and ran to the bunkhouse for his heavy coat. With great haste he haltered his horse and slapped a saddle on it, jumped into the leather, and lit out on their trail. The night was his protection, and he intended to stay well behind, but the two men had set a punishing pace, and he was hard put to catch up.

During their dry ride neither Lenifee or Daly spoke, each man engaged in his own secret thoughts. They were well beyond the settlement and halfway to the west portal when the alert Daly picked up a sound directly ahead, a lone rider, fast approaching. His warning grunt dragged Lenifee from his musings, and they halted in the gathered darkness, drew their guns by common impulse, and waited. The oncoming rider's eyes defined their shadows at the same time that Daly yelled: "Hold up!"

The rider plunged to a stop and called out: "Who is it?"

Daly spurred forward until he was abreast of the man. "Hell," he said. "It's Gil Tyner."

Tyner immediately recognized him. "Hulloa, Pinto. Didn't know you at first. Who's that with you?"

"It's Cat," said Daly suspiciously. "Who was you expectin'?"

"Nobody in particular," said Tyner, his guard up because of Daly's frosty tone. "What the hell is going on? Heard the news?"

"No we ain't," cut in Lenifee, riding out to join them in the road. "What news? And where you headin' in such a hurry?"

"I'm goin' home," said Tyner, "to find out what's goin' on. I hear Ben's dead."

Lenifee was a motionless, black shadow on his horse and his flat, ominous words jumped at Tyner. "Who told you Ben was dead?"

"Miss Joyce did. She just run out the west entrance with Bowley chasin' her. Must've had a lovers' quarrel 'cause they was both mighty upset. When I tried to stop 'em, Bowley took a shot at me."

In a voice soft and deadly Lenifee continued to press his questions. "Anybody tell you how Ben died?"

"No," said Tyner without hesitation.

"Miss Joyce never had time to tell me anything more, and I ain't seen nobody else. What the hell is happening around here? Do you know how the old man died?"

Lenifee relaxed sufficiently to answer him, some of the edge gone, his manner more easy. "G'wan home, and you'll find out. We got no time for talk." He lost interest in Tyner, and his mind turned back to other things. He wheeled his horse around, ready to go, then he thought of something else. "Was Bowley and the girl headed for town?"

"Last I saw, she was runnin' hellbent in that direction," said Tyner, "with Bowley hot on her trail. If you run into Bowley, look out for him. He's gone loco and might throw a shot your way."

He backed his mount away, never letting his glance drop from the two dark figures before him. He cut a wide circle around the pair and headed toward the settlement.

When darkness swallowed him, Lenifee observed dryly with a voice full of disdain: "Seems like everybody's headin' for town tonight." He lifted his reins and brought his spurs down hard, driving his startled beast along the road in a great leaping run. Daly followed at his heels, lashing his own horse in an effort to keep up.

311

Tyner's words had led them to believe that the western approach would be deserted. They were, therefore, surprised, upon nearing the rocky defile, to be stopped by a warning shout that drove forward from the darkness.

"Who's there?" a heavy voice demanded. "I've got a rifle. Sing out or I'll shoot."

Lenifee recognized the caller. He quietly drew his gun and held it before him on the saddle horn. "Bowley," he said with a rough impatience, "put down the damn' gun. What the hell you doin' here?"

"Cat, is that you and Pinto?" Bowley asked, a rush of relief riding on the words. Without waiting, he came scrambling down through the talus, his bootheels dislodging a small avalanche of pebbles that tumbled down the slope. "Glad to see you boys. Pass anybody on your back trail?"

"Nobody at all," said Lenifee smoothly. He holstered his revolver and suddenly leaned forward, scraping a match alight along his trousers and holding the sudden flare in Bowley's face.

It startled Bowley who reared back and batted the light out with his hand. "What you do that for?"

"Wade," grated Lenifee, "you rode up to my cabin with Chester and the stranger,

Allard. They were after us. Then you hid in the trees on the far side and threw a couple of shots at Allard but missed him. Whose side you on?"

Forgotten was the fact that the man in front of him had killed Ben. Bowley's overriding hatred for Allard obliterated everything else. "God damn him, I want Allard dead. He's the reason Joyce has gone cold on me."

Lenifee's voice was a thin, subtle rustle, dry as a thistle. "Still figgerin' on marryin' her, are you?"

"Ben promised," Bowley insisted. "Makes no difference he's dead. But she don't want to go through with it now."

The other's interest in the girl was obvious. "You seen her? Where is she?"

Bowley swung his arm westward. "She's off there somewhere. I was takin' her to Mountain Pass to see the parson, but Tyner turned tough and stopped us. Then she run off, and I lost her in the dark. If I stay here, I got her cornered when she tries to come back."

All at once there was a strange silence around them, thick and disturbing. Lenifee and Daly were two motionless shapes. They had him flanked and were watching his huge shadow with a steady attention. In the deadly quiet the invisible tension seemed to grow greater. Lenifee's jaws ground gently on a cud of tobacco, and he lifted a hand and passed it across his mouth. He was weighing all this in his calculating, secretive way. He seemed to be deliberating something, and then of a sudden the tight readiness left his muscles. He turned, bent, and spat in the dust, and the long interval of suspense passed. "Pinto and me are headed for town," he said. "We run out of whiskey."

Bowley thought that over. "If I can't locate Joyce tonight, maybe you boys can help me round her up after daylight."

His statement struck Lenifee as humorous and brought a coarse laugh from him. "Sure, Pinto and me might give you a hand, right, Pinto?" Then his mind, never still, moved to what had been foremost. "I got some free advice for you, big boy. Don't invite any guests to your weddin'." Before Bowley could grasp the full measure of this remark, Cat turned to Daly. "We're wastin' time, Pinto. Let's go."

The two men spurred off into the night, leaving Bowley in the road, scowling dismally after them. Cat Lenifee's mocking taunt angered and unsettled him. Until now, all his spleen had been aimed at Frank Allard, but Lenifee's barb opened up a fresh, new threat. His hot temper, quick to change, shifted in another direction, and he belatedly saw Cat Lenifee as his most immediate adversary.

The night wind whirled dismally around and plucked at him with icy fingers. He blew on his hands, pulled his lips together and moistened them. It was fruitless to remain where he was, waiting for the girl to slip back into the basin. He had lost her trail and now did not believe she would attempt a return home before daylight. He made a snap decision, turned, and ran around the rocky outcropping to his horse, hauled himself into the leather, and viciously dug his sharp-roweled spurs into the animal, rushing down the road after them.

A hundred yards away, shielded by darkness, Wiley had listened to the low rumble of their talk and heard the departure of the first two horses, followed shortly by Bowley's. He had successfully avoided the fast-traveling Tyner by moving off the road and into the shadows while the man galloped past. Now he returned to the road, kept a safe distance behind Bowley, and continued to follow.

Chapter Nineteen

The road was a barely discernible pale band curving out of timber and then dropping into a pocket of shadow, dark as the blackness of deep water. Therefore Allard, who was unfamiliar with the territory, stuck strictly to its surface, believing that it led to Mountain Pass. The night closed cape-like around him and was so thick he had no concern that Bowley might be lying in ambush, and he pushed onward.

Several miles of steady running brought him within sight of the reflected glow from far-shining lights, marking the village against the hills. The road curled around a timber-clad hillock, the trees broke away, and he raised a glow of lights between the down-sloping shanks of the mountains a half mile ahead. He veered into the forest and rode among the silent giants until he found a spot to his liking, where he dismounted and left his horse tied to a tree. Groping his way out of the timber, he crept along the backside of an unlit building, ending up in the vague emptiness of a side alley, running outward from the center of town.

He drifted up to the alley mouth where it met with the main street and halted there to consider the main thoroughfare.

The night wind was a cold and steady force bearing against him, depositing a clammy dampness on his skin. The constant urgency to find the girl which had pushed him all day continued to gnaw at him, but the town offered a variety of concealments, so he took a moment's time. The little town was astir and full of movement, and he faced a street turned robust and lively, a fact that struck him as odd until he thought about it and realized it must be Saturday night. Horsemen singly or in parties dashed out of the darkness and pulled in at the hitching racks, swelling the restless flow of foot traffic. Halfway down the street the Sage Hen's discordant racket and yellow displays of brilliance cracked the darkness, and the Gilt Edge, diagonally across, vented its own brand of raucous clamor. A solid line of ponies ranged along the racks, and men kept traversing from one saloon to the other. The board sidewalks ran toward him and away from him in two pale, uneven bands, linking the front entrances of bleached storefronts. Their windows were dark and sightless, but at the far end of the street the livery stable's wide entry was framed by the light from its familiar, suspended lantern in the archway.

Few men on the street had the look of townsmen. They were, for the most part, cowboys from neighboring ranches or itinerant trail hands, blowing off steam. He directed his attention elsewhere and studied the other reaches of the town for some sign of unusual activity. His patient survey was rewarded when a tall man, leading a saddled pony, emerged from a cross alley and moved away down the street. When he passed the outflung glare of the saloons, Allard caught him against the light and saw that he was no range hand. He was neatly dressed in dark trousers and coat with a black, narrow-brimmed hat clamped squarely on his head. The man vanished into the livery stable with the horse then reappeared almost immediately without the animal. He made his way back on the opposite side of the street.

Allard took six long strides that carried him from the alley mouth to the facing cross street from which the man had originally emerged, and here he took a position in the shadows and waited. When Henry Tinker drew abreast, Allard spoke.

"A minute," he said softly, "of your time."

They were both in a pool of liquid

shadow, and Tinker saw only the charcoal shape of a man looming in front of him. He immediately came to a stop, his voice cool and guarded. "Who is it?"

"My name is Allard. I'm looking for someone. I take it you live here in town?"

"I do," said Tinker, identifying himself. His voice was edged with suspicion. "Who is it you're after?"

"A girl. Miss Joyce Lenifee from Winona Basin. She was headed this way, perhaps in the company of a very large man." In the short silence that followed, he thought to add: "I mean no offense, of course, but she will want to see me."

Tinker was an old hand in dealing with people and not easily misled. The girl had told him about two men who were seeking her, one from whom she was fleeing and the other whom she wished to see. He also recalled his conversation with Amos Burns and the mysterious tobacco pouches. He had, on occasion, seen Wade Bowley in town and this man was much too small to be Bowley. But he had never met Allard and was unsure of the identity of the shadowy figure before him. He took a cautious route.

"No, I've seen no one from the basin in town today."

"Whose horse was that you took to the stable?"

"Why, damn you," retorted Tinker with some asperity, "that is hardly your business. The horse belongs to my wife. Stand aside and let me pass."

He swung on his heels and stepped around Allard, stamping down the side street to his own doorway. Before entering, he cast an ill-tempered glance behind him, then went inside, and slammed the door.

"Henry," called his wife from the bedroom. "Is that you?"

"Yes," he said, and removed his hat, hanging it on the coatrack. He went into the living room and, standing before the fireplace, rubbing his hands, heard the women moving in another room. He lifted his voice. "Martha, please come out here with Joyce."

He was still there, his hands clasped behind his back, when they appeared. Martha Tinker had combed out Joyce's hair. The room's warmth painted the girl's cheeks faintly pink.

"I stabled your pony, Joyce," Tinker said. "Also I must tell you both it will be a noisy evening in town. Lots of 'punchers in off the range. Even saw a couple prospectors." He turned his attention again to Joyce. "I met a man on the street who was looking for you."

He saw the sudden look of alarm that flashed over her face. "Have no fear, child. He doesn't know you're here. I told him nothing. I couldn't see well in the dark, but this man, although a little taller than average, was not huge. Said his name was Allard."

The girl's hand flew to her throat. "He's come," she whispered. "I knew he would." Then she approached Tinker and put a hand on his arm, her eyes searching his face. "Where did he go? Why didn't you let him know where I was?"

"I'm sorry, but, until I talked to you, I wasn't certain of his identity. Now I'll go back and find him."

Martha Tinker interrupted in a short and exasperated voice. "Henry, I don't want you in that part of town tonight. It's overcrowded and full of drunks. Besides, how can you be sure this man was telling you the truth?"

"Bosh. I can take care of myself in this town. Have I ever had trouble before? I'll find this man, Allard." He glanced at the girl. "Would you like me to bring him here?"

"Oh, yes," she said, her eyes alive and glistening. "Please do, right away."

In spite of the warm hospitality she had

shown the girl and her motherly appearance, Mrs. Tinker had an imperious and obstinate side to her nature and used it on occasion when she felt the situation demanded. She fixed a stern look on her husband, and her voice bore sharply against him. "Be careful, Henry. When you find this man, come right back. Don't you dawdle with Otto Ludwig."

Tinker was normally composed and unflappable, handling the common problems of life with an habitually calm approach, except when around his wife. "I'll do that," he said wearily and went into the kitchen where he was out of sight. He opened a cupboard, pushed aside a canister, and pulled down a half-empty bottle of whiskey from the shelf. He uncorked the bottle and took two generous swallows, then replaced it, and quietly closed the cupboard door. When he returned to the front room, he felt the weight of the women's eyes on him. The edge to his wife's severe glance told him she knew what he'd done.

He opened a desk drawer and withdrew his old Starr double-action Army .44, dropping it into a pocket. "If you think the town's a little wild, I'll take this just in case," he said lamely to his wife. "Be back shortly." He moved toward the door.

Joyce had not taken her eyes from him, her expression alternately lightening and darkening to the play of her thoughts. When he went into the hall, put on his hat, and loudly threw the bolt back, she underwent a sudden change of mind and ran across the room. "Please wait, Mister Tinker. I'm going with you."

Her words triggered an instant reaction from Martha Tinker who crossed her arms over an ample bosom. "My dear, I absolutely forbid it. You would not be safe out there tonight."

Joyce possessed a will of her own and more than her share of backbone. "Missus Tinker, try to understand how it is. If Frank Allard is in town, I must find him. We have been searching for each other, and I cannot take the chance he will leave town not knowing I'm here."

Martha Tinker opened her mouth to remonstrate, then closed it. Somewhere in the girl's eyes she recognized the fire of a spirit as unyielding as her own, but she was moved to dispense some advice. "Rather a whirlwind courtship I should say."

Her imperious tone prompted her husband to rally to the girl's defense. "Martha, if I remember correctly, we knew each other exactly nine days before we were married."

Martha Tinker's jaw snapped shut, and she shot a withering look at him. "Well then, Joyce, if you insist on going, stay in this part of town and wear something warm." She raised her voice, and it followed her husband out the door. "Henry, do you hear me? Go only as far as the hotel with this girl, no farther. If you have to continue on, go by yourself."

Once outside, with Joyce wearing one of Martha's coats, they were bucking the force of what was now a stiff wind. Tinker offered Joyce his arm. His gesture brought a wan smile to her lips.

They had come from a warm room, and the chill current bit through their clothing. Joyce shivered and with her free hand drew the coat about her waist. Together they rounded the corner and paced down the street. Dark shapes flitted before them, as men roamed the street, bound nowhere in particular, aimlessly strolling from one saloon to the other in ceaseless movement. They had scarcely passed the front of Tinker's store when the night was shattered by the crashing report of a gunshot that burst from the doorway of the Gilt Edge. Tinker immediately came to a stop and pulled Joyce aside, as a great confusion erupted at the entrance to the saloon.

When Henry Tinker stalked off, Allard remained in the alley where he commanded a view of the street and considered his options, not entirely sure of his next move. He had no reason to doubt Tinker's word. If Joyce and Bowley were not in Mountain Pass, then he had lost them somewhere between town and the west entrance. His two alternatives seemed to be to backtrack along the basin road and try to pick up their trail — a feat next to impossible until daylight — or wait for their eventual arrival in town.

He was on the point of returning to his horse when a fractional smear of motion disturbed the far shadows and rooted him where he stood. Cat Lenifee and Pinto Daly whirled in from the darkness and swung past him. Allard immediately saw that Lenifee rode the flaxen palomino. He thought about old Amos Burns, waiting in his cabin three miles to the north, totally unaware that the sheriff lay gravely ill at the doctor's office not thirty yards from where he stood.

By the brilliance from the two taverns Allard watched Lenifee and Daly wedge their horses between the packed animals at a hitching rail, tie up, and disappear into the Gilt Edge. He also saw something else as they passed through the lighted doorway. Daly wore his revolver as usual, but Cat Lenifee had strapped on a second gun and now wore one on either hip. A third horseman raced out of the cañon trail and roughly forced his horse into the rack, causing a minor commotion among the animals tethered there. It was Bowley, his giant bulk looming wide in the bronze shine of lamplight. After dismounting, he delayed a moment to make a short survey up and down the street, then followed Lenifee and Daly into the saloon.

Allard drew a deep breath and expelled it. The girl had either broken away from Bowley, or the man had lost her trail and entered town for another purpose. There was a third explanation for her absence, a numbing possibility that froze his heart.

This, then, was the night on which rode his survival and all his hopes for the future. Death waited impatiently for him inside those doors, and the odds were heavily against him. He was aware of it and could not help it. Always before he had had an abiding faith in his own star, in a power that moved events and looked after him in preference to all others. No miracle had been incredible as long as it happened to him. Now this faith had vanished. He could conceive that he was just the same as all other people . . . and he was afraid. This combined with the desperation in him to alter the pattern into which his life had fallen. He had been immersed too long in his own isolation, and so, now that he was here, although he might perish, although he was afraid, he must see it through no matter the outcome.

With three guns against him it would be sheer madness to tackle the Gilt Edge through the front door. Bowley was no gunfighter but was nevertheless a factor to be considered, for he was armed and would shoot Allard on sight. In Cat Lenifee and Pinto Daly he faced seasoned killers, faster than he and to whom the prospect of gun play was a heady spice.

Allard retreated down the alley next to the uneven wall of a store, melting against the boards and feeling his way through the litter of rear lots. In the inky blackness he was guided entirely by his hands. The smell of garbage and fried food laid a musty sourness on the air, and he found himself at the outer end of another lane, somewhere ahead hearing a man's soft groaning. It was a single sound, accenting emptiness, but it stopped him, and he saw a vague shape rise from the earth and stumble toward the main street, steadily mumbling.

After searching the roundabout shadows, he resumed his careful progress, arriving at a closed door from under which a thin blade of light seeped. It was the back entrance to the Gilt Edge, and there was stillness here. He softly tested the knob and put his weight against the door. It gave way. He slipped inside, pulling the door closed behind him.

Otto Ludwig, sole owner of the Gilt Edge, stood in his establishment at the extreme end of the long wooden bar next to the wall and found himself in excellent spirits. He was a short, plump German with a bulldog face who had emigrated to the American West as a young man. Over the years, as one of the first citizens of Mountain Pass, he had watched the little village take shape. His eyes had seen enough of man's subtle devices so that his naturally cultured humor was tempered with hard realism that gave him a wry and cynical view of the human race. His Continental heritage had never left him, and he had his own notion of dignity, favoring more formal dress after dark than the usual western garb. He was clad in a neat, black suit and vest over a white silk shirt and flowing tie. A gold watch chain dangled in a loop from one vest pocket to another across his ample midsection, and on his left hand a large diamond burned its single spot of white fire.

The Gilt Edge was the town's oldest and best saloon. Ludwig operated it above reproach. He allowed no women to cross the threshold, tolerated no card sharps or panhandlers, and his whiskey was honest. Almost every night, sometime after the dinner hour, he could be found at the bar, taking his ease in the fragrance of his third cigar of the day. He had his own peculiar theory that a nightly glass or two of red wine contributed to better digestion, and one hand encircled a long-stemmed glass of claret. The other rested flat on the elaborate mahogany bar, his most-prized possession. It had been shipped in sections around Cape Horn to San Francisco, ferried upriver to Sacramento, and then hauled by wagon over the Sierra Nevada mountains and across the Nevada desert to Mountain Pass. It ran along the back wall, spanning half the width of the room and beyond it was a closed doorway leading to a farther room and the rear entrance.

Behind the bar, in a carved wooden frame heavy with scroll work, was a mirror as long as the bar itself, adding glittering radiance and, by its reflection, doubling the apparent size of the barroom. Spaced at intervals, in polished brass fixtures, the kerosene bracket lamps and crystal chandeliers imposed an overtone of elegance to the place in strange contrast to its soiled and grimy occupants. Through a murky haze the shifting light cast its greasy shine on a sea of faces, and the restless grinding of sharp-heeled boots scrubbed the floor with a ceaseless drum of sound.

It was the time of year for some of the remote ranches to move their cattle off the desert and into cooler summer range offered by the unfenced mountains. Visiting cowhands pushed in and out of the entrance in a moving mass of bodies, wheeling and colliding with each other and pleased to have it so after long and dry days of abstinence on the drive. At the end of the room on a low dais a piano and banjo struggled against the steady racket, the sharp ring of the banjo's strings cutting through the noise. Behind the bar Ed Burrows and two other bartenders labored to keep up with the standing customers and service the packed gaming tables.

Ludwig noticed some of the town's permanent population sitting in a poker game at one table. A few trappers dressed in buckskin stood at the bar with shaggy prospectors from the hills, their hats caked by dust and grime. He laid his cigar in an ashtray and slipped a finger into one vest pocket, bringing forth the heavy gold watch. Later tonight he was expecting some of his old friends to gather for a late night game of cards.

As he slid the watch back, he heard a commotion at the entrance, and two men roughly pushed into the room and elbowed their way to the bar, forcing themselves through the crowd with their shoulders. In the lead was a hard-looking individual with a flat nose above a drooping, black mustache and strings of greasy hair cropping out from beneath his hat.

Cat Lenifee, upon entering, conducted his own quick inspection. Hard living had left its indelible residue in the deeply etched lines on his cheeks, but his murky eyes missed nothing as they scanned the room. For a brief moment his curious glance fastened on Ludwig, then he turned away, hooked both elbows on the bar, and signaled with his hand for a drink. Ed Burrows, the chief bartender, approached with glasses and set a bottle of liquor before them. Daly immediately poured two generous shots which he and Lenifee drained with great thirst in a single, continuous swallow. He refilled the glasses after which they hunkered down over the liquor and began a low discussion between themselves.

The atmosphere in the room was already stuffy and growing warmer, as the horsy smell of unwashed bodies and heavy clothes lay close in the trapped air. A row of 'punchers stood three-deep at the bar, their wax-like faces glistening in the lamplight, and other men stood solidly behind them in small groups, contributing to the hubbub with their rowdy language. Drinks flowed freely and smoke from the guttering coal oil lamps drifted lazily around, strong with the sharp, tar-like odor of kerosene.

Another newcomer arrived, striking the swinging doors with both fists and bursting noisily into the room, pausing just inside. Wade Bowley stood there, his Goliath-like figure dwarfing every other man in the room. When he discovered Lenifee and Daly established at the bar, he began to make his way in their direction. He bucked through the throng, using his raw strength to force a passage, roughly thrusting men out of his path. Several 'punchers, rudely pushed out of the way, turned about, ready to quarrel, but, upon observing Bowley's imposing size, hesitated and grudgingly gave ground, affording him space.

Bowley reached the bar and made room

for himself next to Daly. He caught the eye of a bartender and took a pair of whiskies straight and fast to pull himself together, in the meantime waiting for Lenifee and Daly to acknowledge his arrival. Both men had seen the reflection of his entrance in the back mirror but ignored him, apparently more interested in their own desultory confab than in him, a situation Bowley found increasingly unbearable. The furious anger that had ridden him since the girl's escape was working on him, scraping his temper like the rasp of a file, heightened by a combination of the rowdy atmosphere and fire in his belly from the raw whiskey. He polished off a third drink with a single gusty swallow and ladled himself another. He fixed a baleful stare upon Lenifee's mirrored reflection.

Pinto Daly was saying: "Now that the old man's gone, ain't nobody in your way 'cept Chester, if he ain't dead."

"Forget him," said Lenifee contemptuously. "Even if he makes it, he's no fighter. You and me will head back after sunup and find my little filly."

"What about the stranger?" asked Daly. "Where you think he's at?"

"Him?" Lenifee laughed in sultry disgust. "Probably lookin' for the girl. He's love-sick, like Bowley over there." Thus far, having ignored Bowley, he now turned to him and acknowledged his presence. "Ain't that right, big boy," he sneered. "You couldn't hold her. Maybe your friend, Allard, has located her, and they're holed-up out in the brush somewhere." He laughed in a coarse, suggestive way and swung back to the bar.

A full-size oil painting of a buxom beauty, reclining on a red velvet couch and only partially clad in thin lace, adorned one wall of the Gilt Edge. Her languid gaze embraced the room, and the picture caught Lenifee's wandering attention. His glass was empty, as was Daly's, and he generously refilled each one, then turned toward the painting, and held up his drink in mock salute, speaking to Daly in particular and the room at large.

"Look up there at the fat one, Pinto. Don't she remind you of Big Nose Kate back in Dodge?" He pulled his attention from the painting and placed it on Bowley. "What say, big boy? Don't you think our little Joyce will make me a better bed partner than either Kate or the heifer on the wall? She's goin' to suit me jes' fine."

He saw Bowley's simmering stare. He deliberately made an obscene gesture with his hands, grinned maliciously, and then suddenly ceased to smile. "I'm tired of livin' a bachelor's life. You thought that little tart was yours, didn't you? Well, she ain't any more. Without Ben to hide behind, you're out of luck." He noted something on Bowley's face that grimly amused him, and a thin smile stretched his lips flatly against his teeth. "Didn't I tell you I'm figgerin' on settlin' down? No more night rides for me. I'm goin' to turn into a regular sodbuster. Tomorrow I'm movin' the lady right into my bed."

In the space of those spoken words the nagging suspicion Bowley had been harboring erupted into stark reality. His wire-tight nerves gave way. He forgot whom he faced and abandoned all caution. "The hell you say! She belongs to me. Nobody else gets her. Soon as I locate her, I'm goin' to marry her!"

"You ain't marryin' no one," snarled Lenifee. "The old man's dead, and his promise means nothin'." He set down his empty glass and made a half swing away from the bar so that he faced Bowley squarely. He dropped into an easy slouch and bent slightly at the knees with his weight on the balls of his feet. It was a stance all too familiar to Daly, who had seen it before and knew what was coming. He immediately took a half-step backward, away from his partner, affording him room. "I've had a bellyful of your damn' bellyachin'. I'm takin' the woman for myself. Better dust out of here while you can still walk."

Lenifee was in his element, all his combative instincts sharpened, prodding the other man into a draw. It was a conspicuous fact recognized by every man in the room except Bowley whose wild frustrations, fortified with liquor, boiled over. He had no premonitory hint of the disaster that lay ahead of him, and his heavy lips came apart with a gusty release of breath. "No, you don't, by God! You ain't takin' her from me. Nobody is!"

The whiskey flush on Bowley's jowls had taken on a volcanic twist, and his bloodshot eyes blazed with a savage urge to seize his tormentor with his bare hands and break him apart. He knotted both hands into fists, shoved himself away from the bar, and took a step toward Lenifee, his heavy legs slightly spraddled and his great arms hanging rope-like at his sides. The closest bystanders had followed the heated exchange, and, as it grew, the drone of other talk along the bar dropped off. In the dragging interval of time that followed Bowley's outburst, the surrounding crowd's heavy breathing rasped the still air, and a rising excitement worked its way through the pack.

Cat Lenifee knew this game by heart and rarely entered a gunfight unless he had chosen his own ground and until he knew the strength of his adversary. He hunched his shoulders, and his neck seemed to disappear. His eyes were too closely guarded to be read, and he watched Bowley intently, his body slack and soft in a half crouch, both hands swinging freely at his sides.

"Move toward me again and you're dead, big boy." His voice crackled across the room like a whiplash. "I'm tellin' you to turn around and get out of here. Your last chance. Better take it."

Light from the bracket lamps laid its sallow sheen on Bowley's ruddy cheeks. He had consumed a considerable quantity of whiskey in a short time, but he was not too drunk to forget completely his respect for Lenifee's prowess with a gun and his legendary draw. Over the past minutes he had been carefully plotting his first move to nullify the fatal sweep of Lenifee's hand. He planned to seize Lenifee's right arm and pin it before the latter could level his revolver. Once disarmed and at close quarters, he could twist the life out of the smaller man.

Buoyed by his drinking, he felt confident he could move swiftly enough to stop the downward slap of the other's draw.

As a result of Lenifee's half-step forward, they were standing toe to toe. Bowley could reach out and touch the other man, and his left hand hung only a few inches from Lenifee's right holster. In the space of an instant he knew what he was about to do and that cold purpose showed plainly on his face. Had he been a more seasoned man, he would have observed that Lenifee wore two guns, but somehow that vital fact totally escaped his notice. His deliberate mind locked him into a course of action that, once set upon, could not easily be altered.

Bowley's huge left hand shot forward and seized Lenifee's right wrist as it flashed down to his hip, imprisoning it in a lock of steel. For a split second, with Lenifee's forearm in his grasp, Bowley thought he had achieved his objective and prepared to close on the man and wrap him in a massive bear hug. Too late he recognized his mistake, and it was his undoing. Cat Lenifee had been through similar episodes before, and Bowley's swift grip on his right wrist never separated him from his icy calm. Without hesitation or interruption, in a graceful flow of movement, his left hand flashed to his hip, and the slap of his palm on the leather holster was a sharp smash of sound in the room. A round flare of light blossomed from the muzzle of his revolver, followed immediately by the deafening explosion from the shot as he drew and fired in a single smooth, lightening-like stir of motion.

The muzzle light leaped from the barrel, flashing and fading, and his single shot thudded into Bowley's wide chest, sending him reeling back and knocking out his wind. His broad features convulsed in agony. He clutched himself, took two stumbling steps, and dropped awkwardly on his face with an impact that shook the building on its foundations.

Chapter Twenty

The circle of Gilt Edge patrons had anticipated some excitement, probably a fight, but the cool professionalism of Lenifee's draw and Bowley's sudden, bloody execution had not been expected. The music abruptly stopped and seemed to be the signal for a general uproar. Men sought to clear the room which, once so crowded, emptied rapidly, as customers deserted the saloon in favor of the street, rushing in a hubbub of senseless grunting to the entrance where they met in a confused mass and fought one another to gain their exit.

Suddenly the stillness of the room was intense. Lenifee remained in a hunched posture, his back slightly bent forward and his revolver swinging from side to side, covering a small knot of 'punchers, all that remained of the original crowd. Pinto Daly, his own weapon drawn, ranged alongside, narrowly watching. Ed Burrows and his two assistants stood silently behind the bar. Then Otto Ludwig walked forward without regard for Lenifee's weapon.

"Kind of sudden, wasn't it," he said,

looking down at Bowley.

Lenifee's eyes had been overlaid with a kind of glaze, and they refocused on Ludwig. He saw the man was unarmed but made no effort to reply. He looked down without expression at the great, motionless shape lying at his feet and raised his head to stare straight at Ludwig. As the killing passion inside him slowly subsided, Lenifee's pupils gradually constricted.

Ludwig inclined his head at the corpse. "You had no call to shoot him down. He hadn't drawn his gun."

"He was comin' after me," droned Lenifee. "You heard me warn him, but he always was a fool." Then something in Ludwig's stubborn air of authority rubbed him the wrong way, and his voice all at once became quiet and deadly. "This ain't any of your business. You want to take up his quarrel?"

Ludwig resorted to the saving diversion of relighting his cigar. "No, what happened between you is not my affair." Then his Prussian pride rose up, and he pointed to Bowley's body and the widening crimson pool beside it. "However, this is my place, and that is entirely your work. Take charge of the body and remove it."

His crustiness seemed to amuse rather

than antagonize Lenifee, and he showed his yellowed teeth in a thin smile. "Don't try to buffalo me, old man. Get your swamper to clean up and call the damned coroner yourself."

The swinging doors squeaked from outside pressure, and some of the crowd who had rushed blindly into the street now were edging back into the saloon. They made a cluster at the far end of the bar, their voices low with suppressed murmurs. Daly's gun was still in his fist. It covered the room, and nobody moved against him. Lenifee took two backward steps and reached behind for the liquor bottle, still standing there on the bar. He closed his left hand around the neck and brought it to his lips, tilting it high for a long swallow. Then he corked it and thrust it into his coat pocket. "It's your treat, boss," he said to Ludwig and brandished his gun in a signal to Daly.

Together they backed to the entrance, the room's occupants fanning aside, giving them a wide berth. At the door Cat Lenifee paused, still cool and deadly calm. He was struck by something he had seen and turned to Daly. "There's another bottle of rye on the bar, Pinto," he said. "We'll take it along."

Daly obediently retraced his steps to the

bar and laid his hand on a second bottle, sitting there. He grinned at Ludwig who watched him coldly. "Much obliged," he said with heavy sarcasm, and wheeled to go.

At that instant the door to the back room swung open, and Frank Allard appeared in the opening, one hand holding a leveled revolver. Daly saw him first and let out a howl of alarm. Lenifee had been waiting at the swinging doors, most of his attention on the milling throng outside. Daly's yell turned him around in time to see Daly cast the bottle aside and pull his six-shooter around in front of him. Allard's shot caught him there and dropped him. Then Allard ducked back out of sight. In the space of an instant, although surprised and off-balance, Lenifee sent three bullets whistling through the vacant doorway in a display of the deadly skill that had earned him his reputation. He was able to shoot with both hands, and, like all professionals when his life was at stake, he paid great attention to the odds. Daly was dead. He was alone, and more shots could be expected from the darkness of the rear doorway. He also could not determine, with accuracy, if other hidden marksmen had a bead on him from one of the windows or through the street door.

Ed Burrows and the other barkeeps had

dropped from sight behind the bar and could reappear at any point with one of the house shotguns probably kept there. He snapped two parting shots into the back-room doorway, then plunged toward the street door, diving between the swinging doors in a single leap.

When Lenifee burst from the doorway, a gun in each hand, he saw men slide into alleys and melt into the velvet shadows. The cowhands immediately before him parted, affording him a clear path to the hitching rack and his horse. He covered the distance in three long-reaching jumps, holstered one gun, and leaped into the saddle, his other revolver covering the street. It was an unnecessary gesture, for nobody moved against him, the crowd interested in the action but having no part of it. There were points on the street where light failed to reach, and Lenifee made an obscure shadow as he wheeled the palomino around and rode up the street, vanishing in the darkness.

He had no thought of flight from the town. His one deadly purpose, fixed solidly in his mind, was to destroy Frank Allard, and he would remain in Mountain Pass until he settled that score. He was still unsure of how much help Allard might have brought from the basin and how many hidden guns might be trained against him, but this hide-and-seek was the sort of game he loved, and he had the rest of the night and the entire town in which to maneuver himself into a position where he could confront Allard on his own terms.

No sooner had he left the hitch rack and spurred fifty yards up the street when Henry Tinker, Joyce Lenifee still on his arm, suddenly emerged out of the gloom directly in his path. They were opposite Tinker's store, some little distance from the lights and activity around the saloons, and the deep shadows had sealed them from sight. Tinker reacted first. He heard the onrushing horse and saw the black outline of a mounted man in front of him. He plunged a hand into his coat pocket for his pistol, but he was much too slow. Lenifee merely reached down from his saddle and struck Tinker over the head with his revolver, knocking him to his knees.

When Tinker sank to the ground, a cry of terror broke from Joyce's lips, and she turned to flee, but Lenifee was instantly off his horse and seized her. She flung herself at him, striking out blindly, but he dragged her roughly to the wall of Tinker's store and bent one arm behind her back, forcing it up to her shoulder blades. When she continued to struggle, he pushed her cramped arm higher, increasing the leverage. Agony knifed its way through her until she ceased to struggle.

Fate had handed Cat Lenifee what he needed, and the odds were now to his liking. He felt certain how this night would end. "Scream again, Jo. Make more noise. You're the honey that'll draw the fly."

From the back room's gloomy interior Allard had seen Lenifee's dive carry him into the street. He rushed into the saloon, warily circled the room, and slid laterally along a wall toward the front entrance. Otto Ludwig was a motionless figure at the bar, surveying the wreckage of his place and the two bodies at his feet. Out of the corner of his eye Allard saw a handful of 'punchers tensely grouped around the door, all that remained of the original crowd, their curiosity prevailing over their concern for safety. They neither shifted nor spoke, making it plain they were not a part of the fracas.

Outside the street was alive. Boots scuffed the walk, and inquisitive heads appeared over the swinging doors. Somebody said: "It's a god damn' slaughterhouse in there. Two men dead."

Pressure mounted at the entrance, and

some of the men were shoved inside by those behind. When they saw Allard with a drawn gun, they immediately moved aside, and he went through the door in a driving rush, hooking sharply around the building's corner and pausing there, blending in the outflung shadow.

His eyes unsuccessfully probed the surrounding darkness for some sign of Lenifee. Cowhands cruised up and down, and customers of the Gilt Edge were joined by patrons from the Sage Hen across the way who added to the general confusion.

Allard tried to figure out Lenifee's probable course. He made his guess that the man would fade from town and return to the basin, in much the same manner, he thought grimly, as he had done once before, after skulking in the shadows beneath Amos Burns's window. Banking on that hunch, he slid his gun back in his holster and turned up the street to get his horse. When he was free of the crowd, he broke into a run, leaving the noise and brightness behind him, heading into darkness. It was in his mind to start his search at the edge of town and work eastward toward the basin, beating his way through the timber nearest the road and hoping to pick up some sign.

Scarcely halfway up the street Allard was

surprised by a commotion of bodies shifting in front of him, darker shadows in violent motion. He heard the sound of a blow followed by a man's hoarse cry and a girl's sharp scream. All of Allard's senses responded to that sound.

"Jo," he called, his voice strong and swift. "I'm here!"

He ripped out his gun, lunging blindly forward. He had miscalculated the man he was up against, a man who made a business out of this kind of warfare and who had out-guessed him. Fred Pond, working late in the rear of the store, had heard the disturbance out front and was making his way up toward the front doors with a lamp, its dull yellow radiance increasing as he advanced. The rising glow through the front windows marked the street with long, golden rectangles. By that growing lane of light, Allard saw Cat Lenifee, facing him twenty feet distant, backed against the wall of the building, holding Joyce Lenifee inside the iron hoop of his left arm which reached down across her breasts and clamped her tightly in front of him, effectively screening his body with her own. His revolver was steady in his right hand and leveled point-blank at Allard's midsection. Henry Tinker was on his knees in the street, dazed and barely conscious.

The girl's face was ashen, but she twisted and fought against Lenifee. Allard's own weapon was up and ready to fire, but Lenifee managed to keep her between them. That lack of choice took the sap out of Allard and wiped out his last hope. He had the briefest moment of enormous regret over his short span and then ceased to care, accepting the death he knew was coming.

Joyce threw her strong call at him in sheer, naked fright. "Frank, run, quick."

There was no point in running. There was no place to hide. Lenifee had him flat-footed, and he knew he was a dead man. Lenifee knew it, too. He was in total command and visibly relaxed, holding himself a half-step from the ultimate killing moment.

"Say your prayers, you bastard, and tell your lady friend good bye. She'll be keepin' me warm from now on."

A madness beyond caring, like nothing he had ever experienced, took hold of Frank Allard. "Shoot, and be damned. You hide behind a woman and ambush men in the night. You're a rotten mongrel coward."

"I thought so!" said Lenifee wickedly. "I was right, figuring you was a spy or a lawman when I first seen you."

It was that small conversation, that fractional delay, which spared Allard's life, for at that instant, before Lenifee's tightening finger pulled the trigger, the dry, nasal complaint of a small caliber shot whined through the night, and a bullet splintered the wood next to Lenifee, narrowly missing his head. The report had a strange sound, high and thin and popping, not at all like the blast of a .45. It startled Lenifee and caused him to jump. It broke through his concentration and diverted his attention for a split second. He instinctively swung his revolver in the direction of the shot. His left arm, clasped around and imprisoning the girl, loosened slightly, and she wrenched herself free, spinning to the ground.

The opportunity that presented itself was compressed into an interval no longer than the blink of an eyelid, and Allard in what seemed an eternity took careful aim. When the explosion thundered, the gun recoiled in his fist, powder smoke rolling back into his nostrils.

The bullet struck Lenifee squarely in the chest, the heavy wallop of the .45 dashing the wind from his lungs. His own gun discharged, and Allard felt it as Lenifee's slug sprayed a puff of chalky dirt at his feet. Then the gun dropped from Lenifee's hand. He laced his fingers across his chest. His leg muscles gave way. He buckled at the knees and jack-knifed forward, striking the earth with his face. Then he rolled to one side, his eyes looking up behind a glazed film, his mouth working in an attempt to form words.

The lantern in Tinker's store had arrived at the doorway and bobbed there, held high by the horrified Fred Pond. Tinker's wife appeared from around a corner of the store, out of breath and keeping her skirts above the dust. When she saw her husband's slack form huddled in the street, she screamed and ran to his side, dropping beside him, lifting his head, and making a cradle of her lap. She rocked back and forth, moaning steadily. Joyce Lenifee slumped at the wall of the building, her face turned away from Cat Lenifee who lay, dying, ten feet from her.

Allard's bullet had ripped its way completely through Lenifee's body, and he was twisted sideways without any power to move his arms or legs. A steady trickle of blood pulsed from a hole in his shirt, and blood ran from one corner of his mouth. "God damn your soul," he breathed, his eyes on Allard. "I should've killed you when I first saw you." The bloody foam out of his mouth ran off his chin and on his coat. He coughed in a thick, congested way. He moved his head from side to side, and his eyes widened with a peculiar stare.

Looking down at him, lying bloody and helpless in the street, Allard's thoughts were of another night on this same street, of a lighted office and two men, alive and unsuspecting. Lenifee's eyes now were closed, as if in sleep.

Allard holstered his gun and moved toward Joyce, pulling her up into his arms. As he held her and drew her tightly against him, the tension of fear and the pain of separation combined to make him tremble. "Jo," he said, "I love you."

"Frank, oh, Frank," she said as she clutched him to her.

They clung to each other with a fierceness until their shudders gradually began to subside. When she finally raised her head and looked up, exploring his face with eyes expressive and stirring, he bent down and kissed her tenderly.

Tinker had regained consciousness and, with the help of his wife, rose to his feet. He leaned heavily on her for support, his tall frame bent and unsteady. She wrapped a handkerchief around his bloodied head and was murmuring to him in a low, soothing voice.

Drawn by the gunfire, people were approaching, and the saloon crowd surged up the street now to form a morbidly curious cordon around them. Men brought lanterns and thrust them forward for a better view of Lenifee's body. Everybody was talking at once, and conversation rose to a noisy pitch as a slender figure emerged from the liquid shadows of a side street and tentatively advanced on the scene. It was Wiley, in his tattered straw hat and overalls, his .22 rifle clamped in one lanky fist, making his way forward with no little embarrassment. He felt the weight of the crowd's eyes, but his thin face showed a fixity of purpose, and the ring parted to let him through. He tried to appear nonchalant but was trembling with excitement. He entered the circle, stared down at the lifeless body of Cat Lenifee, then turned to stand irresolutely before Frank and Joyce.

"Wiley," said Allard. "Was that your shot?"

The boy nodded. He smiled shyly. "I thought you were done for. I shouldn't've missed him, but Joyce was so close, I pulled to the right."

Allard moved closer. "Wiley, that shot saved my life."

The boy's freckled face grew red. He kicked at the dirt with the toe of his boot. "I trailed him an' Pinto from the basin. I been watchin' 'em and would've warned you they was in town, but I didn't know you was here till all hell broke loose in the saloon."

Joyce bent near to the boy, put a hand on his shoulder, and kissed him on the cheek.

Frank grinned. "Wiley, you're coming back with me to my spread in Nevada. We're partners in that ranch from here on."

Martha Tinker was a smoldering presence. Her voice rose and came against them. She had her hold of her husband around the waist and had recovered some of her doughtiness. "Henry needs a doctor. I'm taking him to see Sam Webber." With the return of her spirit also came her sharp tongue. "I certainly hope he's there and not in the Gilt Edge."

"We'll all go see the doc," said Allard, coming over to give a hand with Tinker.

Webber's office and living quarters were combined in a single building, a square pine-board affair sitting forlornly on a side street, directly around the corner and two blocks distant from the Gilt Edge. A faded coat of white paint, dusty and flaking, distinguished it from neighboring structures, and Webber's warped shingle dangled at eye level next to the entrance. Somebody had left the door wide open, and under full sail Martha Tinker marched boldly through it. Allard followed with Tinker who was now ambulatory, Joyce and Wiley bringing up the rear.

A table lamp in the room illumined the functional furnishings with a subdued light that shone whitely on the draped sheets of a slender examination table pushed against the opposite wall. A vertical wooden cabinet with several trays of medical instruments rose at one end of the table. Several occasional chairs, carelessly arranged, completed the ensemble.

Two men, choosing to disregard the seats, lounged on either side of a single inner door, leading to a farther room. One was the hosteler, Hank Ennis, who brought with him the rank aroma of the livery stable. In the small room it was strong, thick, and unpleasant, but he seemed quite oblivious. The second man was Gil Tyner from the basin who had been on guard at the west portal when Joyce was fleeing from Bowley. He had come to town with a sorely troubled conscience. When he saw Joyce, a flood of relief rushed over his face and perceptively loosened his tightly held shoulders. He crossed the room immediately and halted before her, awkward and quickly embarrassed, not meeting her eyes and fingering the buttons on his shirt.

"Mighty glad to see you safe, Miss Joyce," he said. "Soon as I got home, my wife turned me right around and sent me after you. Right now I got ten men from the basin beatin' through the hills."

Joyce permitted herself a small smile, and her lips softened as she thanked him.

Tyner looked at Allard, surprised, as if seeing him for the first time and not fully comprehending his relationship with the girl, but he was bursting with hearsay and the excitement poured out of him. "Did you hear about Wade? Cat shot him dead in the Gilt Edge. That's two men Cat's killed today, and he's loose around here somewhere."

Martha Tinker had found a chair for her husband, and Tinker's slumping body fell heavily into it with a deep groan. The sight of him sprawled there, holding a bloody cloth to his head, drew Tyner's curiosity.

"What happened to Henry?"

Martha Tinker had heard the news Tyner brought and also his question, and she thrust out her determined chin. All her attention had been directed toward her husband, but she was painfully aware of Ennis's odoriferous presence and turned toward him, registering her distaste by giving him a cold stare, before speaking to Tyner. "Cat Lenifee did that to Henry," she snapped with acerbity. "I'm surprised you didn't hear the shooting. Cat Lenifee's not loose anywhere. He got what he deserved." She rolled her eyes in Allard's direction. "This man just shot him."

Tyner stared at Allard, and Hank Ennis turned instantly. Before either uttered a sound, Joyce reached out and plucked at Tyner's sleeve. The deep-seated concern she had temporarily pushed to the back of her mind now came rushing out. "How badly is Chet hurt?"

"He's at Maude Crandall's," said Tyner, "with a hole clean through his chest. But he was lucky. Ain't coughin' blood, and Maude says the bullet missed his lungs. She thinks he'll pull through, but she wants Doc. I come special to get him."

"Thank God," she breathed, fighting back the tears of relief welling up in her eyes.

Allard said to the room at large: "Where's the doctor?"

"Yes, that's what I want to know," declared Martha Tinker. "Henry needs medical attention."

Ennis jerked a thumb toward the inner room. "Sam's in there with the sheriff."

At his words Allard immediately withdrew from Tinker and crossed the room in three long strides, entering the doorway. A bed was there, and Amos Burns lay dead under a single sheet. His eyes were closed, and his once ruddy face was as bloodless as marble. Doc Webber sat on the front edge of a chair at the bedside, his elbows resting on his knees, his bowed head staring sightlessly at the floor. He had removed his stethoscope from his neck and was swinging it back and forth between his knees.

Allard approached the bed and looked down at the lifeless form. Webber raised his head to look up, his eyes reflecting the grief he felt, then swung his glance back to the bed. His low voice touched Allard, strangely apologetic. "Amos died just minutes ago. I couldn't save him. It was pneumonia that killed him, not the old bullet wound. But the gunshot opened him up to infection, and his damned fool trip to town was too much."

Allard leaned closer, looking down at the man responsible for his long and solitary pilgrimage, and felt a sadness. "Why did he ride into town?"

Henry Tinker's voice reached them from the doorway. He had risen and limped into the room to join Allard at the bedside. He carried with him a certain dignity in spite of his bloody turban. "I can answer that," he said. "I sent Posey out to Amos's cabin with a load of grub. When he got there, Amos gave him a message for me and told Posey to deliver it soon as he hit town. Amos wanted me to ride out and see him. Posey headed straight for the Gilt Edge and got drunk. Forgot all about any message. When I didn't show up at his cabin, Amos got to worrying and figgered what had happened, so he foolishly got out of bed and rode in here, just to deliver a pouch of tobacco he said you left at his place. Didn't know you had been out there, and I'm damned if I know why it was so important to return your pouch, but he insisted on it and made me promise I'd send it out to the basin with Joyce. Did you get it?"

Allard inclined his head.

Webber interrupted: "I think he knew the ride might kill him, but, before he died, he told me why he felt he had to come in. The night his deputy was killed, Posey saw a man ride a palomino horse out of the alley, right after the shots. Posey didn't know who it was, and he never told anybody, but Amos got it out of him somehow when Posey delivered the grub." He turned his attention directly to Allard. "He sent you a note in that pouch about the horse and rider. Amos told me more. You and Yeager grew up together back in Nevada, and, after Yeager was killed, Amos wrote a letter and asked you for help because he couldn't go after the ambusher himself. You probably been foggin' around without much luck because Amos had no idea who was responsible. Then Posey told him about the man in the alley and the palomino. It must have belonged to Cat Lenifee."

"It did," said Allard. "Lenifee was in the alley that night and shot them both through the window."

Tinker slowly lifted a hand and wrapped his fingers around one bedpost. "A tough way to go out." He leaned down for his own last look at the silent figure. "Amos and I came here to get away from people, back when the land was young and good. I'll miss him."

He pivoted on his heels, winced from the pain in his head, jammed both hands into his pockets, and moved slowly over to the room's single window where he stood, looking out.

Webber rose abruptly and returned the stethoscope to a small valise, snapping it shut. Assuming his former businesslike attitude, he jerked his head in Tinker's direction. "What happened to you?"

"Cat Lenifee gave me a tap." Tinker turned, ruefully fingering his skull.

"I understand he shot a man in the Gilt Edge," said Webber, "and I heard he killed Ben Lenifee earlier, up in the basin. All in a day's work for him, right? I'm the coroner in this town, but he's giving me more business than I want." He glanced at the two men, altogether outraged. "Somebody should shoot him."

"Somebody did," said Tinker. "You've got another customer, so don't close up shop. Cat Lenifee's lying dead on the main street. Frank Allard here just killed him."

Webber turned his head and gave Allard a brief glance of amazement which turned speculative. He permitted himself a short smile of satisfaction. "There'll be no service for Cat Lenifee. I'll dump him in a hole down by the river and cover him with mud. Don't want him in our cemetery."

The three men retreated solemnly into the front room where Joyce and Tinker's wife waited. Hank Ennis had disappeared, but Wiley and Gil Tyner ranged along one wall, their shoulder points braced against the planks, taciturn but rigidly attentive.

Webber guided Tinker to a chair. He re-opened his satchel and began to examine the storekeeper's wound. Martha Tinker hovered at his side, and Webber addressed himself to her. "It's a nasty cut but purely superficial. Ordinarily I would keep Henry here tonight to make sure there is no concussion, but Amos is dead in the back room, and I have no more beds until he's buried. Right now, I have to go out to the basin. Take Henry home and keep him quiet."

Martha Tinker glared at the doctor but found nothing to say. Webber began to dress Tinker's wound.

Gil Tyner spoke up. "Miss Joyce, you comin' back with us?"

The girl looked at Allard. "We'll follow soon. You ride on ahead with the doctor."

"I'm finished here," Webber suddenly announced and turned to Tyner. "Get my horse from the stable and meet me outside in five minutes." Wiley had remained quietly by the door, his presence drawing Webber's attention for the first time. "No need for you to hang around, young man, we have things to do here."

Allard's voice rose up instantly. "Wiley stays. This boy's shot saved my life. Otherwise it would be me bleeding to death in the dust instead of Lenifee. The kid's coming back to Nevada with us."

Webber found his hat.

Martha Tinker cleared her throat with a rasping sound. She threw her husband a wife's exasperated glance and pursed her mouth to say something to him but was stopped by Hank Ennis who thrust his head into the doorway. He addressed Tinker. "I got Lenifee's palomino outside, Henry. What you think I should do with it?"

"In my opinion the horse should go to Joyce," said Tinker, shifting his glance to the girl who immediately swung her head from side to side.

"No," she said softly, "I don't want it."

"Wiley," said Allard, "you need a new bronc' for the trip. The palomino's yours, if you want him."

"Sure, I'll take him."

"Son, you own the best lookin' horse I ever seen," said Ennis. "I'll hold him down at the stable." He returned to the street.

Allard spoke to the others still in the room. "Joyce and I are going back to the basin to bury her father and look in on her brother. Then we're going to get married and make the trip to my ranch in Nevada. Is there a parson in town?"

"We do have such a person," said Tinker, a thin smile creasing his face underneath the helmet of bandages. He had regained some of his dry wit. "Reverend Alonzo Pike is our deacon, and, if you need a shave or haircut before the ceremony, he'll do that, too. Although Missus Tinker and I may not make the wedding, you be sure to stop by before leaving the territory."

Allard assented with a nod of his head, and then all at once fatigue hit him solidly.

Webber saw it happening and said: "You better get some sleep. You're out on your feet." He immediately wheeled from the room.

Allard took Joyce's arm, and they went outside into the street, Wiley following. The night was fresh and keen with now only a slight wind blowing. Its pleasant, cooling effect seemed to drain away all Allard's accumulated tension. The crowd had dispersed, melting into the night, or gathered in the saloons from whence their lively voices could be distinctly heard.

Allard turned to Wiley and laid a hand on his shoulder. "Would you ride out to Sheriff Burns's place and get my packhorse? In his shed . . . a big bay? Spend the night there if it suits you. In the morning bring it out to the basin and meet us." He gave directions and watched the boy disappear.

Joyce again slipped her arm through Allard's, and together they walked back up the street, turned a corner, and strolled into the first line of trees, proceeding in the listening stillness to where he had left his horse. The eager beast, largely forgotten until now, snorted a welcome and pushed his nose in Allard's direction. In the soft shadows the pressure of the girl's palm stopped him, and they stood as one, without speaking.

The memory of their nocturnal meeting in the basin was in their minds, and something rich and eternal ran silently between them. They embraced and kissed with ardor.

When she drew away, she could hear his breathing and feel his eyes upon her through the dimness. It was a small, questioning voice among a riot of thoughts racing through her head, but she knew she had to deal with it. When she had things on her mind, she needed breathing space to sort them out. She withdrew from the circle of Allard's arms and retreated a pace to stand quietly. He made no move to stop her.

She felt life flow through her in a way it never had before. Nothing ever remained stationary — it always keeps moving. The past and the future would join together. The gap would be closed.

"Jo," he said then, "I deceived you when we first met. I came here for one purpose, to find the man who shot my friend, Tom Yeager."

"I know," she said softly. "Before I delivered those tobacco pouches, I looked inside." Then her eyes were laughing at him. She walked up to him and put a hand against his chest. "Any other secrets, Frank?"

"No," he said, "nothing more." But something else was working on him, grinding away at his contentment.

"Frank," she said, "I know, but it's not true. You're no killer. You only did what had to be done. Cat and the others would have killed you."

"That's true enough," he said, "and I'm not sorry. I'd do it again, and that's what worries me. Given enough time, can you forget what happened?"

In spite of the darkness, depriving him of looking directly into her eyes, something in the pressure of her hand, now on his arm, told him that she understood. She had that power. "But," she murmured in a low, amused way, "you've been telling everyone we are to be married. Don't you think you should ask me first if I want to be your wife?"

"You're right," he said then, backing away, burning with embarrassment. "And there's not much to offer on my spread. It's a pretty isolated spot for a lone woman, out in the middle of nowhere."

"Not all my memories of the basin will be good ones," she whispered, reaching up and touching the healing scar on his cheek, "but we'll be together."

"I don't know much about women, Jo," he said, "but I love you. Will you . . . will you be my wife?" He could not see her shadowed face, but he could feel her breath blow gently against his cheek.

"Yes," she sighed. "All this has happened to us so very swiftly, Frank, and we've gone through such a lot of misery before finding each other."

In the enclosing silence, when their lips met, it happened again, their future, suddenly, becoming their memory.

About the Author

Perry Holmes was born in Napa, California, spending his early years in the pastoral and once bucolic Napa Valley. From those years came a love for a rural atmosphere and the outdoors that has never left him. He was attending Stanford University at Palo Alto when the Second World War began. He joined the U.S. Navy and served four and a half years in the Pacific Theater as a Communications Officer, attaining the rank of lieutenant. After the war he resumed his education at Stanford and then entered the world of business with a small contracting firm in San Francisco. He remained with this firm for thirty-nine years, advancing to president and chief executive officer. Retiring in 1986 he undertook his lifelong ambition to write stories about the American West, as had his father before him, L. P. Holmes, author of some six hundred short stories and fifty novels. Today Perry Holmes resides in the small community of Lafayette, California, with his wife, Peggy.